SHARDS OF SHADOW BOOK 3

THE
BALANCE
OF
SHADOWS

JOSEPH R. LALLO

Art commissioned by Joseph Lallo as chapter headings by viiStar.

Cover design: Deranged Doctor Designs

CONTENTS

PROLOGUE

You've got to keep a lot of plates spinning. A lot of pots simmering. It's a good policy for life in general, but it's downright essential for someone hoping to make a living as a freelancer. Alan Fontaine fancied himself a photographer. These days that meant making most of his money doing assignments for Cox Media. It was a company that could be best described as a "paparazzi distribution center." Mr. Cox was somehow clinging to financial solvency using a very old-fashioned business model. Alan tried not to dwell upon the potential for Cox Media to go belly-up at any moment, taking his bread and butter with it. Instead, he did his best to keep his other side hustles simmering. Wedding photography? He'd do that. Professional headshots? Absolutely. Anything at all that required a camera and a skilled hand to operate it was fair game for him. To that end, today he was anxiously excited to be moving a pot from the back burner to the front.

He glanced to the passenger seat of his car. A manila envelope sat snugly beneath the seat belt. A very official seal beside the return address identified it as coming from the American Board of Criminalistics, a suspiciously made-up sounding name for such an important organization. The envelope contained a hard-earned document certifying that he had demonstrated the proper knowledge and skills to serve as an officially sanctioned forensic photographer in the city of Philadelphia and the state of Pennsylvania. After years of earning his living taking pictures celebrities didn't want taken, it was thrilling to finally get a chance to take photos in the name of truth and justice.

A soft slurp shook him from a carefully sculpted daydream of turning in a packet of photos that would put a deranged arsonist behind bars. He glanced to the passenger seat again, this time shifting his eyes a little farther, where a high-quality metal thermos drifted precariously above the envelope, seemingly of its own volition.

"Be careful with that coffee," he said. "The last thing I need is to show up on my first day of orientation with a stained certificate."

The words were directed at the shadow cast across the passenger seat. There were any number of things that would have been bizarre about talking to one's shadow, but in Alan's case, there were several additional oddities. The rising sun was shining in the heavily tinted passenger window, so the shadow was being cast in the wrong direction. It was also being cast in the wrong shape. Rather than matching his weary but fit frame, it depicted a short, impish female form with hair that roiled up from her head like flame. Most curious of all, the shadow had a pair of piercing white eyes that glared wearily back at him. It was Blot, a creature known as a shade who had managed to massively complicate Alan's already complicated life.

"Have you ever known me to spill even a *drop* of coffee?" she asked.

"I'm just saying now would be a bad time to start."

She nodded and leaned aside. Whereas *she* was cast on the passenger seat, the shadow of the thermos was cast where it was supposed to be. Her inky form slid across the car's interior to the shadow and put her lips to it.

A long, slow slurp drained the last of its contents. The emptied thermos dropped down to the cup holder. A light nudge of the shadowy hand caused it to vanish entirely.

"Happy?" she said.

"Very."

"Good. Give me your phone."

"What for?"

"For practicing."

He slowed to a stop at the next intersection and pulled the smartphone from his pocket. It tugged from his fingers before he could offer it, and the button on its side depressed, lighting up the screen. The phone turned this way and that, bobbing lightly as Blot's form fiddled with its shadow. Alan made a turn when the light changed. The shifting light placed the shadow more easily in reach of his passenger.

"Did I ever thank you for installing these dark things on the windows?" Blot asked, glancing at the sun through the smoky-gray coating.

"You don't seem to be very big on vocal gratitude," he said.

"Well, thank you," Blot said. "I was getting sick of the stupid sun whipping me around the car all the time."

The screen of the phone went dark from inactivity.

"By the void, you stupid humans and your touchscreens."

She tapped the power button and started tapping at the shadowy screen again. A few more taps failed to produce any effect, so she held out her other hand. With a magician's flourish, she let the shape of a simple locket slide through her fingers. She held it forward, and, like a sticker peeling from the seat, a bit of jewelry suitable to cast such a shadow emerged. Her eyes narrowed with concentration. Her black-as-night fingers coalesced around the chain, emerging just as the locket had. Her arm followed. Blot's entire upper body pulled forward and achieved physicality. She was still featureless, like a black, imp-shaped void snipped out of the fabric of reality. The phone sat in one hand. The locket dangled from the other. Her eyes narrowed into a look of supreme concentration. Finally, she wrapped her stubby thumb around to the phone screen and smeared a shape on the lock screen. It blinked red.

"Hah! Progress!" she crowed.

"I really wish you wouldn't do the whole 3D-shadow thing in broad daylight."

She rolled her eyes. "I *can't* do it in broad daylight, thank you very much. And if the tint is dark enough to let me do it, it's dark enough to keep the normies out there from *seeing* me do it."

"Even so..."

"You worry too much."

She slipped the locket around her neck and tried the screen again. This time she was able to drag out part of the shape. She wrapped her free hand around the locket and tried a third time. Merely a red flash again.

"I don't think this thing is helping at all..." she muttered, slipping back into two dimensions until only her phone hand remained. "Do you have any idea how frustrating it is to have a Shard of Shadow right at my fingertips and not have it *do* anything?"

"I've held it in my hand, Blot. It burned like hell." He blinked. "*Literally* like hell, for all I know."

"Exactly!" She managed to get half a shape traced. "I know it's powerful. I can feel the power. But I can't get to it. It's like having a big, powerful gun but not knowing where the trigger is."

The phone blinked and blipped a few times as they continued on their way. They reached the police station and pulled into the lot.

"We're a few minutes early. Do you want me to wait here while you give it a few more tries?" Alan asked.

Blot's hand was visibly shaky, like the weight of the phone was steadily becoming too much to bear. She huffed a defeated breath and withdrew the hand. The phone bounced to the seat.

"No. We'll try it later. Now go in there and become a cop so maybe I can get a gun that I *know* were the trigger is."

Chapter 1

He stepped through the front door of the station. Things had been refreshingly slow there lately. Today the worst offenders on hand were a traffic violator and a drunk-and-disorderly. Three people were at the main desk. Two glanced up and gave him a weary nod, less a greeting and more an acknowledgment of his existence. The remaining person on duty shot him a room-brightening smile and hopped from her chair.

"There's our boy!" said Officer Jessie Hearst. She gave one of the other desk staff a slap on the back. "You know who that is?" she said, jostling a gray-haired officer with the sour disposition of an ancient tabby.

"The new photographer," the man rumbled.

"Let's find out if you're right," Jessie said. She hopped the half gate separating civilians from the more official portion of the lobby and held out a hand. "Have you got the paperwork?"

Alan tried to ignore the almost audible eye roll from his shadow and handed over the envelope. Jessie popped it open and perused the relatively terse wording of the printed certificate within.

"Keep an eye on her," Blot whispered. "Remember what happened in the hospital."

He nodded. Blot was invisible to anyone without a shade of their own, which *usually* meant she was free to say and do as she pleased within whatever degree of freedom the light levels allowed. However, an idle observation from Jessie a short time ago suggested the veil of secrecy wasn't entirely impenetrable. She'd yet to repeat the stunt, but Blot was nothing if not cautious.

"Looks like everything is in order," Jessie said.

She tucked the certificate under her arm and reached back to slap the desk. The tired officer on duty reached beneath it and revealed an intra-office mailer tied with a string. Jessie snatched it and unfastened it.

"By the powers vested in me by the upper-office staff who couldn't be bothered to do the job themselves, I hereby bequeath to you the enviable status of..." She tugged a laminated badge at the end of a chain lanyard from the envelope. "Provisional Contract Employee of the Philadelphia Police Department's Forensic Squad."

"Gosh. I feel like a king," he joked, lowering his head for her to anoint him with the lanyard.

She slapped his back and smirked. "You're on the force! Only on alternate Mondays, plus a twenty-four-hours-on, forty-eight-hours-off rotating on-call schedule, but on the force regardless. Come on. I'll show you around." She opened the gate for him and followed him through.

"So what's the plan?" he asked. "Do I get some sort of orientation?"

"Yep! But first, congratulate me."

"Congratulations," he said. "What did you do?"

"You're not the only one who's finally cleared to actually do something meaningful for the department for a change. As of yesterday I'm finally off the stupid painkillers that were keeping me out of the squad car."

"You're back on the street?"

"Darn right I am. Provided I can stay healthy."

They approached a door. She stopped in front of it, then stepped aside.

"Go ahead," she said, indicating a small black box on the doorjamb.

He waved his new badge, and the door clicked open. A smile came to his face. Sure, he'd worked hard, taken tests, and passed assessments. But something about his freshly minted credentials actually unlocking a police station door hammered in the reality of his achievement like nothing else.

"Feels good, right?" Jessie said. "Come on in."

They stepped through the door to what looked a bit like a pawn shop. A wire gate separated the entrance of the room from the rest of the caged-off storage. This was at least the third such room he'd encountered in the police station in the last few months of trying to get on staff. Multiple tiers of locked doors seemed to be a hallmark of station design. The fact that his borderline kleptomaniac of a shadow passed effortlessly through the wire cage and started window-shopping was evidence that such security precautions were not devised with shades in mind.

"This is the equipment room. When you go on duty, either in the office or from home, you come here and you check out your camera and stuff. Sign out there, mark off everything you're signing out. When you get back, everything you used up gets marked down there before you sign the equipment back in." She waggled a finger at him. "Don't you forget this step. Chain of custody, remember? Plus, if you don't mark something as used up, there's this guy Jonesy in logistics who *will* rat you out for theft. You haven't seen spiteful bureaucracy until you've seen a desk jockey in action."

Alan buzzed through the door and grabbed a camera bag that clearly came from the lowest bidder.

"No stealing. Got it," Alan said.

Ostensibly, the comment had been directed at Jessie, but his eyes were firmly locked with the white orbs staring up at him from a lower shelf, where the office lights weren't quite enough to keep Blot from slipping her shadowy hand into a semiorganized pile of assorted police equipment. Blot reluctantly pulled her hand free, but not without the glint of a handcuff key vanishing into her two-dimensional clutches.

"Since it's only my second day back in the saddle, they've still got me on limited duty, but giving you your orientation certainly qualifies."

"There aren't any weapons in here, Alan," Blot griped. "Not even one of those fancy sticks for hitting people in the head. It's nothing but radios and handcuffs and stuff."

Alan ignored the statement. "What does orientation entail?" he asked.

Jessie slid a small notebook from her pocket and clicked out a pen. "Let's see. Equipment checkout procedures. Check. Confirmation of schedule." She glanced up. "Your twenty-four hours on call starts now."

"Got it."

She nodded and checked a box.

"Ask her where the SWAT stuff is!" Blot said. "You think your badge gets you in there? I wouldn't mind getting my hands on a third flash-bang."

"A third?" he whispered.

"What's that?" Jessie asked.

"Sorry, nothing. You were saying?"

9

"Uh… There's a lot of station-specific policy stuff, but we'll take care of that in the car, because the rest of the day is going to be you and me driving around and responding to calls."

"Are there really going to be a ton of calls requiring forensic photography?"

"Pff. Probably not even one. But we'll be treating every call we get today to a full forensic sweep. Sort of a low-impact ramp up to get you familiar with the way things work outside of a simulation."

"I guess that makes sense."

"Don't forget to ask about the SWAT thing!" Blot said.

Jessie, unable to hear the shade's nagging, continued. "We'll also stop by some of the usual day spots. There's a bunch of businesses around town that'll give free drinks and such to the boys in blue. Or girls, as the case may be. I'm not too proud to have a midafternoon snack compliments of the generosity of the local convenience store. You're not in uniform, so I'm hoping me showing up and talking you up will be enough to get you in the club."

"SWAT!" Blot urged.

"Sounds good," he said, finishing up his sign-out form.

"Come on, Alan. This little lull in people trying to kill us isn't going to last forever," Blot urged.

"Hey," Alan said, following Jessie out of the room with his bag over his shoulder. "Silly question, but does this badge work for *every* door in the station?"

"No. Just main entrances and this equipment room. Oh, and the stairwells."

"So I don't get to go grab goodies from the SWAT team's stash," Alan said.

"Ha! No, not with a contractor's credentials."

"I bet I could get in. Ask her where they keep the stuff!" Blot said.

Alan ignored her.

"Spoil sport."

Alan rolled his neck and checked the time. A day on the job doing crime scene shoots was, by every subjective measure, far better than the celebrity stakeouts he was accustomed to. He got to see more of the city, people didn't immediately curse him out if they spotted him, and sure enough, he could score a free iced tea now and again. But it wasn't what he'd call interesting. In seven hours, they'd photographed a grand total of four scenes: one home break-in, one automotive break-in, and two vandalisms. He wasn't going to be getting the key to the city for his carefully framed shots of leaky spray paint cans. But there were two things that made the day one of the best he'd had on a job in a long time.

The first was Blot. Though traipsing around in the sun wore on her nerves, she was beyond excited about the possibilities afforded by this position.

"Did you see how that guy with the painted wall treated you? 'Yes, sir' this and 'no, sir' that. We're getting respect! That's a nice change of pace. And people just *let you in* places. This is going to give us access to so many places. Plus, there's already been a crime there, so who's to know if we help

11

ourselves to a little bit of this or that? *You're* the one taking pictures of the evidence. Just don't take pictures of that." She laughed. "Not that I'd leave any. You guys are all about fingerprints and I don't have any. No footprints either. You should have gotten this job a long time ago."

"Mmhmm," Alan said giving his shadow a quick glance.

"You ever eat at this place?" Jessie said. "They're supposed to be known for their gyros or whatever, but let me tell you—I could eat about ten pounds of their falafel. I ever tell you about the first time I had falafel?"

He shook his head and leaned back. No one could make the hours fly by like Jessie. She had the glorious ability to make a meal of the tiniest story. Even back in college she could spend fifteen minutes at a party and leave with three hours of anecdotes. But after a few years on the police force, the characters she'd met and worked with made for an endless barrage of the most enthusiastically told stories he'd ever heard. As though she had a sixth sense for it, the very instant Alan started to feel as though the sea of words was getting old, she'd switch gears and pry a fresh story out of him. No one was more interested in who you were and how you were than Jessie Hearst. He had a feeling those free snacks and beverages from the locals were less about the badge and more about the gem of a human being wearing it.

"... don't know how they fit all that sauce in that container, but I managed to get every last drop of it on my shirt. Third day on the job. *Nothing* makes a mess like Mediterranean food," she said. "But I've been yammering. What's up with you? You've been quiet."

"Just fresh out of stories," he said. "My life isn't as eventful as yours."

"Liar," Blot jabbed.

"Liar," Jessie said at the same moment.

"Whoa," Blot said, shrinking a bit behind Alan. "Did she do it again, or was that a coincidence?"

"You had a hand in uncovering that election scandal, which would have been plenty, but then you were nearly killed in a prison riot. I bet you've been plagued by folks looking for the story."

He shrugged. "I was the one with the camera for most of it. My face isn't really out there in association with it, you know? I mean, have you noticed anyone hounding me for an autograph?"

"No, but we're dealing with folks having a bad day. That's the job description. You either help the people who are having a bad day or give a bad day to the people who deserve it. It tends to be the first thing on their mind. 'Hey, aren't you that guy?' gets pushed right out of their heads." She gave him a nudge to the ribs. "But at parties? You gotta milk that thing."

"That will require me to go to parties."

"You don't like parties?"

"It's been a while since I was invited to one that I wasn't being paid to photograph. If you count those, then I went to sixteen weddings last year."

"Yikes. You couldn't pay me enough to go to that many weddings."

He shrugged. "One of the better gigs. Most folks are expecting to end up with a heap of debt after them, so most of them don't try to talk the price down. Plus, free dinner."

"You get to eat with the guests?"

"Sure. And if you're nice to the kitchen staff, they'll send you home with leftovers. You'd be surprised how long you can stretch a couple of servings of prime rib."

"But when's the last time you went out for a good time, off the clock?"

"When I went to take shots of the eclipse."

"A night in a frozen field with a camera watching a shadow creep across the moon. You wild man."

"You'd be surprised what sort of trouble a fella can get in during a night in a frozen field during an eclipse."

She raised her eyebrows. "Do tell."

"Don't tell," Blot said.

"You know," Alan said. "Bears and stuff."

"Were there any bears?"

"No."

"Cool story, bro. Listen, I've got to get you some phone numbers. You're bumming me out," she said. "There's a group I'm a part of that does a karaoke night, if you—"

A squawk of the radio cut off the offer. "Cars in the vicinity of Pier 70 Boulevard, please report. Possible homicide."

Any joviality vanished from her face in an instant. The shift from Jessie to Officer Hearst was almost jarring. Her attention turned fully to the radio. Alan felt a wave of anxiety and anticipation. Pier 70 Boulevard was halfway across town, so they were almost certainly not intended to respond, but he was on the clock for forensic matters, and homicide was certainly a forensic matter.

"Officer Hearst, you have Fontaine with you, correct?"

She grabbed the radio. "That's an affirmative."

"Lieutenant Stockton wants him on hand for this one."

"On our way, ETA seven minutes." She hung up the radio handset and switched on the siren. "Guess orientation is over."

From the first glimpse, it was clear this crime scene was different from the others. Police tape cocooned the area, holding curious onlookers at bay. The scene of the crime was a motel with the exterior doors for each room. An acrid metallic stink filled the air, subtle but penetrating. It was the sort of smell that sent alarms blaring out of the deepest parts of the human mind. Something bad happened here. Something messy. They were the third squad car to arrive on the scene. An ambulance was on hand as well. The two officers were looking green and unsteady. The EMTs were simply looking tired.

"We ready for photos?" she said.

The younger of the two nodded, as though if he opened his mouth, more than words would come spilling out. Jessie motioned to Alan. Lieutenant Stockton was already on hand, and from the looks of it, the place had already gotten a round of photographs from more senior personnel. Alan didn't bother asking the forensic lead why someone on their first day on the job would be working on such a major crime. Now was a time for getting the job done. Questions could wait.

He could feel the pit of his stomach start to lurch and quiver, but he focused on dredging his fresh forensic education to the surface. Step here, not there. Wide shots first. Establish context. He wasn't sure if the ever-present specter of Lieutenant Stockton and his crew hovering in the doorway monitoring him was helping or hurting his nerves. Trying to stay cool and detached was a little difficult, though, with Blot in his ear.

"Wow..." she said, awe in her tone. "This is brutal."

He clicked on a flashlight and stepped gingerly inside. Blot stretched around the beam once she was no longer at the mercy of the evening sun.

"There's so much blood, Alan," she said. "I didn't know you people had this much blood *in* you."

He took a deep breath, hoping to steady his nerves, but a whiff of the fresh blood wasn't terribly calming. Instead, he focused on the voices behind him. The sureness and confidence that made Jessie's stories so enthralling also served to make her an island of stability in this mind-rending scene.

"What do we know?" Jessie asked.

"People next door complained about a disturbance. Knocking around and such, but it stopped before motel staff could step in, so they decided to leave it until morning. By then, there were complaints of the smell," the older officer explained. "They found the latch there. Fresh install on the outside of the door. None of the other doors have it. The manager couldn't state with any certainty when it was installed, just that it wasn't there during their last inspection."

"So it wasn't hotel staff that did it."

"No. There's a matching latch on the inside. The cleaning staff say the external one was latched. We had to bust the door open. Looks like the interior one was latched too."

"Interior *and* exterior doors were latched?" Jessie said. "So they were locked inside. Possible suicide?"

"This wasn't a suicide..." Alan said, his voice a notch lower than it should have been.

It didn't take a detective to make that determination. The body was in the center of the room. It looked like every blade, every piece of glass, everything within a hundred yards that could hold an edge had been put to work on the victim. No one could have done that much damage to themselves. They would have been dead before half of those cuts had been made. It wasn't just excessive, it was sadistic. Grotesque.

"Well if it wasn't a suicide, how did the killer escape?" Jessie said.

"It wasn't through the windows," Blot observed, stretching about the interior of the room. "There's boards screwed across them. And some sort of metal foil over the boards."

"Why is there foil on the windows?" Alan asked, his brain seizing on the one non-horror-movie detail.

"This is starting to sound familiar," Jessie said coldly.

Alan placed more markers and snapped more pictures.

"The bulb in the lamp is smashed," he said. "And the bathroom light is out too. There's candles on the nightstand. Half-burned. An awful lot of effort was put into keeping strong light out of this room."

Blot slid in front of him. "I suppose you're going to blame this on my people, aren't you?" she said. "Just because the room has been rendered perfectly dark, and someone was murdered while locked inside with no means for the murderer to escape beside the crack under the door, doesn't mean it was a shade that did it."

"Who could have done this?" he asked.

"I'll bet those white-suits could figure out how to do this. How come you never blame *them*?"

"What do we know about the victim?" Jessie asked.

"Wallet was on the end table. Open. Ran the license. A Mr. Gene Neusome. Real piece of work, this one. There was actually an open warrant from New Jersey for being delinquent on his child support payments. He's been caught with prostitutes. Three priors for domestic abuse..."

"Domestic abuse," Jessie mused.

"Yeah..." the older officer said knowingly.

"Can you please fill me in on this?" Alan said, stifling a gag. "I think I just saw my first human kidney, and I... really need a distraction."

"This is starting to sound like the Metro Ghoul," Jessie said.

"Metro Ghoul," Alan repeated.

He didn't recognize the name, which was clear from his tone, but mostly he just wanted to say something to try to click his brain out of the horrid little circles it was spinning in.

"I'm not surprised you haven't heard of him," Jessie said.

"Or her," noted one of the other officers.

"We're talking about a serial killer. The odds are heavily in favor of a him," Jessie said.

"What's his deal?" Alan asked, crouching to adjust an evidence marker and snap another picture.

He'd taken to breathing through his mouth to avoid the smell, but now he could swear he could taste the coppery tinge of blood in the air. His stomach was beginning to slide downhill.

"Notorious serial killer on the East Coast. The original goes way back. Jack the Ripper era, I think. Or just after. They caught him back then. Full confession. Witnesses. No doubt about it. But since then there have been something like half a dozen copycats. Whoever it is lures deadbeats and other bottom-feeders somewhere, blocks out all the light, and... well..." She gestured. "That."

"He likes blades. Sharp things," Jessie palmed her forehead. "Damn copycats."

Alan continued his documentation at Stockton's direction. Bit by bit, every speck of blood spatter was recorded. New details emerged as he was directed farther into the crime scene. The quest to eliminate light was far more thorough than they'd first thought. Two of the outlets were hanging out of the wall, ground wires pulled free. The rest of the outlets, while still in place, had evidence of tampering. Rolls of industrial aluminum foil and duct tape were in the bathroom. This was planned and executed with clear skill and experience.

Doing the forensic job properly took hours, particularly when a more experienced crew ducked in to do more-official documentation for every fresh bit of evidence. Word spreading about the murder, on the other hand, took minutes.

By the time Alan finally got a chance to step out for fresh air and swap out his camera battery, a news crew had given three separate breaking news updates. A middle-aged woman with a microphone was just finishing up a borderline bombastic account of the crime scene as he snapped nitrile gloves from his hands.

"Watch it around these people," Stockton croaked, eyes glaring at the camera crew. "Vultures. They show up whenever someone dies and they feast."

"Uh-huh," Alan said, his mind elsewhere.

The sun had fully set while they were inside. This would have given Blot freedom of movement, except that the crew had brought their own lights. Alan stepped into the shadow of the ambulance to spare them both from the glare.

"Why are they still here?" Blot asked. "What could they be waiting for that they haven't seen or said in the last few hours of watching us?"

Alan felt a tinge of shame for knowing the answer. "The money shot," he said, watching the EMTs enter with a gurney. "If you bring a camera to an event, you don't leave until you get the shot that wraps it all up. If it's a wedding, you'd better get the first kiss. If it's a birthday party, you'd better get them blowing out the candles. And if it's a murder, get a shot of the body."

Flashes flickered as the victim, cocooned in a black plastic bag and draped in white cloth for the purposes of sanitation and decency, was loaded into the ambulance.

"Speaking from experience?" Stockton asked, assuming the words were meant for him as he clicked through the camera roll.

"Only for the weddings and birthdays. This is my first murder," Alan said.

"And you didn't lose your lunch? You might actually last in this department."

"I'm saving it for later, sir," Alan said. "I prefer to be sick in private."

"I'd recommend getting it over with. Everyone loses it the first time. Heroes like you usually end up messing up the squad car."

Alan could hear the broadcast signing off. The lights of the camera clicked off, and the news machine, now well fueled for the next cycle, moved on. All the talk of being sick had Alan's stomach doing flips, and his mind was helpfully flashing through some of the highlights of the horror he'd just seen.

"If it's not one thing, it's another," Stockton muttered. "Who are these yahoos now?"

Alan was leaning on the wall of the motel just outside the police tape, so he didn't quite see to whom Stockton was referring. When they spoke however, there was no doubt.

"We are here from Headquarters," said a cool female voice.

"We need to speak to Mr. Fontaine," said an eerily similar male voice.

Alan turned to see three individuals dressed in white. The first two were in crisp white business suits. The third was dressed in white overalls. They were collectively who Alan had come to call the "white-suits," and they were the straw that broke the camel's back when it came to Alan being able to control his nausea.

"With the exception of Mr. Fontaine, would you all direct your attention elsewhere?" directed Dina, the woman in white. "We need a word in private."

"We are certain you all have more pressing business to conduct," Gabriel, her male counterpart, assured them.

Everyone within earshot, from the police to interested bystanders, simply obeyed the instructions. Their actions were smooth, natural, and absolutely not of their own free will. The remaining member of the trio,

Angel, stepped forward and helped the wavering young photographer stand straight.

"That looked unpleasant," Angel said. "Would you like a mint?"

"Get away from them," Blot said shakily. "Get away from them before they start playing with your head."

The shadow stretched as far from the newcomers as she could manage. Dina and Gabriel stepped up. The former glanced in distaste at the mess Alan had made.

"Really, Alan. You simply must demonstrate greater intestinal fortitude," she said.

"You were quite industrious and dedicated in your pursuit of this career," Gabriel added. "Now is no time to discover you do not have the stomach for it."

Alan spat and wiped his mouth. "I assume you're here because you came to the same conclusions I did."

"You are welcome to your own conclusions," Dina said.

"But if you believe this... little event is the only reason we've come, you betray a poverty of insight," Gabriel said.

"Let us step inside, away from prying eyes and ears," Dina suggested.

"It's a crime scene," Alan said.

Gabriel raised the police tape. Dina stepped through.

"You will recall, Alan, that our primary concern is to interfere in matters only when circumstances require," Dina said.

"We are quite capable of leaving things undisturbed," Gabriel said, ushering Alan under the tape and through the open door of the motel room.

In the minutes since he'd been inside, Alan's mind had already helpfully glossed over some of the more chilling details of the room as a defense mechanism. The smell hit him with a force that, if he'd not done so just seconds before, likely would have prompted another "outburst" from the unsteady young man. The removal of the dead body had done little to decrease the horror of the setting. And somehow, having the pristinely dressed outsiders on hand served only to underscore the gritty, rancid feel of the place. Their outfits seemed to bring their own light, actively resisting the darkness of the room and repelling the layer of grime that had existed long before the crime was committed. Blot crept up the far wall. Her white eyes gazed with raw distrust and animosity at the white-suits.

"I trust you are enjoying the handiwork of our dear," Dina grumbled under her breath, "*Angel* here."

"Our benevolent gifts. The ones that have kept you and your parents safe for these last six weeks," Gabriel said.

"Gifts? I was running errands for you to earn those wards. That's not a gift. That's gig work. Take it from a guy who's been doing it since college," Alan said.

"Oh, no. You are mistaken," Dina said.

"If they were payment, they would have been withheld if we were unsatisfied," Gabriel said.

Dina leaned toward Alan. "And we are *not* satisfied."

"I found out what was going on. And I *did* something about it," Alan said.

"No one asked you to do something about it," Dina said.

"If you had a fraction of the insight you *thought* you had, you would know that we very specifically wished for nothing to be done at all," Gabriel said.

"Yet what did you do?"

The matched set of white-clad individuals started alternating their points, counting them off from some unseen list.

"You involved yourself."

"Stuck your nose where it did not belong."

"You endangered lives."

"Produced chaos."

"Unleashed a *ritual* within a mundane setting."

"Took sweeping action against the shades."

"And produced a massive power imbalance."

Angel nodded and added, "And those are just the things you *know* you did."

"We try to make it a point to be direct."

"Verbosity, prevarication, and loquaciousness are hallmarks of deceit," Gabriel said.

"So we will be blunt. Something is wrong."

"And we blame you."

"Why? What's happening?" Alan asked.

"As you have likely been made aware, we considered you to be a curiosity, but one unworthy of our personal, ongoing attention," Dina said.

"A rare failing in our own insight, as it happens," Gabriel said.

"The key individual in the area..."

"Provided 'area' is broadly enough defined..."

"Is a shade by the name of Stigma."

Blot's eyes widened a bit. "They're never going to stop Stigma. Stigma is the best of us."

"We were watching him closely," Dina said.

"Following his actions," Gabriel said.

"But something unforeseen occurred."

"Almost certainly a ripple of your own ill-advised vigilantism."

"It has made tracking the local shades far more difficult."

"Bordering on impossible."

Dina crossed her arms. "That is a new and unacceptable development."

"One that is clearly, and demonstrably, your doing," Gabriel said.

"Maybe they just learned to hide. Maybe it just happened," Alan said.

"Natural changes are evolutionary," Dina said.

"Evolutionary changes are small," Gabriel explained.

"This is sweeping. This is revolutionary. Nature does not create revolutions."

"People unwilling to accept the natural order do."

"We actually know precisely the source of their new abilities. And it is absolutely your doing," Angel said. "Not on purpose, mind you. You played a role in another person's plan."

Alan narrowed his eyes. "Of course I did. Apparently, that's all I ever do these days."

"Well then, it should come as a comforting and familiar discovery that you shall now be playing a role in one of ours, yet again," Dina said.

"We are no longer able to reliably track Stigma and his ilk," Gabriel said.

"But we can quite easily track *you*."

"And as you have a shade of your own..."

"And we know that shades can track their own..."

"You may be able to supplement our surveillance."

Angel nodded. "At least long enough to find out how they're hiding so we can defeat it."

"So we have an assignment for you and your... partner."

Dina gestured vaguely toward Blot. She wasn't terribly accurate, but Blot shifted aside as though a gun were pointed at her regardless.

"You want me to find Stigma."

Both Dina and Gabriel laughed. It was a chilling, mirthless sound. Like a scientist delighted at the antics of a creature slated for vivisection.

"Heavens no, Alan," Dina said.

"Dun played you like a fiddle," Gabriel said.

"I hesitate to think what would happen if you were to end up anywhere near Stigma."

"Hey! I defeated Dun *twice*," Alan said defensively.

"That enduring misapprehension is evidence of its own inaccuracy," Dina said.

"What's that they were saying about being too wordy?" Blot said.

"Consider the fact that if you've had to defeat him twice, you didn't really defeat him the first time, did you?" Dina said.

"Miscalibrated victory conditions." Gabriel removed a pad and a silver pen from his pocket. "Back to the actual matter at hand. It should be clear that the mess made of this motel room was the work of a shade."

"Of course they blame us," Blot snapped. "That's projecting. I still think *they* did it."

"We were unaware of this shade's motion as well," Dina said.

"It is a reasonable assumption that this shade is among those who has learned this new trick," Gabriel said.

"As you have clawed your way into a law-enforcement-adjacent field, it seems apt to assign you the following task."

"As a test, you will find this killer."

"What you do with it is immaterial."

"Likewise for the host."

"All we require is that you determine the means being used to evade our gaze."

"If it proves useful in allowing us to follow the activities of Stigma once more, that will be considered sufficient to restore the balance."

"More specifically, it will be adequate to allow more skilled hands..."

"*Our* hands..."

"To restore the balance."

"You will be permitted to carry on as the aberration you are."

"Provided you cease your meddling."

"So you want me to find the killer," Alan began.

"An error in your first three words," Dina said.

"Not a good start," Gabriel said.

"We *require* you to find the killer."

"We *instruct* you to find the killer."

"Fine, fine. But aren't you forgetting something?"

"Unlikely," Gabriel said.

"What about the Shard of Shadow?" Alan asked.

"Would you shut up?" Blot hissed. "It's bad enough they can order you around, don't go reminding them of things they can take from us."

"Bah," Dina said.

"Keep it," Gabriel said.

Alan raised an eyebrow. "Really?"

"Someone like you or your shade with a single Shard of Shadow..." Dina began.

"One recently drained by a ritual..." Gabriel added.

"...is like an ape with a rifle."

Alan blinked. "Unpredictable and dangerous?"

"Yes. To the other apes," Gabriel clarified.

"The shard came from the Dawn. Now you have it. A lateral move," Dina said.

"It does not affect the balance."

"And so it is none of our concern."

"We've taken enough of your time," Dina said.

Gabriel handed Alan a note from his pad. "And more crucially, you have taken enough of *our* time."

"Time that would be better spent in pursuit of Stigma."

"Is he up to no good?" Alan said.

"We do not know what he is up to," Dina said.

"That was the entire thrust of the conversation," Gabriel said.

Dina looked to him. "My confidence in this individual continues to erode."

"But are there terrible things happening that are going unchecked? What's the urgency?" Alan asked.

"On the contrary. Things have gone quiet," Dina said.

"The goal is to restore surveillance before they get loud again," Gabriel said.

"You have your assignment."

He looked over the immaculate handwriting on the note. It simply restated "Find the killer" and "Uncover the means of concealment."

"Wait," Alan said. "Refresh my memory. What do I get for doing this?"

Dina and Gabriel both looked aghast.

"Really now, Mr. Fontaine," Dina said.

"You will earn redemption," Gabriel said.

"You will restore the status quo," Dina said.

"More importantly, you will avoid the consequences of failure."

"You will retain our protection."

"You will not earn further ire."

"That should be *more* than enough motivation."

"Fair enough," Alan said.

"Good. Then we are through."

The white-suited visitors marched back into the motel parking lot.

"You may resume your prior activities," Dina instructed them.

Attention gradually began to reaccumulate upon the crime scene. Angel lingered as the others marched away.

"They will be indisposed. You will, as before, be reporting to me," Angel said. "Please understand that it is crucial you treat this with all seriousness."

"Who exactly *are* you people to just show up and order people around?"

"Just regular humans like you, Alan."

"Humans don't have the power to compel obedience!"

"They don't have intelligent, autonomous shadows either," they said.

"Touché."

"Work quickly," Angel said, as the other police officers approached. "I hope to hear from you soon." Angel turned to the police. "And none of you will recall seeing me here."

With that, the mysterious overseer marched away, completely ignored by Jessie, the other police, and the entire forensic staff.

"I think we've done all we can do here, Alan. Let's get back to the station and fill out the reports." Jessie leaned forward and passed him a stick of gum. "You're going to need this."

"You've got newbie breath, kid," Stockton pointed out.

Alan nodded numbly and stuffed the gum in his mouth. Right now he had an awful lot to think about. No sense adding newbie breath to the list.

Whoever came up with the idea for the heap of paperwork at the end of the average police day deserved far more credit for their psychological expertise. Alan had seen the aftermath of a horrific crime. There were images that would probably haunt his dreams for years, and it was his first day. And yet by the time he was finished with the mind-numbing, soul-deadening tedium of reporting his findings, frustration had managed to dislodge horror as the prevailing state of mind. Thus, he climbed into his car drained rather than emotionally inflamed. That was good, because while it was the end of his in-station hours, he was still technically on call for another sixteen hours, and some pressing personal matters wouldn't have waited for him to shrug off the horror show.

"Stop at Vice Versa," Blot said.

"I don't know if they're open," Alan mumbled.

"It's Thursday. They're open late on Tuesdays and Thursdays because Lamar wanted to see if it was worth giving it a try to go twenty-four–seven, remember? It was when they were talking about doing that app delivery thing, too."

"... I don't remember any of this."

"Well, it's true. So go! If we give them enough business, maybe they'll decide to give it a shot and we won't have to worry about them ever closing."

Alan's inner skinflint told him to rebel, but the allure of well-prepared caffeine proved too strong for him. He made a turn and headed in that direction.

"If you know the business plans of our local coffee shop, it's possible we're becoming a little too dependent on it."

"Oh, you want to talk to me about being too dependent on things?" Blot said. "How about how you're being led around by your nose by a bunch of white-suited demons because we literally can't live without the protections that we *thought* we'd earned, but apparently they'd simply *loaned*."

"Demons?"

"If people can call shades demons, then shades can call those things demons."

"Yeah, but demons are creatures of darkness, and they're—"

"Which one of us is more likely to know something about demons, Alan, me or you?"

"You."

"Right, and I say they're demons. End of discussion. But *not* end of argument, because thanks to our dependence on them, I'm now put in a position to hunt down one of my own."

"So suddenly you're on board with the theory that the murderer is a shade?"

"*Of course the murderer is a shade!*" she said. "You've got to learn to tell the difference between legitimate disagreement and contrariness to defend my frequently indefensible kin."

"What kind of coffee are you getting? The usual?"

"No, I've got a new order. I want a large sixteen-shot Americano."

"Sixteen shots."

"Yeah."

"That's *pure* espresso."

"Right! Did you know they've been mixing water with it? If I wanted two ounces of coffee in my coffee, I'd order a two-ounce coffee!"

"You're not getting a sixteen-shot espresso. You're getting a double shot like normal."

"What does it matter to you?"

"Because *I'm* the one ordering, and I don't need the drive-through lady remembering me as the guy exceeding the recommended daily maximum for caffeine, Blot! That *can't* be healthy for you."

"... Quad shot."

"Fine."

"Good, so can we get back to the subject at hand? I'm not done being mad at you for it coming to this."

"Proceed."

"It's bad enough there's fifty-some-odd shades who are effectively helpless, clinging to the carcasses of prisoners rotting in jail who lost their abilities because of *my* actions. Now I'm supposed to head out there and hunt down one of my own who's managed to do something that, if we could do it, would have meant we wouldn't have needed the white-suits in the *first place*." She huffed an agitated breath.

"You still want that coffee black? I seem to remember you liking that sip you stole of Jessie's latte with the French vanilla creamer in it."

"Black! ... Maybe a *little* French vanilla. And quit avoiding the subject."

"I'm sorry, Blot," he said earnestly. "I never meant for anything like this to happen. We owe our lives to each other a dozen times over at this point."

"More like six for you and three for me."

"Fine, but we've kept each other alive, is what I'm saying. It's not right that you've been the most moral and most reasonable shade I've encountered by *far*, and all you've gotten for it is infamy and no-win situations. I'm sorry. I really, really am. But what choice do we have?"

Blot muttered, "No choice. Which is very irritating because I not six weeks ago decided to take my life into my own hands, or at least take *our* life into my own hands, and stop following my training—and now here I am, backed against a wall, forced to do what someone else wants me to do. Free will is a joke."

"It sort of is." He pulled into the drive-through.

"Welcome to Vice Versa. How may I serve you today?"

"I'd like a large double-shot Americano, black, and a large sixteen-shot Americano with a splash of French vanilla."

"Sixteen shots on the second one?"

"Yes."

"That's going to cost as much as eight regular espressos, you know."

"Oh, I know."

"Okay, pull ahead. It'll be a few minutes."

He nodded and pulled up. When he glanced in her direction, Blot's white eyes were fixed firmly upon him. Alan shrugged.

"Free will means you should at least get your coffee the way you want," he said.

A flicker of a smile twisted the white line of her mouth. "You make it very hard to stay mad at you sometimes, Alan."

"Don't underestimate me. After all, I *have* ended up in a job that'll mean loads more time with Jessie."

"Yeah..." Blot fumed. "At least she's armed. If you're going to have one of your own yapping your ear off all day, given how many people wouldn't mind seeing us dead, having that person have a gun and lots of training is the best I could hope for."

The window slid open and Alan handed over his credit card in exchange for a pair of coffees, one of which probably should have been classified as a controlled substance. He slipped Blot's coffee into the cup holder, as handing it to his shadow while a barista was watching probably would have raised questions. Once they were on their way again, Blot eagerly produced her brushed-aluminum thermos and popped the lid off.

"We need to decide what's next," she said, deftly transferring the piping-hot beverage from one container to the other.

"Ideally, we'd be working with the police for this. They're going to be investigating anyway."

"But they haven't got a chance to find the killer if it's a shade, so we can't just wait for them to do the job and swoop in at the last minute." Blot sipped her coffee and nearly purred. "Vanilla is good once in a while..."

"Actual investigations aren't my area. I'm not going to be able to just tag along. That's not how these things work."

"All you have to do is get close to the right places. I'll get what we need to know."

"You can't keep doing that, Blot. There are records. People are going to figure out something's up."

"Do you think they're going to blame your shadow?"

"No, but—"

"So you'll just need an alibi and we'll be golden."

"I don't want to rely on supernaturally defeating well-intentioned security measures."

"For as long as our task is a supernatural one, our tactics will be supernatural." She slurped her coffee. "Phew. This might be a little too much coffee all at once."

"Then take your time."

"Moderation is for the weak, Alan." She slurped again. "Can you get back into the police station so we can get back to this right away?"

"Uh, I think there's limits on how long I'm allowed to serve in the station as a contractor."

"Go back anyway. They'll just think you're a go-getter."

"I think I'd rather go home for now."

"The sooner we get back to this the sooner—"

"I saw the inside of a human being today," he snapped.

"Fine, fine. We'll avoid any potentially gruesome stuff for a while. But when's the next time you can get in the station properly?"

"Sunday morning. Until eight a.m. tomorrow, I'm still technically on call here, and then by nine a.m. I'm due at Cox Media for the photo pool."

Blot considered this. "So you put together a work schedule that technically runs from eight a.m. on Thursday to, what, six p.m. on Friday? With a one-hour gap?"

"Uh-huh."

"Excluding the assignment from mysterious demons to hunt down a metaphysical killer."

"Yep."

"What was your plan for sleep?"

"Hope no crimes are committed for the rest of the day."

His phone chimed. He glanced at the screen. It was Stockton. Blot held up her thermos.

"You might need this more than I do."

Chapter 2

T here were only two more calls during Alan's first shift with the force. Both were relatively innocuous crimes that probably wouldn't have called for his attention if he weren't in the midst of orientation. As a result, he was able to get six solid hours of sleep before showering, shaving, and hauling himself off to Cox Media.

The morning scrum was unusually light, less than a dozen photographers waiting for Cox to emerge with the precious pile of index cards assigning this spot or that to stake out. Even Cox's personal favorite, Marie-Anna, was notably absent.

Blot peered up from where the lights of the meeting room pinned her. "Not as popular as it used to be."

"Mm-hmm."

"I take it that doesn't bode well?"

"Mm-mmm."

"It's for the best. You had too many jobs anyway."

"The credit card company doesn't see it that way."

"What?" said a man beside him.

"Mmm? Nothing, sorry," Alan said.

"Fontaine! Office!" reverberated a perpetually irritated voice.

"At least Cox is still giving you the personal treatment," Blot remarked as his trot down the hallway started nudging her this way and that.

He stepped into the boss's office and took a seat. Normally, Blot would take this opportunity to dim the light and pillage Cox's stationary, but for once he was actually *in* the office when he'd summoned Alan, rather than having sent him there while dealing with the others.

From the looks of the red-faced media mogul, Mr. Cox had come to a similar conclusion about the current state of his business as Alan and Blot had. This trimmed his already unnervingly direct means of doing business far more so.

"I need big-ticket photos, Fontaine," he said, without so much as a hello.

"I'll certainly do my best to give you quality work."

"Like hell. The quality isn't the issue. Ansel Adams would be busing tables these days. No one cares if what they're looking at looks good. They care if what they're looking at makes them feel angry or superior."

"Okay..." Alan said. "I'm not sure why you're telling me this."

"Because you just had your first day in the police force. That place is an outrage factory. What've you got for me?"

"I can't share photos I took for the police. There's policies."

Cox waved his hands. "No one's asking you to do anything illegal. I am officially, on the record, instructing you *not* to do anything illegal. But what have you got for me?"

"Nothing."

"You don't get to keep taking pictures for me if you keep bringing me nothing, Fontaine."

"With all due respect, sir. I have delivered two massive exclusives for you already."

Cox pointed his hand vaguely to the scrum room. "You see all those people out there? You know why all these upstart internet outfits don't do that? Because it takes buckets of money to keep a bullpen like that stocked, when you can just wring out the local content creators for a fraction of the price. But I don't do my business that way. I run things the way I want to run things. Your exclusives gave us a few months in the black after a lot of months in the red." He leaned back and chewed a thumbnail with the same gusto as someone puffing on a cigar. "A man can get used to actually *making* money."

"Tell him about the serial killer. I bet he'll be very interested in the serial killer," Blot suggested.

"I can't tell you about the serial killer," Alan said.

"About time you brought that up!"

Cox flopped a newspaper onto the desk. It somehow seemed fitting that this man was one of the handful of people in the city who still read their news in print. Two obsolete business models shoring each other up. The headline read "The Metro Ghoul Back from the Dead?"

"This'll be all the people want to read, and see, until the next sexy or bloody thing to splash across the headlines. You're in on this, right?"

"I took photos of the crime scene, which I can't—"

"Right, fine, fine, but you're in the loop. Liable to know when and where developments are occurring."

"There's rules against this stuff. I can't just—"

Cox leaned back and spread his hands as though conjuring words into the air. "According to a trusted source within the police force, dot-dot-dot. There's a reason we have anonymous sources. Now I don't do reporting, but I work with people who do, and this sort of a thing is a great way to a firm partnership."

"I'm sorry, sir."

Cox grumbled. "Fine. With my luck we'd get nailed with a lawsuit on day one. On my budget, these things can only go as far as the first cease-and-desist."

He pulled open a drawer and started to sift through some handwritten index cards. Alan cast a meaningful glance down at Blot.

"Well?" she said. "I can't ask him for you."

"You make it seem like you've done this sort of thing before."

"Never with an informant. Windfalls like that don't come along that often."

"But you've pursued breaking stories from the outside?"

"What do you think private detectives are for?"

"They still exist?"

"If one person's got a check made out to cash, there will always be another person willing to do a job to claim it. Big bucks, though, you're asking someone to do an end run around the police. Which is why I am so keen on the confidential-source angle." He slapped an index card on the table. "There. That's your assignment."

Alan grabbed it.

"The same artsy-fartsy types who ran that film festival last year are looking to make Philadelphia the de facto off-off-off-Broadway place to see theater. Big renovation just finished up and they're showing off the repertory company they put together, or something like that. Head down, get some shots. Don't come back to me without a name."

"I didn't even realize you people still did stuff in theaters. I thought it was all the television and other big screens and stuff," Blot said.

"I think if you tack that many 'offs' onto the word Broadway, we're not going to have very many 'names' to choose from."

"Theater is where washed-up movie stars go to burn out. Good place to find bitter has-beens. Bitter has-beens are good for an embarrassing shot now and then."

"That's a bit of a long shot."

"Are you going to stick around here and keep pointing out the reasons why I need big money from your stuff, or are you going to get out there and do the nickel-and-dime jobs that we're stuck with?" Cox barked.

"Sorry, sir. I'll do my best."

Cox released a sound in reply that barely brushed the English language and set about sorting the remainder of his stack of index cards.

Four hours later, Alan slipped back into the driver's seat after feeding the parking meter for a second time. The official press event announcing the new cast wasn't due to happen for another few hours, but one of the tricks that Cox had passed on to all his photographers was to show up early, because the people they want to show off have to show *up*, and getting a glimpse of them on the way in is a good way to scoop the more official, and less unscrupulous, press representatives. Thus far the pseudo stakeout had not borne fruit, beyond giving Alan and Blot the opportunity to brainstorm a bit more.

"I really like this private detective idea," Blot said, doodling in a stolen pad.

The tinted windows made for a much more pleasant experience for her when they were stuck in the car for hours at a time. By Alan's count, she'd filled up easily twenty notebooks with steadily more intricate sketches and doodles.

"We can't afford to hire a private eye, and they wouldn't have any more luck at finding a shade than the police."

"No, no. Not *hiring* one. Becoming one. That might be even better than this forensic thing. Fewer rules. I'm much better at doing jobs that have fewer rules. If we can't be *spies*, which is still my favorite idea, then maybe we can be private detectives."

"I'll take it under advisement."

She flipped a page on her pad. "You sure know a lot of wishy-washy ways of saying no."

Alan raised his camera and snapped a picture.

"Anything good?" Blot asked, peeking her shadowy form up high enough to glance out the windshield.

"Trent Street. Used to be a big dramatic actor. Local boy. Makes sense he'd want in on something like this."

"Is he doing anything salacious or embarrassing?"

"He's signing autographs."

"Five dollars," she murmured.

"If that. Not worth getting out of the car for a better one."

It was slightly embarrassing how quickly Blot had mastered the fine art of estimating bounties on assorted types of photos. At this point she could more reliably guess how much a shot would sell for than he could.

He glanced aside at her pad. Blot had become less secretive about her doodles of late, no longer angling the page away from Alan whenever she felt his gaze shift. As such, he was keenly aware that what she was working on now was quite different from her usual fare. Far from the haunting and unearthly animals and landscapes she liked to sketch, this page was covered with carefully rendered runes. She traced them out in threes, scribbling out the last set each time she finished the next one.

"What are you doing?" he asked.

She glanced at him, then went back to the work. "Stigma's able to hide from those white-suits. Which means that if they can't already, everyone serving under him will eventually be able to. That means there's a way to do it."

"Do you think you can figure it out?"

She angrily scribbled out another set of runes. "I'm starting to think my whole education was to make sure I *couldn't*."

"What's supposed to happen?"

"The only thing I know for sure is that *something* is supposed to happen, and it isn't." She stabbed the page. "There are spells, rituals. They're high-level stuff, not intended for cannon fodder like me. We learn little fragments of them, mostly so we'll know properly formed spells when we see them. But I just don't know enough to *do* anything. It's like they taught me an alphabet without vowels. A language without verbs." She sketched out another few runes. "Do you remember the spell etched on the prison? The one that was enough for Angel to send us in to investigate? The one that confounded the *Dawn* too?"

"I remember that it existed."

"Well, I remember every swoop and swirl of every shape. It's my specialty, noticing and remembering things. But I can't get those runes to *do* anything. And now the others have got something even better, something so good that even the smarter, better white-suits are hoping we can crack them, because they can't. But I can't even get *these* to work. I'm going to end up as the only shade in this whole wave who can't hide from the white-suits. It's frustrating. It's frustrating that they didn't even warn me about the white-suits, and now I'm at the mercy of them while the whole rest of the wave isn't. And do you know what's *more* frustrating?"

"What?"

"I know exactly why they kept me dumb. *That* much they taught me. 'It is in the best interest of those in power to control and ration information. This makes the many more easily led by the few, as the many require information controlled by the few. The humans will do this, and so the humans sow their own weakness.' They went on and on about how it would make it that much easier for us to take over, because we'd only have to get a hold on a handful of people to control the rest. But I was too *stupid* to realize they were doing it to all of us too."

"Masterminds are clever like that. It's what makes them masterminds," Alan said.

"Yeah, well, I'm not going to sit here and take it. I'm not going to just accept that they didn't even teach me how to be *me* properly. I mean to find out more about my abilities, the things they never wanted me to know. I'm going to get *better*. And one way or another, I'm going to figure out how to keep the white-suits from spying on me. Mark my words."

There was a knock on the window.

"Let me guess," Blot rumbled.

Alan turned. On the other side of the tinted glass was the not entirely unexpected face of Angel. The androgynous individual in white overalls was beginning to feel like some sort of supernatural parole officer.

He rolled down the window.

"May we have a word, Alan?" they asked.

Alan looked to Blot.

"It's not like we have a choice in the matter," Blot said.

He popped the power lock. "Back seat," he said.

"Not the passenger seat? I... Oh, yes. Your shade. My apologies." Angel opened the back door of the car and carefully shifted some of the camera gear aside before taking a seat. "Would you consider moving to a more secluded location?"

"I'm on the job," Alan said. "Such as it is."

"Move the car, please."

The engine had started almost before Angel had finished speaking.

The car puttered to a stop in a more secluded place. It was an alleyway a bit closer to the theater, but around the corner from it. As such, it offered no good view of the place. The shadows cast by the buildings *did* make for a very Blot-friendly parking spot, however.

"Thank you, Alan," Angel said.

"How could I refuse such a polite request?" he said.

"Keep them talking. I'm going to see if they have anything worth stealing," Blot said, subtly slipping between the seats.

"I want you to know that I do not enjoy compelling your behavior in that way."

"Well you could have fooled me," Alan said. "You do it an awful lot."

"It is simply because these matters *require* your action."

Blot was curling her malleable shadow form around where Angel sat, inspecting them from all angles. Her fluid motions and gingerly avoidance of any direct contact put one in mind of a particularly cautious house cat inspecting a new visitor.

"I don't feel any protection wards, but then I don't usually feel them until after I do something," Blot reported.

"I need to inform you, first, that you need to tread lightly," Angel said. "You are clearly aware that you are being watched, but you do not always choose your words with the care of someone who is in danger of offending those watching you."

"Are we still pretending that you're a perfectly normal human, or are we going to admit you have unexplained powers?" Alan asked.

"Heavens no. I am a standard, everyday, run-of-the-mill human." Angel fetched a notebook from their pocket and flipped through it.

"Oooh, I want that book so bad..." Blot said, curling her fingers toward the book but giving it the same careful space as one toying with a live wire.

"Any words or phrases that indicate otherwise are either misinterpreted by you or the listener, or intended in jest," Angel said.

"Great. Just wanted to be clear that all this 'you are always being watched by all of us' talk is hypothetical."

"Well, even hypothetically, you wouldn't *always* be observed by *all* of us. Focus is by definition limited in scope. The best evidence of this is the fact that you are currently dealing with me rather than Dina and Gabriel. They would be less inclined to treat the situation with civility and leeway."

"But they're too busy failing to find Stigma," Alan said.

"I like that you're getting some edge to your words with these people," Blot said. "It's about time."

"Correct," Angel said. "They are having trouble remaining fully apprised of his activity. Shades, however, must have hosts. Hosts are conventional beings and thus are capable of being tracked by conventional means. A shade's abilities may complicate that, but cannot erase it. Thus, they are focused and dedicated, and not *wholly* ignorant of his motion and action. But they will look back to you from time to time, and it would be best if you were visibly cooperating and contributing at those times."

"Or else?" Alan asked.

"I invite you to fill in the consequences with your imagination. Or better yet, take steps to avoid having to even consider them."

"Are you here just to put the fear of god into me?"

"I do not believe supreme beings were a part of the conversation, nor should you muddy the waters by including them."

"I think you know what I meant," Alan said.

"Terrible deception skills. Pathetic," Blot said.

"I simply wish to avoid confusion," Angel stated. "And as for why I'm here, it is to impress upon you that you *must* take this seriously. A terrible disease can be treated painlessly if it is treated early. If things are allowed to fester unseen, just below the surface, for too long, treatment can become more traumatic. More destructive. Those dedicated to treating infections will do what needs to be done to restore health and order to a patient. It is in the best interest of the patient to do whatever is needed to ensure the treatment comes quickly, when it is the most minor."

"It seems to me you could save a lot of time if you'd stop speaking exclusively in analogies."

Angel tipped their head to the side. "I know you are under a great deal of pressure, Alan, but I'm concerned that this situation has negatively affected your attitude."

"Oh, it has. It definitely has."

"As long as they're being evasive, I've got a question for them," Blot said. She held out a shadowy hand and bobbed it slightly, dropping the silver locket down into reality.

"Oh my heavens," Angel blurted, leaning away from the bit of jewelry dangling in midair. "A word of warning would not be out of place."

Blot shut her eyes and drew her mind to the task of more properly joining the conversation. Her arm looped up into full, inky depth, followed by her shoulder and head. When she was leaning out of the seat as though it were merely a beaded curtain to a hidden room, she spoke. "What are these symbols on the locket?" Blot asked, holding it toward Angel.

The mysterious overseer leaned not so subtly away from the locket as it was presented. "Decoration," Angel said, eyes squinted as though a light was being shone into them. "The silver itself has been treated. The rest is decoration."

"You don't seem to like it."

"I don't." Angel gently nudged the locket away with the back of their hand.

"What's so scary? You made it," Blot said, swinging it toward Angel.

"I am not overly fond of Shards of Shadow," they said, leaning back into the seat.

"Cut it out, Blot."

"But there's nothing to *worry* about," Blot taunted. "It's wrapped up in a locket. Perfectly safe. See?"

She thrust it forward. Angel slapped Blot's hand with the pad. A static flash filled the car, and Blot squealed in discomfort. She snapped back into the shadows and took the locket with her.

"Kick them out of the car!" Blot said between shaking and blowing on her hand.

"You sort of had that coming," Alan said.

"So? It's still a reason to kick them out."

Alan turned to Angel. "Sorry about that. She's feeling extra rebellious today."

Blot crossed her arms. "What's the point of baiting someone into an assault if you're not going to take advantage?"

"This little intervention is not going as well as I'd hoped. I fear the consequences I've been forced to imply may have soured our relationship somewhat." Angel put the pad away. "But regardless of your feelings about me, please consider what I've said. You need to act with haste."

"Look, we're doing everything we can."

"I appreciate that you haven't done nothing, but you are most certainly not doing *everything*. You have spent the day sitting in this car. That time could have been spent searching."

"Unfortunately, I live in the real world, where if I don't earn money, things like investigation become kind of difficult, what with the homeless-ness."

Angel nodded. "Yes... Yes, financial concerns *would* apply additional pressure. You are hoping for a notable photographic opportunity, correct?"

"Yeah, and we're not going to get one here."

"One moment." Angel opened the door and stepped out of the car.

"Wait. Wait, what are you going to do?" Alan asked, jumping out of the car as well.

"Bring your camera," Angel said.

Blot, still shaking her hand, grinned. "Okay. Now I'm intrigued."

Alan rushed from the car, camera in hand. Angel strode confidently into the open and made their way toward the theater.

"Hey!" Alan said. "Seriously what are you going to—"

"Video or photograph?" Angel interrupted.

"Video, exclusive!" Blot urged.

"I don't want Angel doing something drastic just for an exclusive video."

"Exclusive video. Just one moment." Angel addressed the small crowd still lingering around Trent Street as he finished up an autograph session. "Mr. Street, follow me please. The rest of you, ignore this!" Angel led the way into the nearest alleyway, with Trent Street, Alan, and Blot in tow.

Trent had the classic look of an aging actor. Once immaculate black hair now had a peppering of gray around the temples. His physique had slid into "dad bod" territory, but his taste in clothes made up for it.

"Right, right, no, I'll talk to *you* later. Stay classy," he called over his shoulder, Angel's supernatural compulsion not quite enough to fully overcome a lifetime of schmoozing. When he turned back, he said, "I have no idea who that was. Seemed familiar. You gotta make everyone feel special, though. That's always been my policy." He clapped his hands.

"So! Are you from the PR firm? They said they were sending someone for glamor shots and an interview."

"No. I am sure they will be along shortly," Angel said.

"So what's this about then?" Street said.

He was clearly quite accustomed to being "handled" by a contingent of managers and concierges, so the simple command to join someone in an alley had a longer-lasting effect than most.

"Mr. Fontaine here would very much like a one-of-a-kind, viral-worthy video," Angel said.

"It really isn't necessary," Alan assured them.

"No, no. I am dedicated to maintaining and restoring balance, and our task is putting you at a financial deficit. I insist I act to restore it. Mr. Street, if you would be so kind, perform an age-inappropriate song, in its entirety, complete with some manner of choreography."

The actor's expression wavered a bit. To his minor shame, Alan didn't hesitate to raise his camera and get Mr. Street properly framed. Somewhat mechanically, he removed his jacket and tossed it to Angel.

"This is 'Oops!... I Did It Again,' by Britney Spears." He clapped. "Here we go."

The actor launched into a spirited rendition of a song and dance intended for a woman a fraction of his age. Alan ensured the camera was capturing the moment.

"Okay. Maybe Angel isn't so bad after all," Blot said with a grin.

Alan got back to his apartment and flopped onto the couch. He had rightly suspected that any further time spent on the assignment would be wasted, as what was destined to be called "Trent's Diva Turn" was going to be worth more than the next ten assignments combined. The amount of shameless glee evident in Cox's expression when Alan dropped off the footage was enough to make Alan a little uneasy. Some faces just weren't meant to show joy. But he had a check, and he had mental permission to skip the next few assignment meetings. For better or worse, he had the time to focus on the assignment.

"Hey, do you think that whole 'incredibly persuasive' thing the white-suits do is just them, or is it a trick they learn?"

"I don't know," Alan said wearily. "I just wish I knew why they didn't use it to solve their own problems instead of making them *my* problems."

"It'd be a *really* useful thing for a shade to learn. Basically, you people would just be puppets for us at that point."

He gave her a look. "Try not to sound so enthusiastic about the idea of stripping away my humanity and using me as a human-shaped suit to do your bidding."

"Oh, I didn't mean for you," Blot said, stretching into the kitchen to fiddle with the coffee pot. "I mean someone less pliable and obliging."

"That's me. Pliable."

"Hey, don't act like having those powers wouldn't make your life easier too. If you could just ask a reality TV star to kick an influencer in the knee a few times a year, you'd be able to spend all your time taking photos that are actually beautiful."

He rubbed his eyes. "It *would* take the pressure off." Alan shook himself, mostly to dislodge the unacceptable idea of exploiting dark powers for financial gain. "Come on," he said. "Let's start really planning out what we're going to do about the Ghoul. If we waste too much time, Angel is going to come knocking again."

They both paused for a moment. When no knock came, Blot chimed in.

"We should probably start with those photos you took. The whole idea is that they might have clues, right?"

"The whole idea is that they *definitely* have clues."

"Right, so we should get them and start looking over them. I remember a lot about the crime scene, but I don't remember *everything*."

"Let's start with what you remember, then."

"If I had anything useful to say, I'd say it. I didn't figure anything out that we both don't already know."

"Then just shout it out. We'll list the important stuff. Maybe one of us noticed something the other didn't. Maybe my questions will help you figure out something you didn't realize was important."

"Worth a shot, I guess... So, what was there? The lights were broken. The wiring was cut."

"There was foil on the windows," Alan added as he pulled out his laptop.

"All things that would help a shade," Blot said.

"What about the stabbing?" Alan shuddered.

"What *about* the stabbing?" Blot asked over the sound of percolating coffee.

"Is there anything particularly shade-like about that?"

"No. It's just an effective way to kill someone." She paused. "Come to think of it, that's a particularly *unshady* thing to do."

She slid back into the room and gradually shifted into her seldom used but still quite intimidating combat form. Even without hefting out into reality, her twisted features and vicious talons conjured images of past battles Alan had been a part of.

"We don't need knives and glass to do our stabbing," she said.

Alan tried not to look directly at her as she glided along the walls. It was almost comical, seeing this demonic form arching up onto the wall and ceiling, yet slouched down and cupping her chin like Holmes considering a clue.

"There were plenty of knives on the floor."

"Plenty," Alan repeated.

"And they were certainly used."

"No doubt," he said, eyes shut.

"Why would *that* be?"

"Maybe this is a shade that can't do the combat form?"

She shook her head and snapped back to her impish shape. "It's instinctive. Half of the wild animals can do it if threatened. Some of us are better at it than others, but a *baby* can do it to some extent. Maybe it was an attempt to keep people from suspecting it was a shade?"

"But people don't know about shades. You may as well try to avoid having someone suspect it was a vampire. Even if someone worked really hard to make it look like a vampire did a crime, people would assume it was a human pretending to be a vampire. We are quite incredulous as a species."

"Not from what I've seen of the internet."

Alan nodded and rolled his eyes. "With the exception of the in-evitable group of people that will always believe what they want to be true, we're pretty good at ruling out things that we don't think are possible."

"What about the Dawn? The Dawn knows about us. A murderous shade would certainly take pains to avoid doing something shady if they thought it would get the Dawn after them." She snapped her fingers. "Maybe this isn't a shade. Maybe this is someone who wants someone to *think* it's a shade."

"That doesn't explain how they got out of a room that was latched and barricaded from the inside."

"What's more likely? That a shade did something that would get a secret society of shade killers on their trail, or that a human figured out how to escape a locked room?"

Alan covered his eyes again. "It really bothers me that I now live in a world where both of those are equally likely." He pulled out his phone. "The Dawn..." he muttered, thumbing through his contacts.

"Wait, you're not going to *call* them, are you?" she said.

"We're most likely tracking a killer shade. That's their entire purpose. For all we know, those amulets they use to track us will still work on the shade we're after."

"I don't like you working with the Dawn, Alan."

"It turned out pretty well last time," he said.

"You almost died and so did a couple dozen shades and the humans hosting them."

"But they didn't die." He tapped a contact and held the phone to his ear. "Almost dying but not dying has basically become my new definition of success."

After a few rings, a wizened voice answered. "You..."

"Hello. Listen, I don't know if you've been watching the news, but—"

"The Metro Ghoul. I know."

"We've been given a very good reason to try to track it down, and we thought—"

"Listen, Fontaine. We've got problems of our own right now."

"Bigger than a serial killer on the loose?"

"They will be, if we don't take care of it. We've had break-ins, thefts. Someone's digging through our organization. I'd suspect you, but most of the attacks have hit things you didn't know about. I think we've got a leak, and until we plug it, the Dawn is locked down and on high alert."

"But this could really—"

"Goodbye, Fontaine." He hung up.

"How did that go?" Blot said.

"They're dealing with their own stuff, apparently."

"I can't say I'm sorry to hear it."

"People can always find the time to threaten us and give us assignments, but when the time comes to help, the best we can hope for is someone with plans of their own."

Blot slid back out into the kitchen. Glasses clinked and coffee poured. "Are you hungry?" she said.

"Not terribly."

"Better question, do you have room inside you for food?"

"Why are you asking me this?"

"Because we've got a whole afternoon where all we're going to be doing is speculating, and Jessie is at work so she's not going to be coming over, so I want to try that pie recipe we watched them screw up last night."

Alan tried to find the words necessary to correctly encapsulate the absurdity of idly honing one's baking skills while attempting to figure out the identity of a killer on the loose. When he realized it wasn't even in the top five most absurd things about his week, he shook his head and hauled himself to his feet.

"Fine, I'll set up in the kitchen so it'll be easier for you to reach."

"Yeah, but we only *think* that. We don't *know* that," Blot said, pulling open the oven. "As far as we know, no one searched the surrounding rooms."

Time enough to prepare some handmade pie dough didn't see them through to any breakthroughs. Even the thirty-five to forty minutes at 400 degrees Fahrenheit, long enough to make a pie, was not long enough to untie the knots a serial killer could tie. Truth be told, they'd probably run themselves in more circles than they'd thought themselves out of.

"That's true."

"We could go back to the crime scene. There might be some clues we could find."

"By now they'll have started the cleanup."

"Still. You never know what we'll find."

He nodded. "It's not the worst suggestion. I really, *really* don't like the suggestion, but it's not the worst suggestion."

"Maybe we'll find a secret hatch and learn it wasn't even a shade that did it."

"I've got to believe the white-suits wouldn't have put us on the case if they didn't *know* it was a shade. We shouldn't have to prove it's a shade."

"I wouldn't put it past them to make fools out of us just for the fun of it." Blot reached into the oven and clutched the pie dish by the shadow. It drifted out, filling the kitchenette with an odd, bitter scent.

"Don't you need oven mitts for that?" Alan asked.

"I'm holding it by the shadow. There's no such thing as a hot shadow," she said. "We've got to let this sit for a while before we cut it. And then you have to tell me if it was a good bake." She set it down on a trivet and slid to the wall behind him to gaze over his shoulder. "What have we come up with?" she asked.

He brought up the notes. "According to everything I could find online, this is a picture-perfect imitation of the last Metro Ghoul attack, which was in the early nineties. The last time, there was some confusion over puncture wounds that were 'inconsistent with weapons found at the scene.'"

"Because they were probably talons," Blot said. "We're going to want to know if that happened this time."

"Right."

"Which means we'll want the pictures."

"They'd be useful."

"So let's go get them."

"They're property of the police department."

"Yes, so let's go get them."

"We aren't allowed to."

"I know that. So let's go get them."

"We're not going to break in to the police station to steal evidence."

"Of course not. We don't have to break in, you've got the key. And even if you didn't, you're supposed to be there every few days. And we won't *steal* evidence. We'll copy it. They'll never know."

"It's not like the evidence will just be lying around."

"You want to bet we'll be able to get to it?" She waggled her fingers. "I've been getting pretty good with keyboards, and I've memorized at least seven different names and passwords since we've been going to the precinct. If there's one thing I've learned about the world you people have put together, it's that all you need to get whatever you want is the right computer, the right password, and a few minutes with no one watching you."

"That's true, but we're not going to do that, because if we screw up doing that, we go to jail. And need I remind you, the prison is filled to the brim with people who really, *really* don't like us."

"The jail is also full of bars, which aren't terribly good at keeping a healthy shade and her host locked up."

He gave her a hard look. "Are we really going to go down this road again?"

"Fine, fine. What do you suggest?"

"I suggest we talk to the people actually doing the investigation. We're due back to at least sign in on Sunday. We head to the precinct. We see if we can get additional information out of them. We find out how they're going to go about things, what they might know about the last time the Metro Ghoul struck that might not have been in the papers... Basically we just listen and ask questions and learn, and whatever we learn, we act on."

Blot nodded. "Sounds good."

Alan looked at her suspiciously. "That's it? No more arguing?"

"No need. Both of our plans require us to go back to the police station. In fact, both of our plans require us to go to the very person who we'd have to copy the evidence from. So while you're doing one, I can do the other."

Again, Alan tried to find the words to properly articulate why that was wrong and why they shouldn't do it. The reasonable, balanced argument eventually found its way to his lips as, "I guess I can't really stop you."

"See? That's what I call a perfect compromise."

He slumped a bit. "Just do me a favor and do it while I'm talking to someone who can testify I was talking to them at the time."

"Of course! What do I look like, an amateur?"

She slid a knife from the block beside the stove and deftly sliced the pie. He was treated to the bizarre view of a gleaming blade dancing about in the air, a plate sliding from the cabinet, silverware popping from the drawer, and finally the steaming slice of pie being served. It was all in perfect choreography with the shadow cast on the wall, but in its absence, it looked like a culinary poltergeist had taken over his kitchen.

"Well?"

"You're not having any?"

She waved her hand. "Solid food is more trouble than it's worth."

In what was becoming an unpleasantly common occurrence, any of the very reasonable observations he might have made about the idea of sampling recipes amid a murder investigation were discarded in favor of just giving in to the moment. He cut the pie with the fork and blew on it.

"What kind of pie is this?"

"Improvisational."

"Oh, that bodes well."

He sampled the pie. For a moment, Blot's face looked uncharacteristically fragile. She played with her fingers and shifted about as if pacing.

"Well?"

"Um..." He swallowed and stirred some crumbs on his plate with a fork. "Are these coffee grounds?"

"Uh-huh!" Her eyes gleamed with pride. "What do you think?"

He coughed a bit. "That's... um... novel."

"Okay, okay." She nodded slowly, internalizing the critique. "But how is it?"

He wiped a tear from his eye. "... Challenging."

"Good bake or bad bake, Alan?"

A lifetime of training from a mother who staunchly believed in saying something nice or nothing at all served him well. "The crust is perfect."

She clapped. "Great! Maybe once we catch this Ghoul, we can look into finding a place with a real kitchen and I can try some bigger stuff."

Alan hurriedly poured himself a glass of milk. When he'd downed enough of it to mitigate the intensity of Blot's little experiment, he took a breath. "Baby steps, Blot."

"My grandmother taught me a lot more savory dishes than pastries. But you don't have any of the same ingredients here."

"I don't understand. If your grandmother did so much cooking, why don't you eat here?"

"Back home, having a body was the default, and bodies need to be fed. Around here, coffee is plenty to fuel whatever physicality I need. So, do you want to finish your pie? Or should we return to the scene of the crime now?"

Alan weighed the two options. It didn't take long to find the one he preferred.

"I'll get my keys."

The motel, despite having recently become the scene of the latest gruesome addition to a pattern of murders stretching back more than a century, didn't look any less scummy now than it likely had the week before. The police tape was gone. In place of it was a sheet of hastily trimmed plywood festooned with warnings of men at work in a number of different languages. Alan could swear he could still smell the blood in the air, though it was entirely possible that was just psychological aftershocks from his last visit.

Alan fiddled with his camera, flicking back and forth between two roughly equivalent settings to give his fingers something to do.

"You're looking a little tense," Blot said as Alan stepped into the light of the setting sun and cast her across the ground.

"Yeah."

"This probably won't be your last murder scene, if you're going to be doing this forensic job. You're going to have to toughen up."

"Whether it is or isn't my last, it is still my *first*. Give me some time to build up an emotional callus, would you?"

He took a deep breath. If there *was* still the scent of blood, it was hidden three or four layers deep in the far more generalized funk of a decrepit and disreputable motel parking lot.

"I really should have argued harder against this," Alan said. "You're eroding my good sense."

"I'm distilling your good sense," she said. "Boiling away the bits that are just useless filler. Now, open those eyes. We're looking for something useful."

He scanned the parking lot. "We're not looking for anything a human would do. The police have more experience than us in that stuff. They'll have covered those bases. We're looking for shade stuff."

"Right. It's a few hours earlier than the crime was committed, so the sun would be about... there... I'd want to be right there."

She didn't have to fight the sunlight much to point in the proper direction. Not surprisingly, it was the alley east of the motel, and thus the very direction all the shadows were already pointing. He marched into the cool darkness of the alley, which brought a brand new level of stench to the kaleidoscope of aromas in this place. Blot gratefully pulled herself off the ground and slid along the wall.

"Oh, yes. This is much better," she said.

She ran her fingers along the cinder block of the wall. It was tricky, but Alan had learned the difference between simply moving and actually interacting. There was something in how deliberate her motions were. Though she was still just a silhouette on the wall, her fingers were kissing physicality, as though she were feeling the surface of the wall from the other side.

"He spent a lot of time here."

"He?"

She nodded. "Definitely. There's a residue. An echo. It's like he left a bit of his... I don't know, flavor? You don't have the sense I'm relying on here." She shut her eyes. "I can practically see him. This doesn't happen by accident, either. It's like marking your territory. This wasn't a heat-of-the-moment thing." She slid down to the ground and slid her palms across it. "This was days. Maybe longer. This was his home for a time."

"But he has a host," Alan said. "So it'd have to be the kind of person who would not only be willing to linger in the alley behind a motel, but that no one would question if they lingered in the alley behind a motel."

"No shortage of people like that, I'd wager."

"Drug dealers," Alan mused. "Prostitutes... Those are the only two that spring to mind."

"Back up against that wall. On the far side," Blot said.

He did as she asked. She used the extra slack to slide up along the wall until she just teased the shadow line of the roof. Her eyes squinted at the roof of the buildings across the street.

"A few more hours..." She snapped back down to him. "Is there any way up to the roof?" she asked.

"Uh... I don't think so. It's a one-story building. It's not like they'd need a fire escape. Why?"

"Because that'd make it a great place to hide if you needed to. You people never seem to look up, particularly when there's no way for someone like you to *get* up. The corner of the roof is already in the shade of that building across the way. Come on."

Alan glanced to the front of the alleyway. The fear of being seen came and went fairly quickly. The whole point of this little maneuver would have been that no one would have seen the killer do it, so there was little fear that anyone would spot him. But he still wasn't overly fond of the method he knew Blot had in mind. Still, there was a certain logic to it. He knew for sure no one had checked the roof while they were here last time.

"Make it fast, and be subtle. Someone in one of these buildings might see."

"I excel at subtlety," Blot said.

He stepped up to the motel wall and placed his back against it.

"Deep breath," she said.

Alan shut his eyes and held his breath. Fascinating as the view was whenever she did this, he didn't feel like giving his spatial reasoning skills a bracing dip into the surreal at the moment. Delicate arms pulled into a gentle embrace around his chest. Blot pulled him tighter against the wall, then smoothly past its surface. A short sensation of bizarre coldness and motion scrambled his mind for a bit, then he abruptly emerged onto the rough, still-warm rooftop.

He opened his eyes and climbed to his feet. "It still screws with my head every time you do that. A shadow pulling the thing that's casting it into the shadows along with it."

"It doesn't have to make sense. It works by the rules of my world, not yours."

The roof was what Alan liked to call a mini-mall-style roof. The facade of the motel reached up about two feet higher on the front of the building than the sides or back, and the roof itself was flat and black. The stretch he was on now was fairly clean, but much of the roof was goopy tar paper. Blot had dumped him far enough from the edge for him to be in no danger of falling, but he took another light step or two for good measure, taking care not to leave the clean patch of roof.

"Aren't you going to go any farther?"

"We don't know what, if any, evidence is up here. We do our searching from here until we're sure there's nothing we're going to foul by stepping on it."

He crouched down and raised his camera. The extreme angle at which he was viewing the roof wasn't ideal for seeing minor details at a distance, but just because he wasn't on the clock for the police didn't mean he didn't have to follow their policies.

On the other hand, Blot could quite easily take a much closer look without any fear of fouling physical evidence. She stretched along the darkened slice of roof as far as she could, which was quite far indeed.

"Can you get a shot of the roof over there?" she said, pointing a dark finger toward a patch still lit by the sun.

He zoomed in and swept slowly. There was an odd shape in a tarry puddle. It was roughly half-moon shaped, with a second, shallower, spade-shaped depression in front of it.

"What *is* that..."

He snapped a picture, then scrutinized the view through the camera as he slowly swept the surrounding area. Three more matching pairs of marks trailed away, toward the back edge of the roof. It wasn't until he'd seen them all in a row that it dawned upon him what they were.

"That's a high-heeled footprint," Alan said.

He swept forward and found another pair of footprints, and beside them, a very recent bit of tackiness on the roof. The tar had formed little shiny peaks, like something had been stuck to the puddle and was pulled away. It was beside a small, swirling vent.

"Can you get a little closer?" she said. "I can't quite get to the vent. I think I see the end of something behind it."

He scanned the roof. At this point he knew there was evidence up here, and he was in very real danger of contaminating it. A thin strip of roof—closer to the edge than he would have liked—was clean and free of tar. If he edged along that, he could probably get close enough to get a better angle without leaving any evidence of his own. He gritted his teeth and inched as close as he was willing to dare to the edge of the roof.

"What's taking you so long?"

"I'm on a roof, Blot," he grumbled.

"So? You didn't seem like you were afraid of heights the *last* time you were on a roof."

"Yeah, and I fell off the roof the last time I was on it. That has a way of hammering home the consequences of a misstep."

"You and I have very different definitions of 'fall.' As I recall, you jumped. And by the way, you survived."

"Not pressing my luck."

He made his way just close enough to see what Blot had spotted, which meant that Blot was able to get a fairly close look at it.

"Is that what I think it is?" he asked.

"Do you think it's a bloody hotel towel?" she asked. "Because that's what it is."

He snapped a picture.

"Let me see if there's something under it."

"No! Don't touch it. This is for the police to deal with."

"Fine, fine."

"Get over here and get me down," he said. "We're calling the cops before it rains and washes this stuff away." His phone was already in hand.

"Wait!" she said.

"What?"

"Aren't you forgetting something?"

"... No?"

"If you are ever doing something questionable, ensure you have the proper lie," she recited like a nursery rhyme. "How did you spot that piece of evidence?"

He considered it for a moment. "I guess I can't just say intuition."

She shook her head and gave a sigh just this side of condescension.

"Why don't you let me handle this one, hmm?" Blot said. "It's very simple. You just have to convince people it was thanks to something they would never question. You're that weird photographer. It just has to be a weird photographer thing. Let's say you... You wanted a record of all of your major crime scenes for posterity, so you got permission to get a rooftop photograph of the *whole* scene from the superintendent of that building across the way. And you spotted the evidence when you zoomed in."

Alan squinted at the rooftop.

"Do you think people will buy that?" he asked.

"Let me answer that question with this one. Are you looking at that building and thinking about what a nice photo you could get from the roof right now?"

"... Sort of."

"Then they'll believe it."

Alan sighed and pulled out his phone to see if he could find the info for the building staff. "I'm starting to worry you know me too well."

"You're not exactly a riddle, Alan. Now let's go get that photo, just to make our story nice and solid."

CHAPTER 3

On Sunday morning, Alan made sure to arrive at the station bright and early. He had no idea how much of his time would be spent on the road, responding to calls for forensic photography, so he needed every moment of access to the station in order to continue his research.

"Now remember," Blot instructed him. "If you ask a question and someone has to log in to a computer to get the information, make sure I can see the keyboard when they do it. Not the screen, the keyboard. Because screens do that thing where they just put dots."

"Yeah, it's not going to be that easy. Overhead lights, so you're going to be on the floor. I'd have to get really close, and then they'd be worried that *I* could see."

"Then get them to turn off the lights."

"How am I supposed to do that?"

"I can't do *everything*, Alan."

He pushed open the main door and stepped inside. Eight in the morning was fairly early for most businesses, but a police station was more or less an all-day affair, so the place was thoroughly staffed up. Alan felt a flutter of disappointment that Jessie wasn't there to greet him as she had been on his first day. Evidently the one-day-on, two-days-off nature of his schedule meant he had weird overlaps with other shifts when they occurred on a weekend. Jessie's schedule didn't perfectly line up with his.

He didn't recognize a single face in the station, and until Jessie showed up in a few hours, there was no one to introduce him. This meant that not a single face in the station recognized *him*. He had to flash his badge six times and bleep it twice before he actually reached the equipment room to officially sign in on the call sheet, sign out his equipment, and start his shift.

As luck would have it, his timing was excellent. The one decent spot to fill out the equipment form was already occupied by a bleary-eyed uniformed officer finishing up his own shift with the equipment.

"Hello, er," Alan leaned forward to check the badge, "Officer Ford."

"Hey," the older man said mechanically.

"You were in the assessment with Stockton, weren't you?" Alan said.

Officer Ford took his eyes away from the paperwork long enough to actually process Alan's presence. "That's right. You're the contractor, huh?"

"That's right."

The officer turned back to the sheet. "I hear you had a rough one yesterday. Had to do shots of the Ghoul's handiwork."

"Yeah..."

"Did you puke?"

"Yes."

"Good to get it out of the way."

"So they tell me."

The officer finished the paperwork and slid it toward Alan. "Well, if you are going to use the same rig, you'll need to restock on markers and swap for a fresh battery. I'm not a pro on the camerawork, so I ended up basically killing it with all the tries it took to get good shots."

"Right. Good. Will do."

Ford started to walk away, but Alan stopped him.

"Hey, listen, I'm new here. Do you know the name of the detective who's working that case?"

"That'll be Detective Barnes. Homicide's up on six."

"Is he on duty?"

"Beats me. What's it matter? We report to Stockton with this stuff. Different department."

"Yeah, but I'm new here. I'm sort of interested to see what'll happen with my pictures."

The officer gave him a suspicious, sideways glance. "You're not a buff, are you?"

"A buff?"

"Look, if you got this job because you're one of those people who is 'into' murder investigations, that's not going to fly."

He waved his hands. "No, no. I just want to see how my pictures get put to work. Maybe see what I could do to improve."

Ford shrugged and handed over the pen. "You're on the clock. Just so long as it doesn't cut into any of your calls or take too much of their time, go nuts."

A few minutes later, Alan found his way to the Homicide Department. Unlike the lobby, this place wasn't quite as staffed up. It had the same layout as most of the departments he'd seen so far, in that a handful of the higher-ranking officers were in offices around the edge, but most simply had desks. Barnes, it turned out, was at the one in the far corner, nearest to the east windows of the building. He was clacking away at a much-abused keyboard and sipping coffee from a stained mug.

"Excuse me?" Alan said, stepping up to him.

Barnes looked up. Now that he could see his face, Alan remembered him from the crime scene. He wasn't the actor Alan would have cast as a detective. Though he was probably in his forties, he had one of those faces that likely still got him carded at bars. As if in an attempt to artificially inflate his maturity, he had made the questionable fashion choice of wearing a vest and suspenders. Jessie hadn't been kidding about the amount of paperwork associated with police work. Despite having a laptop up on his desk, he was filling in a printed-out form and had a great deal of longhand notes on a yellow legal pad. The computer was in sleep mode.

In what had come to be the standard greeting procedure these days, Barnes squinted at Alan's badge and recited his name.

"Alan Fontaine. Right, right. The new camera. What do you need?"

Whereas his face didn't accurately portray his years on the job, his voice and tone were certainly those of a man who had made a living out of wading through the aftermath of violent crimes. It had a steely edge, and every word struck Alan's ears like Barnes had been repeating it all day and this was the absolute last time he would say it.

"Nothing, sir... Detective? I'm sorry, I don't—"

"Just Barnes. What do you need?"

"I wanted to discuss the photos from the scene."

"What about them?"

"Did they serve the purpose?"

"You're new on the job. You made some mistakes. But nothing that will hurt the investigation. What you tripped up on, the senior guy handled."

Alan flinched. "Wait, mistakes?"

Barnes dragged his laptop a bit closer.

"Quick!" Blot blurted.

Alan slid in front of the window a bit, such that the rising sun cast Blot across the desk as Barnes tapped out his credentials.

"Got it," she said.

A complex surge of accomplishment and shame twisted through Alan's soul.

"Why do so many of the passwords these people use have the word 'eagles' with some garbage before and after? Am I missing something? Do people worship these animals?" Blot asked.

Alan disregarded the question he couldn't answer out loud. Blot's white eyes narrowed in their attempt to view the screen at a rather oblique angle. Barnes navigated to a server, then through a complex file system to where the evidence for the ongoing investigation could be found.

The red-splashed crime scene was displayed in thumbnail form on the screen. Barnes picked a few and opened them to full. "See, here? How you have the overview image, then tight on these three individual elements?"

"Yes."

"I'd like a transitional image to give a better indication of proximity and orientation. Levels of detail are important. I want to feel my location in space at all times. There's no lost information. We can get it all from the overview photos. But get a midlevel next time to streamline analysis."

Alan pulled out his phone and made quick note of it. "I'm sorry about that. It wasn't in the material and training."

"Training never gets everything," Barnes said. "Other than that, good work. It doesn't seem like you missed anything, good detail. Thorough. And I understand we've got you to thank for that extra set from the roof, indirectly."

"Right, right. What did they turn up?" Alan said.

Barnes brought up some photos with visibly less polish than Alan's own.

"It's a towel. From the motel. What appears to be fresh, size-seven high-heel footprints. Analysis suggests they date to approximately the time of the crime. There are some older footprints, similar-size ladies sneaker."

"Has anything come of that?"

"We're less than a week into the case. Nothing's come of anything yet."

"We at least know it's a copycat of the Metro Ghoul, right?"

"We try not to rely upon that. It tells us a few things about their potential mindset, but the profilers can do their own work, I'll do mine. For me, this is just another murder. And we'll treat it as such."

"And how *is* that?"

Barnes gave him a familiar sideways glance. "You're not a buff, are you?"

"I can tell this is going to be a problem for us," Blot said.

"Just trying to get a handle on things," Alan replied.

"I'll tell you that it doesn't quite work the way the movies and shows would have it," Barnes said. He stood and approached a small pile of files and notes arranged atop the filing cabinets lining the wall beneath the windows. From the looks of it, Barnes had claimed the surface as a sort of auxiliary desk. He turned his back to his computer.

"Two steps to the left and hands behind your back like you're thinking!" Blot said quickly.

Alan silently obeyed the bit of choreography. The sun was too bright for Blot to have freedom of motion, so she was stuck matching Alan's position, at least broadly. She could choose if she was matching the direction Alan was facing or flip it, but otherwise she could manage only subtle changes from his position. Placing his hands behind his back took them out of his silhouette. This meant Blot could tease a bit of dexterity out of them with enough effort.

He resisted the urge to glance over his shoulder to see what she was up to. There was really no need, though. It was the same thing she was up to with every unsupervised computer they encountered. She was nosing through the files, picking things she thought were important, memorizing them, and generally being an information security specialist's worst nightmare.

"Step one is to contact friends and family of the victim and establish their whereabouts at the time of the crime. Nine times out of ten, the perpetrator will be one of the first five people you question. In this case, we're spoiled for choice. Three prior charges of domestic abuse. That's part of the Metro Ghoul MO profile, but even if it wasn't, it'd give us strong leads. Deeper digging suggests that number should probably be higher than three. Numerous complaints from neighbors. He's pretty light on family. Parents dead. No siblings. We'll wait until the facts support it before we start speculating seriously, but I think we're going to find it was an ex who was pushed too far."

He flipped to a new page. "Barring that? He's got a history with prostitutes, and there is plenty of that sort of activity going on at the Eagle's Rest Motel."

"There's that eagle thing again!" Blot remarked.

Barnes continued. "It would be a genuine surprise to me if we had to go any further than that."

"So the serial killer thing?"

Barnes waved his hand dismissively as he turned to the computer. Blot closed the window she'd opened before he could see what she'd been doing.

"That stuff is for the papers and the evening news. It isn't as though we're dealing with the original Metro Ghoul. He died in prison, what, two hundred years ago? This is a brand new murderer. Trying to draw parallels is just going to draw focus from the facts. Even if the Ghoul's copycats are more prone to do their homework than most."

"How so?"

Barnes took a seat. "Most copycats are broad strokes. The sexy parts of what the real killer did, but always flavored by their own particular psychoses or what have you. With a couple of exceptions, the Metro Ghoul killings are distinctive in their accuracy. Same type of victim: someone with a history of violence and poor impulse control. Someone who takes advantage of others. Same type of setting: shrouded in darkness, in an isolated space with no obvious means of escape. Same type of murder weapon: edged weapons, some improvised, to ridiculous excess. The really surprising bit is that the specific details aren't always the same, but the spirit is. Darkness is always the focus of the setting, but the methods of maintaining and ensuring darkness evolve. That stands out, as either a typical copycat would do *precisely* what the last killer did as though it was some sort of ritual, without really understanding why it was even being done, or else they'd just skip the parts that don't appeal to their darker impulses."

He double checked his notes, then locked his computer and shut the lid. "But this is exactly why I don't want to focus on that aspect of the crime. I care about who did it and how I can prove it. The rest just gets in the way. You want to dig into that stuff, there's plenty online."

"Yeah, I've read a fair amount of it. But it seems weirdly sparse."

"And you say you're not a buff?"

"It's my first major case. I'm taking it seriously."

"Mmm..." Barnes murmured doubtfully. "In a situation like this, where for some reason people can't get enough of repeating this guy's MO, we try to keep the finer details out of the public eye. In the short-term it keeps people from calling in with tips they *assume* are true but aren't, and in the long-term it hopefully makes him a less attractive killer to copy, since there's big gaps in the record." He shook his head. "But people keep managing to fill them in."

"Is there a more official police record on it?"

"Of course. But we haven't had a copycat here in Philadelphia. You'd have to hit up a different department. Now, if you'll excuse me, I've got calls to make."

"Right, right. Thanks for your help. Say, this being my first major case, I was wondering if I could be kept in the loop on—"

"Nope. That's not how it works."

"Okay. That's fair. Thanks again." Alan paced down the narrow aisle between desks and headed for the elevator.

"I know where the photos are and his log-in information. How should we copy the photos?" Blot asked.

"I'd really like to make it through my first full week without stealing any files," he whispered.

"You can't always get what you want."

Alan's orientation was officially over because, while there was no shortage of work and buzz in the station itself, he'd not been called out for any official crime scene work. According to the sign-in sheet, he wasn't the only one on duty. This seemed like it was the sort of place where seniority would hold a lot of sway. He just wasn't sure if that meant he'd be doing way too much work or way too little work as a result. Near as he could tell, the hours of puttering around in the station were a pretty good indicator that the Philly PD liked to give the interesting jobs to the veterans.

A police station wasn't a great place for a newbie. It wasn't as cliquey as, say, high school had been, but the body language on display was less than welcoming. Heads were down, jokes were primarily of the inside variety, and every time he lingered anywhere for more than a few minutes, he started to get distinct you're-in-my-spot vibes.

Alan was confident that would pass in time, but not having a place of his own and everyone else being very mindful of the new guy made Blot's personal quest to pillage the evidence files basically impossible. Beyond some idle chitchat, their investigation had hit a wall.

"Stupid police and their stupid security skills," Blot muttered to herself. "What in the name of darkness does a shade have to do to get enough privacy to steal some photos?"

"You can't always get what you want," Alan said.

He'd taken to leaning on the wall beside the fire escape on the first floor. Half of the bulbs in the overhead fixture there were dead, so it was nice and dim, and it was at the end of a short hallway, so he could get away with having a coffee in each hand and not turn too many heads.

The stirrer sticking out of the second cup jostled a bit as Blot slurped at its shadow. "They need to change the coffee filter," she said.

"Yeah, they kind of burn it, too."

"I don't mind the burnt taste."

He shook his head. "I don't understand how you can legit have an appreciation for good coffee, but then guzzle this motor oil."

"I am a creature of diverse and specific tastes."

A distant door opened, and a voice echoed through the hallway. Even before he could make out the words, he knew it was Jessie. She passed through a crowded place like a fresh breeze, perking everyone up along the way.

"Try not to wag your tail too hard," Blot muttered, crushing the empty cup in his hand into the shadows.

He trotted down the hallway toward the main lobby. Jessie had been pretty busy out in the squad car for most of the day. She'd been hung up on the other side of town during lunch. Thus, with just a few minutes left in her shift, she was *just* crossing paths with Alan.

"Hey! Alan!" she chirped, leaning in for a hug. "How's the second day on the job?"

"Uneventful. No calls at all."

"That's good news. In a police station, a slow day is a good day," she said. "I've got to do my homework. After that, you want to go get dinner?"

Years of keeping to a budget, pinching his pennies, and attempting to avoid eating out didn't stand a chance against the thought of sharing a meal with Jessie after the mess of the last few days.

"Absolutely," he said.

"Great. Let's get to my desk." She led the way. "So what'd you do today, if you didn't get any calls yet?"

"Tried to educate myself and drank a bunch of coffee."

"The internet in here is the worst, isn't it?" she said.

"I wouldn't know."

She gave him an incredulous look, then turned, as if to address the whole of the station.

"Are you people honestly going to tell me that *no one* got this man on the network?" she said.

Most of those within earshot ignored her. A few pointedly avoided eye contact.

"Come on, same equipment room as the cameras. We'll get you a department laptop. Seriously, how did they expect you to get anything done on the terminals upstairs?"

"The what where?" he said.

She gave him a blank look. "Clearly, I have been remiss in my duties. Come on. We're going to bring you into the information age."

"Okay, Deborah, thanks!" Jessie said as the resident IT lady handed off what was now Alan's computer.

Alan stared at Jessie, dumbfounded.

"What?" she said, squirming a bit at the intensity of the attention.

"You just got a network administrator, within an hour of quitting time on a weekend shift, to get me set up with new equipment, in less than a half hour. That's, like, faster than the speed of light in tech support time."

She laughed. "You just need to know who to sweet talk and where to send the bottle of wine come Christmas time. You owe her a bottle of rosé, by the way."

She pulled open the drawer of her desk and flopped a fresh form onto it. Alan's PC was perched on the corner of it, with the borrowed network wire plugged in.

It had rolled past the end of the shift, so the somewhat more lightly staffed swing shift had started, leaving a number of the desks empty. This fact was not lost upon Blot, who was well aware there was now no one between Alan and the far wall.

"Let me at it!" Blot squealed.

Alan debated leaning away and keeping Blot from the computer, but it was only a matter of time before she found a way to get at it. She didn't need to sleep and he did. Better to do this while he could keep at least the corner of an eye on her.

"Talk, I need something to drown out the button presses."

He glanced across the desk, where a small radio sat. "Hey, does that work?"

"Yeah, you want some music?" she glanced around. "There's no one to complain."

She clicked it on. It was tuned to a jazz station. As soon as there was enough stand-up bass and trumpet to cover it, Blot went to work. The keyboard clacked quietly like a player piano.

"There really isn't anyone here," she said, scratching at her paperwork. "I never realized how quickly this place empties out. I guess because I'm usually one of the ones who's out of here in a hurry."

"Having spent a full eight hours here without very much to fill my time, I can absolutely sympathize."

She was quiet for a time. Almost quiet enough for Alan to worry she might hear the keys. When she spoke, a layer of the brightness was missing from her voice.

"Alan, remember when I said I'd had a rough five years since college?"

"Yeah. You didn't want to go into it."

"Right. Well..."

"You want to go into it?"

"I don't *want* to go into it, but I should, so I'm going to."

"Should I be ready to run away?"

She laughed. "Might be worth making sure your shoes are tied. As I think you know, I got this job here right out of college. Did you meet Jack?"

"Uh... I think that was after our last class together. I didn't see you much, toward the end."

"I know," she said flatly. "Jack was... we'll just say that these days Jack is a bad word. Looking back now, it's so clear he was no good. Controlling. It started slow, but before long he got me off social media, didn't want me hanging out with friends without him there... I mean, did you know I was married?"

"What?!" Alan said.

"Two whole years. It's hard for me to talk about it like it wasn't a hostage situation."

"He didn't hit you or anything..."

"No. No, it wasn't that kind of situation. But he... I'm going to start slipping into therapy terms if I dwell on it. Long story short, 2014 to about 2018 are basically lost years for me. Found ways to cope. Some of them chemical. Finally dumped him. Got a restraining order. Got a therapist. Started healing."

"What finally did it?"

She looked up from the page. "What finally did it? You're not going to ask about the chemicals? About the therapy?"

"Look. This is stupid and childish, but it's stuck with me. When I was a kid, if I was upset, I'd cry. I was, as every bully from kindergarten through about sixth grade would observe as often as possible, a crybaby. And if I was *just* about to finish crying, and someone asked me what was wrong, it'd start back up. So I'm very careful about where I poke."

"And you've chosen to poke the straw that broke the camel's back?"

"That's the healthy decision you made, right?"

She smirked. "It is, but I've got to say, you'd be a heck of a riddle for my therapist to untie. Anyway, stupid as it might sound, what finally did it was him cheating on me. It wasn't even a new thing. He'd been doing it almost since the start. One of those 'secret family' things, which always sounded so absurd to me. It's why he had to bolt down so hard on who I could talk to and how. In this day and age, a long-term affair is a tricky thing to hide."

"It turns out you can just log in as someone else. I'm in as Barnes now," Blot said.

Alan's eye twitched. Jessie scratched out a few more lines on her form.

"You know what's the worst part?"

"Jack was the worst part."

"Ha! Yeah, but the thing that still wrecks me is that it wasn't that he was so controlling. It wasn't that he stole years of my life, damaged friendships, separated me from family. What finally persuaded me to get rid of him for good was that he *lied*. I might still be with that pile of trash if I'd never found out that it had all been a lie, that he'd been hiding so much from me."

"Whatever it takes to get out of a bad situation," Alan said.

Blot piped up. "I've got the photos on here, but Barnes transcribed a bunch of his notes here. I'm getting them too."

Alan felt a flicker of concern about whether what Blot was doing was going to be traceable, and how exactly she got so good with computers, but at the moment Jessie was his greater focus. "I just can't picture the person I know ever letting that happen."

"If you'd asked me before, I never would have believed it would happen. But it'll sure never happen again. I've got a couple of months of therapy under my belt, and I'm just starting to piece together what I can of my old life. You'd be amazed how many people won't answer the phone again after you ghost them for a few years. But you did."

She huffed a breath and finished her form.

"Thanks, is what I'm saying."

"I don't think I really earned that, but you're welcome."

Alan expected to see tears in her eyes after the intensity of what she'd been saying, but her expression was steady. It was something that had all been said before. This particular bandage had been torn off already. She paused for a few seconds, and the leaden seriousness in her expression lifted like a curtain being drawn. Her sunny demeanor returned. The speed and ease that her attitude shifted betrayed a great deal. It revealed practice at the transition. It made Alan wonder how much of a mask her smile really was.

"Well. Enough of that. To the diner? Maybe some soup du jour? Provided your computer's at a place where we can shut down."

Alan parked the car and walked Jessie into the diner that was swiftly becoming the primary contributor to Alan's caloric intake. Any moment that Alan and Jessie weren't talking, Blot was filling his head with her assessment and findings. For once she didn't appear to be irritated at having to sacrifice her limited moments of freedom for the sake of Alan's social life. She was far too busy sinking her teeth into the stolen information. In fact, she'd come perilously close to being discovered when she'd slipped into the back seat and conjured up a pad and pencil to transcribe some of her findings.

"I should ask," Jessie said, "what's with the limo treatment on the windows? I know your name got out there a little bit with that riot thing, but I didn't notice any groupies hounding you at traffic lights."

"I've found myself a little sensitive to bright light lately," Alan said.

"That's right," Blot said. "The best kind of lie. Impossible to prove, and too innocuous to question."

"You should get that looked at. Lots of bad stuff starts as light sensitivity," she said. "Have you been having migraines? I know those are related sometimes."

Blot glared at Jessie. "Unless they're a nosy busybody."

Alan assured her there was nothing deeper than the desire for a little shade as they worked their way inside. The usual booth was taken. This late at night the lack of bright light outside made it less crucial where they sat. Alan and Jessie slid into another booth and started to scan the menus.

"Give me your phone," Blot said, slipping into the darkness beneath the table. "I want to start looking things up."

Alan casually slipped his phone onto the seat beside him as the waitress stepped up and set two coffees and an iced tea on the table. After a short discussion regarding daily soups, a chicken-and-orzo and a matzo-ball soup were ordered, along with a chopped salad and a chicken Caesar.

"He may have said he's not interested in the Metro Ghoul, but not only did Barnes have tons of notes on it, he's got a note about wanting to get the full case history from other precincts," Blot said. "That means *we* are probably going to need that. Find out how that works."

Alan sipped his coffee. "Hey, I had a question about police procedure and stuff," he said.

"Always dressing on the side," Jessie said.

"...What?"

"When you order a salad, always get the dressing on the side. Not just because it'll save you calories, by the way. It'll give you something to dip your fries in, if you have any later in the meal."

"That's not really the sort of procedure I was curious about."

"With salads on the way, it's the only procedure that *this* police officer finds relevant at the moment."

"Right, but if someone, say, wanted the files on the Metro Ghoul."

"Ugh," she said, rolling her eyes. "Now there's fun dinner conversation."

"Okay, that's fair, but, like anyone else then."

She sipped her iced tea. "Realistically, archived records like that will have to be officially requested. There's forms, of course. And *official* requests come only when the investigation determines they are warranted. They take time to process, clear, and fulfill. Weeks. And that won't happen in this case, because we can speak with complete certainty when we say that this is *not* the work of the same killer as last time. It's practically part of the Ghoul's MO that each copycat has been reproducing. Eventually, definitive and concrete evidence lead to the arrest and imprisonment, followed some short time after by death while in prison."

"But would someone be able to—"

"Alan, pretty please don't turn into the kind of person who eats and breathes this stuff. You've got to let it slide off at the end of the day or you'll never get any peace."

"That's fine. It's all we need to know." Blot giggled fiendishly. "We're going to have to 'borrow' that information too."

Alan shot a glance downward and shifted uneasily.

"Barnes's notes say the good info is all going to be in Boston's records. He says the last big investigation back in the nineties happened there and should have duplicates of all the other info..."

"See, that's what I'm talking about," Jessie said.

Alan jumped a bit as he realized he'd let his focus shift from Jessie. During his lapse in concentration, she'd leaned across the table a bit to lock eyes with him.

"You got lost in your own head there, right while I was watching. You're looking twitchy and hunted. Haunted, even," Jessie said.

"Haunted is for ghosts, not shades," came Blot's unheard correction. "Hunted is at least moderately accurate."

"This is a danger everyone runs, but people like us more than most. When it comes right down to it, no matter how social we are, no matter how friendly the support and how much we have, when we close our eyes at night, we're alone with ourselves."

"Ha! Shows what she knows," Blot added.

"If you're not comfortable in your own head, there's no getting away from it. So take care of yourself, okay? Tell you what. Moratorium on talking about serial killers and prison riots for the rest of the meal. What else have you got going?"

Alan drummed his fingers on the table. "Um... Did you see that Trent Street video?"

"Darn right I did. That man's got moves!"

Alan poked his chest with his thumb.

"No way! Tell me all about it."

After as healthy a meal as he was likely to have at a diner, Alan pulled up to the parking lot of the police station so Jessie could drive herself home. The conversation had stayed light through most of the rest of the meal, but the lightness was beginning to feel a bit labored toward the end. He parked a few spaces away from Jessie's car.

"You don't have to park. I'll just hop out and we'll both head home," Jessie said.

"Before you go. Uh... back at the station, you said some heavy stuff. I've been thinking about it."

"Don't worry. It's the past."

"Right, I know that, but I didn't want to part ways without addressing it. I'm not... *great* at handling stuff like that properly. We'll call this practice."

"Okay, shoot. I'll grade you on a curve."

"If that sort of thing starts to happen again... if *any* sort of thing starts to happen again... don't forget my number, okay?"

She smirked. "That's the general idea, Alan. You've seen me in the station. You know how I am. You better believe I know everyone's first name, middle name, and beer of choice. I'd call any one of those guys and gals if I needed help moving. But... I think some author or something called it 'the dark teatime of the soul.' If I feel myself putting on the kettle for that, the boys and gals at the station aren't a good fit. You passed the audition." She slapped his shoulder. "Good job."

It didn't really feel like a smiling occasion, but for some reason he couldn't keep from grinning at the assessment.

"Glad to hear it."

"And that goes both ways. If I keep seeing that look in your eye, like you're slipping into your own head in the middle of a conversation? You'd best believe I'm going to intervene."

"I'm fine."

"Alan, I've been in therapy for a bit, and one of the side effects is a tendency to become something of an armchair analyst. You are simultaneously not fine and too fine. On the surface you're soldiering on, keeping up appearances, but the cracks are starting to show. For heaven's sake, Alan, you ended up unconscious on the floor of a prison during a riot, and, except for the mandatory seventy-two hours of observation, you haven't been back to see a professional. I know they recommended one."

"It's fine."

"No one's just magically fine after something like that. I don't think you even took the time to *feel* it. Three days isn't enough. It isn't *not* going to hit you. Lightning struck a tree outside your house. The right thing to do is take it down before it comes down faster and harder than you want, and in a place you can't handle."

Jessie reached into her pocket, fishing out a business card with suspicious ease. "This is the lady I go to. She's good," she said.

"Therapy seems like a big step."

"The first step is always a big one. I felt the same way. Of course, it helps that I had an idiot telling me he didn't want me going to therapy because 'they're just going to blame me' for a couple of years. But go. It's like a personal trainer for your mental health. Work out those emotional muscles before you get a brain cramp. If you're not going to do it for you, do it for me. Gotta have you in fighting shape for when I need you, right?"

She gave him another slap on the shoulder and started to get out of the car. "Good talk. You're back on Tuesday, right?"

"Wednesday."

"Great! I'm off Mondays and Tuesdays for a while, so we'll line up for the next couple. See you then! And hey, enjoy the rest of your shift."

"Heh, yeah, it's going to be a few more hours. With my luck, just as I'm ready to doze off, I'll get a call."

"You'll get used to it." She shut the door and paced away.

Alan lingered long enough to be sure she got to her car and got it started, then followed her out of the parking lot. Jessie turned left, Alan turned right. Despite the intensity of some of the conversation, he found his chest wasn't quite so heavy, his mind wasn't quite so clouded. And the smile that still seemed so strangely out of place for the topics at hand stubbornly refused to leave his face.

He glanced to the passenger seat. Where Jessie had once been, now shadow with very judgmental eyes was glaring back at him.

"She's trying to fix you," Blot said.

"What?"

"You're a project for her now. She got bruised by the last guy, and so she's picking out a bruised guy to put back together into the shape she needs."

"Calm down," he said.

"Oh sure, calm down. You can say that. But it's bad enough that we're three or four dinners away from the two of you sharing a bed."

"Now you're just being paranoid."

"It'll be her home, by the way. Take it from someone who has had her life completely defined by controlling, authoritarian taskmasters. She's taking control back for herself, and she's not going to give it up for you. She's going to make sure the next step is into *her* territory." Blot sniffed. "But as awkward as that's going to be for me... I don't even want to think about having to watch you things mate."

"Whoa, easy!" he said.

"My big problem is, if you let her or that doctor of hers dig around in you long enough, they're going to decide that what's wrong with you is *me*."

"Yeah. I don't know that much about psychology, but I'd bet you'd be a great symptom of all sorts of mental disorders. I'm *sure* if I brought you up in therapy, I'd walk out of there with some heavy-duty medications."

She sat up a little taller. "You can't get rid of me with medicine."

"Well, I mean, you seem to have a pretty positive reaction to caffeine, so you've got some sort of chemical susceptibility."

"Yes, when *I* drink it. You can drink any potions or remedies you want. I'll still be here. They were very clear about that when I was being trained. 'They will try to be rid of you with herbs and treatments, but they will fail.'"

"We've gotten pretty good at medication, but I suspect you're right about a supernatural symbiont being more than a match for Big Pharma." He drummed his fingers on the steering wheel.

"What are you thinking?" Blot asked with the same tone of voice you'd use on a baby who was eying a power outlet.

"I'm just thinking about how hard it would be to convince a therapist that you were a real thing."

"Oh, trust me, if it started to be a problem, I'd be able to convince them *real* quick."

"But that would just—"

Blot swiped a hand through the air. "I don't want to talk about it. We have more important things to talk about. This search for the Metro Ghoul is going to get harder in a hurry, and we need to act fast."

The warm, buoyant afterglow of his much-needed conversation with Jessie vanished with a leaden thunk in his chest. "Why..."

She produced her notebook with a flourish. "And I quote. 'In the case of the original Metro Ghoul, and in what we have come to label as 'faithful' imitations, there are a handful of observations which have proved to be extremely reliable. There will be no fewer than three killings within the initial four weeks of activity. Following those four weeks, the Ghoul will go dormant for a time, resurfacing to repeat the process in another metropolitan city. There seems to be little pattern in the selection of the new location. Only that it will be on the East Coast, and will be in a large city.' So we've got to act fast."

"Before he kills again," he said.

"I was going to say before he *moves* again, but I suppose both are pretty bad."

"So what do we do?"

"This is being done by a shade. Probably all the others were, too. I don't know if all those line up with eclipses. It feels like the last eclipse that we sent people through was longer ago than, what, a few decades? But it may be that among the many things that they didn't teach me were a half dozen other trips that weren't successful enough to tell tales about. The point is, this feels like a ritual. We take rituals very seriously. Even when something doesn't start as a ritual, if it goes well, we'll *make* it one. That's why it would be so similar for each of these. And that's why we need to find out *exactly* what happened the last time, because it will happen as near as possible to that way this time."

She slapped the pad. "And what Barnes dug up isn't enough. We need the whole story. Every little detail."

"You aren't suggesting…"

"How soon can we get to Boston?"

"They're not going to just give us the files. You heard Jessie."

"That's why we're not going to ask for them. They can't say no if you don't ask."

"You want to steal from a police department."

"Sure! At this point I've got some good practice. It should be easy."

"You're not… this is… do we even know where to *find* the files?"

"I have a phone number and a name for the records person. There's a department name. That's enough, right?"

"I don't know! I guess they'll probably…" He shook his head. "I am *not* planning a heist from Boston PD with you."

"I'll plan it on my own, but it'll probably go smoother if you help. You know your world a little better than I do."

"There are proper ways to do this!"

"And those ways don't make allowances for shades or white-suits. They sure don't operate on any sort of an urgent timeline."

Alan took a few deep breaths and squeezed the steering wheel.

"Look. We launched an all-out assault on my people because you couldn't tolerate any loss of life. We know to a near certainty that if we don't act fast, someone else will die. That's just the global consequences of dragging our feet. The personal consequences are that every moment we wait, we run the risk of getting the white-suits angry enough to revoke our protections, and then if and when some other shades who are after me or you decide we're worth their time, we're fighting for our lives."

"Maybe we can just ask the white-suits to help us!" Alan said. "They could just *ask* for the files."

"Oh! Maybe!" Blot said.

He glanced at her. She was inching up a bit more to eagerly look out the windshield.

"I would have thought you'd be against that idea."

"Oh, I don't trust them as far as I can throw them, but they have a habit of showing up whenever we mention them, and right now we're moving at high speed in a car."

Alan considered the statement, then widened his eyes and slowed down a bit.

"You're terrible."

"A shade can dream, can't she?"

Alan's phone rang. He tugged it from his pocket and threw it on what would have been Blot's lap. It was an unknown number. Before he could tap the speakerphone, Blot's hand darted out of the shadows and poked it for him.

"Hello?"

"Alan! It is Angel."

"You can just call me?!" Alan said. "You appear out of nowhere and scare the life out of me, and you can just *call* me?"

"Circumstances sometimes require it. Do not bother adding this number to your contacts, however. I am borrowing the phone of the nice woman who lives next door to you."

"You are in Ms. Levitt's house?" Alan said.

"Yes. You don't have a home phone I can use, and besides, you made it quite clear you do not like me entering your home unannounced."

"Tell them to do something mean! Tell them to take the milk out of the refrigerator and hide it under her bed!" Blot said.

"No!" he said.

"Fine. I'll do it tonight after you go to bed."

"Were you talking to me?" Angel asked.

"No. Sorry. I assume you're calling because you, somehow, overheard what we were talking about?"

"No, no. Of course not. I am, after all, a simple human. However, if I were to speculate, I would guess you were considering asking me for help."

"What an amazing guess," Blot said flatly.

"We need access to some police records to help us track down the Metro Ghoul. Blot can feel that it is a shade, but there's no trail for us to follow."

"I see. It certainly does make sense that police records would help you."

"So can you get them for us? You'd just have to tell them to go get them."

"It is entirely within my capabilities. I am, however, prohibited from doing so."

"Why! You got a movie star to strut like a pop star to get me some cash."

"Yes. The task I had assigned you would have cost you money. I took action to restore the lost money. Balance. This is a very different request. I cannot interfere."

"Convenient," Blot said.

"I do, however, endorse this course of action."

"Hah! See!"

"You endorse me breaking in to a police department to steal criminal records?"

"I endorse you taking every necessary action to hasten your discovery of the shade and his methodology for evading our observation. The sooner you do, the sooner further questionable acts can be avoided, and the sooner proper surveillance can be restored. If you are feeling conflicted, do not be. This is the correct thing to do."

A shrill voice faintly rang out across the phone.

"If you will excuse me, it would appear I failed to give Ms. Levitt sufficient instructions. She is really rather unreasonable. We will be in touch."

Angel hung up the phone. Alan stared at the road ahead like it had called him a dirty name.

"There is an awful lot of supernatural peer pressure going on."

"That's how you know it's the right thing to do."

"Well, your honor, I knew I *had* to break in to the police department, because the voice in my head *and* the mysterious person who always tells me what to do agreed!" He tightened his jaw. "If we're doing this, we're not doing it until my shift is over. That gives me another fifteen hours or so to try to come up with a better solution."

Chapter 4

The next day, after some fitful sleep interrupted by a convenience store robbery he had to snap some pictures of, Alan was packing his car. He'd completely exhausted the various means at his disposal to tease the details of the other Metro Ghoul murders out of the internet and books. Sure enough, large, specific gaps in the details had been kept from press and researchers alike. The *only* place he was going to find the information he was after was in the files that awaited him at the end of a five-hour-long road trip.

There were a few things that needed to be done in order to minimize the chance that his absence would become conspicuous. First, he removed himself from the Cox Media photo pool for a few days. This prompted no small amount of shouting over the phone from Cox himself. Alan had reattained his golden boy status in Cox's eyes, but failing to show up and score another viral video the following day was enough to remove that status immediately. He also called his parents and said he was going to be heading out to the country for some nature photography and wasn't going to have reception for a while.

Alan and Blot brainstormed the details of the heist for a few hours, trying to plan out what they would need and when it would be best to show up. By the time they were heading to the car, it was already seven in the evening and looking like a midnight arrival, which ideally would give them a relatively good chance of successfully infiltrating.

"I can't believe the first time I get to use my ski mask will be for breaking and entering..." he muttered as he tossed his duffel bag into the car. "This is still crazy, you know. There's got to be a better way."

"There might be a better way, but clearly this is the best way *we* are going to come up with," Blot said. "It will be fine. We will slip inside. Perhaps unlock some doors, I've been practicing that. I'll do all the work. It is old information, which means we probably won't need computers. Easy!"

"Honestly, I'd feel a lot better about this if you weren't acting like we were about to go to a theme park."

She crossed her arms as she settled into the passenger seat. "I will not apologize for being excited about putting my training to its intended use. I didn't chide you for being happy about getting the forensic job. This is the same thing."

"It isn't even close to the same thing, but point taken."

"You are going to be in very good hands, Alan. No one will ever know what happened. All you need to do is get me there."

He started the engine and the navigation on his phone. "Just so we're clear, when you suggested that we should try to be spies, aside from that not being the sort of job you can just *get*, this here is precisely the sort of thing I didn't want to be doing."

"How do you know you won't like it if you haven't even tried it?"

"Because it's espionage, not broccoli."

Five hours is a long time to spend in a car. Alan's anxiety had more endurance than most, but even he couldn't stay acutely anxious for the entirety of the car ride. By the time they'd made it through the state of New Jersey, he'd managed to push the forthcoming felony to the back of his mind and actually begin to enter the zen of the long-haul drive.

"Your world is really beautiful at night, you know," Blot said, eyes blinking at the view through the tinted windows.

"You might be the first person to voice that opinion after driving through the Garden State."

"I know you don't see things the way I do. Philosophically *or* literally. But I can see so much farther into the darkness. You still douse everything with whatever light you can manage, but out there on the long stretches of road, when the cars start to thin out and the cities are off in the distance. It's just so *big*."

"Maybe one of these days, if we can get out from under the thumb of the various people giving us odd jobs, I can take you up north to Upstate New York again."

"I've been there, remember? It's where we first, uh, *met*."

"You've been there, but you haven't seen it. Not really. I've got to talk to Mom and Dad. I think that land deal is still covered in question marks. There's half a chance we'll be able to head back there." He tipped his head. "I guess it doesn't have to be that land. It's not like there's anything that makes it any different than any campground. It's just the one I remember."

"It's special. It's where the gateway tree was."

"That's true. I guess that means it's got a lot of your people lingering there, huh?"

"No. It means it's probably the only place in the area *without* any shades lingering there. It's the entrance. Our goal is to get as far from it as possible to maximize our influence on the world. That I ended up linked to the man literally sleeping next to the tree is the sort of thing that would make me a laughingstock if my people knew."

"Jokes on them. We've made a darn good team."

"By your standards. By their standards I'm infamous."

"Infamous is still famous."

Her lips curled into a reluctant grin. "There is that, I guess."

"So what makes the view beautiful?"

"Color. We just don't have it at home. Not like here, anyway. There it's all blacks and whites. Barely any gray. It's beautiful in its own way, I guess. But here... so much more."

"I wonder why you can even see color, if there's so little of it there."

"Dun taught that it was proof we were meant to come here, that we were created with all the tools we would need to navigate your world. Considering the way he and the others sculpted stories to their whim to inspire us to join the cause, I don't know that I believe it anymore. But it was answer enough for me while I was still there."

Alan glanced in the rearview mirror, then the side mirror.

"You keep doing that," Blot said.

"You're the one with finely tuned observational abilities. What do you think is making me anxious?"

"The blue-green car with the garbage bags on the windows," Blot said. "I was hoping you hadn't noticed it."

"It's been in my rearview mirror for over a hundred miles. Including at least one rest stop. How am I not going to notice it?" he said. "And how are *you* not worried?"

"At this point, with the people who we've angered, so long as they aren't trying to ram us off the road, I'm happy."

He squinted at the car, which had one headlight. It was weaving just a bit more within its lane than seemed healthy.

"I'm pulling over."

"Don't. We've got coffee. You've got snacks. Just keep moving," Blot said.

"I'm not talking about a rest stop. I'm pulling over right now. On the side of the road. Simultaneous rest stops might be a coincidence. Pulling over to the shoulder is definitive."

Blot narrowed her eyes. "I can think of an awful lot of places I'd rather have a showdown than the side of the highway."

"Would you rather it happen in the police station while we're trying to break in?"

"I suppose not." She shifted a bit, as if limbering up. "If this is going to be a fight, try to time it so it happens between the headlights going by."

Alan switched on his hazard lights and pulled over to the shoulder. The garbage-bag-festooned car cut across two lanes of traffic to pull onto the shoulder a dozen yards ahead.

"Either this is a particularly conscientious driver worried we might need help, or mission accomplished on forcing their hand," Alan said.

"I can't imagine which one it will be."

Alan sat behind the wheel, car shuddering with the wind of other cars rushing by. At this point, the car could easily contain anything from a white-suit to possibly a member of the Dawn, or even an enemy shade. Perhaps someone from the Philly PD had noticed Blot's rummaging through the network. It could even be a rival media company angry that he'd been making such a splash lately. He wasn't comfortable with the vast array of rivals and enemies he'd accumulated, but he was at least familiar with the feeling of waiting to see which one he was dealing with.

A full minute passed with no motion from either car. No door opened. No window rolled down. Just the blink of hazard lights and the anxious drum of Alan's fingers.

"We are on a schedule, Alan," Blot said. "Either see who it is, or ram them and speed off. We can't just sit here waiting all night."

Alan glanced into the back seat. He'd taken the precaution of acquiring a handful of semipotent self-defense items. The pair that seemed best suited to handle the widest array of would-be attackers was a fresh can of pepper spray and a four-D-cell aluminum-body flashlight. Experience had taught him that the one-two punch of disorientation and a thump from a blunt object had a way of turning the tide of the average battle, at least long enough for a quick getaway.

Properly armed, he popped the door open.

Blot shuddered as headlights whipped by. Headlights were a particularly irritating light source for her. As far as she was concerned, *any* electric light was brighter than it needed to be, but headlights were punishing in their starkness and intensity. Worse, they were frequently moving quickly. The combination led to disorienting swings and slides. She'd been gathering strength for a number of months now. If she braced herself and dug in her fingers, she could just barely hold her ground, but for now that effort was better placed elsewhere.

She focused on the car ahead. As Alan paced closer, the door had yet to open. Garbage bags on both the inside and outside of all windows save the windshield meant they couldn't get a good view of who was waiting for them. She gathered her mind around the metaphysical senses at her disposal, trying to get a sense for the foe. The deep, instinctive fear she felt when the white-suits were near had yet to flare up. The distant tug of another shade was missing as well.

"I think it's the Dawn," Blot said. "Be ready for thumping instead of shining."

Alan nodded and shifted his grip slightly, flipping the heavy tail end of the flashlight forward. As he approached, the door popped open and swung out to roughly grind against the guard rail. A scraggly leg with shredded clothes barely clinging to it stepped out. A few crumpled beer cans clattered to the ground.

"Come on..." Alan said.

A bearded man with a round beer belly and an odor that fought its way upwind to Alan's nostrils hauled himself from the car. He brushed himself off and stretched, then offered a broad, gap-toothed smile.

"Hey, kiddo," he said.

"Todd?" Alan said.

"Rive..." Blot said.

A twisted shadow moved with purpose, slithering out of the car and glaring back and forth between Alan and Blot with ragged, curling eyes. In the rare but notable encounters they'd had before, Todd had never been a paragon of good health or good grooming. The last few weeks since their last encounter hadn't treated him well. He looked more ragged than usual. His eyes were half-lidded and red. He had a waver to his stance that threatened to require the support of the roof of the car to keep him from keeling over.

"I thought you said it was the Dawn," Alan said, flipping the flash-light into shine-ready position.

"I didn't feel him. Whatever that trick is that's hiding the rest, he knows it. And it works on us. At least a little. I can feel him *now*." She tightened her fists. "That's going to complicate things."

"How did you get out of the prison?" Alan asked. "The last time I saw you, you were getting your butt kicked by Brink."

The fragrant drunk tapped his nose. "You get thrown out of as many bars as me and you start to get a feel for when it's time to drag yourself out," he said. "It helps that what's-his-face got his hands on—"

"Silence!" Rive hissed.

Todd looked down to his shadow. "Look, you want me keeping secrets, you lay them out beforehand."

"What's this about? Why are you here?" Alan said.

"Just keeping an eye on you. I guess you've been talking to some folks that make the bigwigs nervous."

"But who have you been getting your orders from?" Alan asked.

"That guy in... wait, where is he?" He looked around until he spotted his shadow. "This guy here. That's just about all I need. Doesn't much matter how far downhill the crap had to roll."

"Why you? If this is any indication, you aren't the best at trailing people."

"Followed you this far, didn't I?"

"In the most conspicuous vehicle on the road, and the most obvious way possible."

"I suppose they aren't spoiled for choice, since you two went and hamstrung all those shadows back in Philly," Todd said. "Point is, I still found you."

"Yeah... You found me," Alan said, squeezing his flashlight a little tighter.

Todd glanced down at Rive. "What do you say? We going to go again? What is this, round four?"

Alan tensed up, but Blot's eyes flicked aside. There was a better way.

"Keep him talking," she whispered.

"We're on the side of the road," Alan said, keeping his eyes carefully trained on the pair of foes in front of him as Blot crept aside. "People are going to see whatever you try to do. You'll probably cause an accident. Presumably, you're still trying to keep this whole invasion a secret."

Rive's eyes started to wander, possibly seeking Blot. Alan clicked the flashlight on, locking Rive behind Todd.

"Would you cut it out with that light? Come on. What else are we going to do but fight? It'll feel good after all this driving. Get the blood flowing." Todd looked back at his shadow. "You always go with something big and stretched out. Let's go with something with a low center of gravity this time. Reach isn't everything."

"We are to follow. Fighting him on the roadside won't solve anything," Rive said, eying Alan angrily. "No matter how therapeutic it would be."

"It'll get me closer to even. I'm not the sort who holds a grudge, but this newsy or whatever has been making a chump out of me." Todd snorted and spat on the ground. "A man's got to have his self-respect."

"No fighting," Rive said.

"What if he starts it?" Todd looked up to Alan. "Come on. You know you want to throw a punch. Remember when I was heading out to kill your dad?"

Alan's eyes narrowed.

"There, see? He's just dying to come at me. This'll be self-defense. Let's just make sure we self-defend so hard everybody'll know which one of us won. Claws are good, let's do claws."

"We are not fighting. We are watching, and we are waiting."

Todd gritted his teeth. "Look, Rive, I'm doing what you say because you keep me good and pickled. But now you've got me driving, so the best I can do is half a buzz, and now you're not even letting me fight. What's in it for me, exactly?"

"I will make your life hell if you even think of resisting me, Todd," Rive warned.

"So, 1990 to 2015 all over again? Not much of a threat."

"I could abandon you. You'd die."

Todd shrugged. "I don't think I've got too many years left with you pulling the strings. Tell you what, how about I just rough him up au naturel and you keep the squirrely lady he's teamed up with busy?"

"I have a better idea," Blot said.

A passing car shoved her back to her proper place beside Alan. At the same time, a huff of released pressure caused Todd's beat-up sedan to slump down. She flicked her shadowy hand, and a strip of black rubber flopped to Todd's feet.

"To the car, quick," Blot said.

She needn't have bothered with the instructions. Alan had already turned and broken into a sprint before she was done saying it. Among the many bizarre skills his life had taught him since Blot's arrival, one of the most important he'd picked up was how to keep a flashlight roughly trained on someone who was behind him. A reverse grip on the flashlight kept Rive behind Todd. For his part, the drunk host of the flesh-sculpting shade confounded expectation by bursting into laughter rather than leaping into pursuit.

Alan didn't look a gift horse in the mouth, taking full advantage of the lack of a twisted monstrosity chasing him to hop in the car, start the engine, and sling gravel on his way back onto the highway.

It took a few minutes of driving before Alan was willing to stop glancing desperately at the rearview mirror. Coincidentally, it also took that long for his pulse rate to drop out of the triple digits.

"We're not being chased," he said.

"I should hope not. I tore a hole in two of his tires. Cars *do* need tires to drive, right?"

"You can limp on the rim if you're a nut. And considering who we're dealing with, I wouldn't have put it past him to just come galloping after me, stretched into some sort of horrifying flesh-horse."

Blot nodded. "Ah, yes. I'd almost forgotten about that. He wouldn't have been able to keep up for very long though. Todd doesn't strike me as the sort of person with really strong endurance."

Alan scrunched his face up.

"What's wrong now?" Blot asked.

"My imagination conjured up a flesh-horse, and now I can't stop thinking about it."

"Oh, a horse isn't nearly the worst thing he could throw at you. If Rive's as good as they say, he'd probably be able to do wings."

"Thank you, Blot. That's really helping."

"Don't think about how scary it would look, think about how funny it would be to see a drunk guy with no experience with wings trying to fly."

He shook his head. "Nope, still horrifying." He glanced at her. "That actually went pretty well, though."

"All things considered, yes. It doesn't bode well that I couldn't feel that it was Rive in that car, but we're definitely better off without him on our tail. All it would have taken was him kicking up a little bit of a fuss while we were in the police station, and in the *best* case we'd have failed to get the goods."

"And we got out of it without blood being spilled on either side."

"Yep."

"We might actually be getting good at this."

"I'm telling you. We would make excellent spies. Just wait until you see how well the heist goes."

He gave her a harder look. "Heist? It's bad enough we're robbing someone, can we maybe avoid calling it a 'heist'?"

"We can call it whatever you like," Blot said. "But really now, when you look back at things when it's all said and done, when you write the story of your life, wouldn't you rather have a chapter entitled The Heist?"

"If this chapter makes it into my autobiography, it's going to have some really interesting footnotes."

Just past midnight, Alan parked his car. Boston was similar to Philly, at least insofar as the parking situation. It would have been pure idiocy to park his car right out front before attempting to slip inside to rob the police station. Fortunately, there was little hope of that happening. Like most of the older cities in the United states, big swaths of Boston still had the twisting, narrow, confusing layout of a city built around horse paths. Even at midnight on a weekday, he had no choice but to park a fair distance away and walk to the police station.

"This is going to be perfect. I've got it all planned out," Blot said. "First, up to the roof, then down through the vents. You've got gloves on, right? No fingerprints. Not that you should be touching anything anyway. I'll check for cameras along the way, and witnesses. We'll need to find the records room, shouldn't be hard. You people always put signs up..."

Alan hefted the small messenger bag with his gear in it. "Could you maybe tone down the enthusiasm a little?"

"This is the sort of task I *dreamed* of getting, back when I was home. It isn't under the circumstances I was expecting, but it's still perfect! Deception, stealth, observation, infiltration, education. Subverting authority.

And all in the dead of night. I'm in my element, Alan." She gazed up at the approaching building. "Pieces of this place even look the way I was told they'd look. Big, fancy hunks of stone with statues and stuff."

She rubbed her hands together. "That's it up there, right? That's the place we're headed for."

"Yeah," Alan said, expression conflicted.

"Great! Back up, into the shadows there. Start getting ready."

She spoke with the certainty and authority of a maestro preparing musicians for the performance of their lives. Alan stepped off the narrow sidewalk and into the alleyway. He pulled on some black cotton gloves and, after a moment to chase away the icky feelings associated with the act, tugged a balaclava over his head.

"I can't shake the feeling that if you're going to be a robber, you're not actually supposed to *look* like the robbers look on TV," he said.

"You have to hide your face, just in case, and you have to cover your hands."

"All that's missing is a black-and-white-striped shirt and a bag with a dollar sign on it."

"White stripes would be easy to spot, Alan. Don't be silly." Blot peered aside, eying the building. "Now, when you were documenting the murder scene, you were interested in footprints, right? So we don't want you leaving very many footprints, so from this point on, you stand still. Don't even take a step. If you need to move, I will move you. We're not going to leave a trace, but if we do, we'll leave traces that they won't be able to explain. Scattered footprints with nothing linking them. So just stay calm, stand still, and..."

"I know, I know. Deep breath."

He backed against the cool stone of the alley wall. Her hands slid out of the darkness and pulled tight around him. Other times, Blot's embrace of the darkness felt a bit mechanical, executed with all the emotion of giving someone a boost to hop a fence. This time it felt more like a playful pounce. She yanked him into the shadows and giggled gleefully as she slid along them toward her goal.

"Give me some warning when you're going to need to come up for air," she said. "I'll have to plan our stops."

He nodded, not entirely certain if the motion would read properly while they both were reduced to two dimensions. Sliding along the rippling cobblestones, fighting against the constant force of artificial light, the journey toward the station was even more of a roller coaster than usual. Alan had his eyes shut tight, but the stirring put him in mind of a marble rolling and bouncing its way through the innards of some Rube Goldberg contraption. He swirled and orbited, curled, and twisted. He felt himself thread between narrow passages and curve around pillars. When his mind decided he'd waited long enough between breaths, he gave her hand a light tap.

"Breather, coming up," she said. "Um... You're going to want to be crouched down, we'll be behind some trash cans in the alley."

She quickened her drifting and, when the time was right, loosened her grip. Alan popped unsteadily back into reality, crouching as he'd been instructed. Even so, the reassertion of the laws of physics came at the expense of his equilibrium. He almost pitched over, but inky black hands reached out of the darkness to steady him.

"Don't blow this for me," Blot said.

He gave her a hard look, but got his bearings and looked about. They'd closed the rest of the distance to the station and even slipped about halfway down the alleyway beside it. The only light here came from the windows of the station, which was the first piece of bad news.

"The place isn't empty," Blot said. "I didn't expect it to be, but I'd hoped it would be. It looks like most of the top floors are dark. We'll be able to get in just fine. You ready for another breath? We'll make it a short one, heading up to the roof. It doesn't look like any strong light is up there, so we should be able to regroup and discuss any new plans."

Alan nodded.

A quick yank pulled him into the shadows again, perhaps a bit before he was ready. He'd not closed his eyes before she was rocketing up along the wall of the building. He'd not taken the time to count how many stories the building was. After watching the strange, incorrect perspective of the city slide past his vision, he decided that whatever the number of stories it was, it was too many.

Their transition over the edge of the roof gave a surreal punctuation to the journey, with his two-dimensional head folding over the corner of the roof and shifting to an equally dizzying view of the sky that then rippled into a more natural view when she released him.

He skidded a heart-stopping half inch on the tiles of the roof. There was no danger of actually falling—he was several feet from the edge and there was a lip separating him from the drop—but logic didn't have much of a say in situations such as this.

"Are you okay?" Blot said, a dash of concern tempering her enthusiasm. "You're super tense."

Alan released a sharp breath.

"You can talk. There's no one nearby."

When he spoke, it was with the careful, deliberate tone of a person who would be yelling otherwise. "Blot, I realize we have done this sort of thing a number of times before."

"Yes! I'm getting faster, and my endurance is getting better."

"And I realize that it's often under much more dire circumstances."

"Yes. No one was trying to kill you this time."

"It turns out adrenaline and desperation have a way of taking the edge off suddenly appearing on a roof."

"Really? You seemed fine on the motel roof."

"Sometimes I'm better at faking 'fine' than others."

"Oh. Do you need a minute?"

"I do need a minute, yes."

"Okay, that's fine. I'll scout out our next steps. I should be able to reach pretty far into the vents without you moving."

"Good, yes. Do that."

"It's extra important that I scout well, because we'll be sliding through vents and there won't be any room to pop you back out if we get into a situation where—"

"The details aren't helping, Blot," Alan said sharply.

"Okay. Sit tight! Time to scout!"

Now satisfied he would be "fine" without her, Blot giggled with delight as she stretched away.

It took three more deep breaths before the shadow slides started to feel less jarring. Though there was a surprising amount of activity in the station, there were no shortage of dark corners for them to hop, skip, and jump through. They fell into a rapid pattern of scouting out a darkened camera-free place to pop into, slipping into that place, and gathering themselves for another iteration. Sure enough, there was plenty of signage leading them to the likely home of their target, Case Report Archives.

A pitch-black void of shadow leaked across the ceiling from a vent. White eyes blinked open and scanned the room. Blot drew longer and thinner as she slipped toward a single security camera mounted in the ceiling. Two hands emerged behind the camera, one clutching a simple pack of sticky notes. She peeled one away, popped it over the lens, then retracted into the vent. A moment or two later, a larger shadow unfurled from the vent and found a clear spot against the wall, and out popped a breathless, ski-masked Alan stepping into three dimensions.

"We're here," she said.

Alan widened his eyes. "Where exactly are we?"

"This is the Deep Storage Records Room," Blot said. "If the sign on the door can be believed."

Alan swept his eyes across the room. The only light in the room came from the illuminated exit sign. "Is it safe to use a flashlight?"

She crossed her arms. "We've got to do something about your night vision. Hold still, I'll check." Blot stretched across the room and under the door. When she snapped back, her bright eyes were just as gleefully excited. "No one outside or in the nearby rooms, but I hear a voice down the hall, so no talking above a whisper."

Alan nodded and withdrew a palm-size flashlight from his bag to sweep carefully across the room.

The place looked and smelled like the stacks at an old, unpopular library. The air was heavy with the musty scent of aging paper. Sturdy steel shelves stood in rows close enough together for it to be impossible for more than one person to fit between them. Rather than filing cabinets, cardboard bankers boxes covered the shelves. Handwritten notes on the outside of each box labeled its contents. They were organized not by anything as sane as date or alphabetical name, but by case number. Beyond the shelves were two large windows, firmly shut and blocked by vertical blinds.

"How are we going to find what we're looking for..." Blot said. "I could go box-diving, but it'll take forever."

Alan scratched his head and slowed his scanning. "My college library was like this for some of the more obscure periodicals. Kind of, at least," he whispered. "There's going to be an index... There!"

A small locking cabinet, directly beneath the security camera, had been carefully labeled with an old label maker: *Case File Catalog and Reference*.

"Why would they lock the index but not the files?" Alan whispered in disbelief.

"I guess they figure if you can't find what you're looking for, you can't steal what you're looking for. Stand aside. I've been practicing this."

He stepped out of her way. Blot's shadowy form flowed up the front of the cabinet. She twiddled the fingers of one hand, then gently eased them into the lock. Already lacking any depth, it was simple enough for them to pinch into the tiny space of the lock. Her lips tightened and her eyes shifted about. Soft clicks came from within the lock.

"You've been practicing this?" he said.

The cabinet clicked open.

"Obviously," she said proudly.

"*Where* have you been practicing it?"

She raised her chin haughtily. "Never mind where."

He pulled out what he hoped was the appropriate book from within and set it down on the top of the cabinet. Unlike the vast majority of the boxes, the book was clearly used rather frequently. In addition to the location of the box containing the associated case, each entry had the location of the sign-out sheet for the data. It was a nesting doll of access control. To do this properly would probably require three different keys and four different books.

Alan flipped through the pages. "It's not going to be under *Metro Ghoul*. It's going to be under the name of whoever was the suspect for that case."

"Oh! I have that. Barnes listed it." Blot produced a pad of her own and flipped through. "It was... Vincent Staccatto. And there's the date, I think."

He flopped the book to the appropriate page.

"Okay. It's row seven, shelf four, box two..."

"I'm on it!"

"Box three, box four, box five..." He turned the page. "All the way to box eleven."

He followed the thin band of shadow connecting him to his accomplice and sidled between the shelves. There wouldn't have been space enough for two people to observe the boxes if not for the fact that one of them had no depth. He shined the flashlight on the offending boxes. Each was precisely as deep as the shelf itself. Probably the shelves had been designed with the boxes in mind. All told, the amount of information wasn't going to be measured in pages. It was going to be measured in reams.

"We were supposed to copy the information and put it back," Alan said slowly. "That was the plan!"

"It's not my fault you people take so many notes," Blot said.

"We should just quit before something goes wrong. We'll find another way. Maybe we can figure a way to streamline the official request. Push it through the proper channels quicker."

Blot pointed back to the cabinet. "You just saw the proper channels. Does any part of that look like it can be streamlined to you? This isn't a problem. This can't *all* be useful information. We'll just go through it and find what we need and copy that."

Alan's jaw tightened, but he grabbed the first box. He'd known Blot long enough to know that riffling through a few thousand pages of evidence in a dark room while under threat of discovery was still faster and easier than trying to persuade her to do otherwise. He moved quickly and efficiently, flashlight in his mouth and box in hand. Once the box was on the one table available in the room, he slid one of his smaller cameras from his bag.

"I can get clear pictures, but there are going to be flashes."

"Don't worry about the flashes. I'll let you know if we need to stop. Just get to work."

Blot's form slid over the edge and down into the box. She rummaged through pages. Every few seconds a page would pop up and she'd shout a point of interest.

"Address! Name! Photograph!"

Each decent bit of information earned a snap from Alan's camera, which Blot had to brace herself through.

Alan learned a lot of things as it progressed. Handling sheets of old paper with gloves on was difficult, as was handling a camera. Doing something under duress while wearing a heavy ski mask didn't help matters. But the primary lesson he learned, and one that came almost too late to be of any use, was that when desperately trying to triage and record useful information, it is difficult to *also* keep tabs on the approach of a curious police officer.

"Wait," Alan said, his voice almost silent.

Blot stopped moving long enough for them both to realize footsteps were approaching.

"Someone's coming!" Blot squealed.

The pair of them snapped into action, hastily stuffing the current set of pages into the box and slapping the lid back on. He sprinted for the shelf and slotted it back into its place. Before he could turn, he already felt her arms around him dragging him down into the shadows.

"Wait! The cabinet!" he whispered.

They both turned. While they'd slipped the index back into its place, the cabinet was still ajar. Blot darted to it and slapped it shut. A key slid into the lock of the records room. Blot snapped back to Alan. She pulled him down into the shadows. The door clicked open. A uniformed officer stepped inside and flipped on the light.

Fluorescent illumination struck them like a wave, rushing the pair back until they were pinned to the far wall between the windows. The designers of the room had done a frustratingly efficient job of aligning the lighting. Banks of lights aligned perpendicularly over the shelves, meaning the only real shadows were beneath the shelves themselves. Blot held Alan tight and fought against the pressure of the light until they'd slipped into the impossibly thin space beneath the nearest shelf.

Alan held his breath and waited, his mind-twisting view showing only the spiderwebs beneath the bottom shelf. Footsteps clicked in his ears.

"Could've sworn I saw a flash..." muttered the officer.

The policeman lingered, taking slow, thoughtful steps. He was probably peering up along each of the rows. Blot eased them back so that they could curl back up along the lower edge of the far wall to keep an eye on the officer. No sooner had she done so than both she and Alan noticed a legal pad they'd set aside during the information triage. It belonged in the box they'd stowed. It certainly didn't belong on the table. And it was only a matter of time before the officer noticed it.

Alan started to twitch. His mind was rather urgently informing him it had been far too long since he'd taken a breath, and a far harder to define additional sense was more urgently reminding him that neither of them had been properly anchored to this world in that same amount of time. The lurching feeling in a pair of lungs that arguably didn't exist layered with the withering sensation in a soul that may not exist either started to layer with the increasing likelihood of discovery. It was not conducive to clear thought.

The policeman lingered. Alan tapped at Blot's hand. Her eyes looked to the vents along the corner of the ceiling. She gathered herself, lurched out into the light, and laboriously hauled herself toward the vent.

Alan could feel the light scouring at them, as if every photon were a snowflake in a howling blizzard. Somehow, she managed to reach the vent and curl inside. From there, she flowed like a torrent into the next room. It was similarly set up, though for some other sort of record-keeping. Before she'd even reached the floor, she released Alan. He unceremoniously returned to physicality a few inches above the linoleum and, somehow, managed to catch himself against the wall. He did not, however, do so silently.

The already suspicious officer audibly exclaimed. Thumping footsteps raced out of the neighboring room. Alan teetered on his feet. His legs felt rubbery, like they were just awakening from falling asleep. It didn't matter. Something had to be done or this was going to turn into a chain reaction of leading the police officer through a sequence of rooms in search of the source of the intrusion.

His darting eyes scanned the room and locked on the windows in the adjoining wall. Long vertical blinds hung in front of them, just as they did in the other room. Alan stumbled toward them, flipped the window lock, threw the window open, and gave the blinds a good hard slap for good measure.

"Back to the other room," Alan said, his mouth dry and his words slurred.

He took his place against the wall. Blot gave him as much time as she dared to let him recover and to remind the universe that at least one of them belonged there. When they heard the key turn in the lock, she pulled him into cold shadows and yanked him back into the vent.

They dropped down in the still-lit archive room. The light threw them against the wall. Blot released Alan and went sprawling onto the floor. He scrambled to his feet. Another pair might have been shouting instructions to each other, but they each knew the many tasks that needed doing and the terribly limited time to do them. Alan scrambled to his feet and shut off the lights, then grabbed the stray pad. Blot stretched to the windows to give them the same excuse for noise. It wasn't a good excuse, but it only had to last long enough for the police officer to stop caring about it. With the window open and the slats clacking, Alan turned back to the shelves. He'd expected to see Blot waiting for him, ready to make their getaway. Instead, he saw the cardboard boxes they'd been hoping to raid rattling one after the other.

"What are you doing?" he hissed.

"I'm stealing the evidence. We'll copy it and come back to put it back."

"Are you crazy!"

"They won't know unless they look for it. The boxes will still be here."

"But they are *going* to look for it because Barnes is going to request it!"

"Then we'll bring it back before then."

"But we—"

"Too late, what's done is done."

She emerged from the shelves. Despite the fact that he knew she was weighed down with seven boxes of case files, there was no sign of any of it. By now the person in the other room would be on the way back. There wasn't time to undo what she'd done. He stuffed the legal pad into his bag and stepped against the wall. She pushed him into it, slid up to snatch away the covering off the camera, then reached down to flick the light back on.

By the time the police officer had arrived to inspect the window they had opened, Alan and Blot were back on the roof. By the time he'd shrugged off his confusion and locked the rooms back up, Alan and Blot were back in his car.

Alan took a few cleansing breaths. It took fifteen continuous minutes of being an actual physical being before the empty, cold feeling of disconnection finally faded.

"That could have gone better," he said.

"It still went really well, though!" Blot said.

He slowly turned to the shadow cast on his passenger seat.

"What? We got what we were after. We didn't get caught. There's no screaming sirens or anything, so they probably didn't notice. Now we can take the stuff home, take our time with it, bring it back in a couple of weeks and—"

"No," Alan said.

"No what?"

He reached into his bag and pulled out his camera. A flick through the recent images showed he'd gotten good shots of what little they'd been able to go through.

"No, we're not coming back. Start laying out the evidence. We're copying it tonight."

"There's thousands of—"

"I've got the battery, I've got the storage. We're not getting caught with this stuff, and we're not getting into a situation where we're going to have to speed through three states to return stolen evidence."

"But—"

"It's what we're doing."

Blot raised her hands. "Fair enough. Let's get going."

Chapter 5

A lan sat on his couch with Blot beside him, head tipped back and arms spread wide. He shook his head a bit.

"Something wrong?" Blot asked.

"Nothing. I was just sort of... daydreaming about driver's ed for some reason. How many pages did it end up being?" he asked.

"Drivers ed?"

"No, the evidence."

"Two thousand, seven hundred," she said.

"Four pages at a time. That's like... what, six hundred photos?"

"Almost seven hundred," she corrected. "And they came out nice and sharp. I flipped through them."

"Ha! See that? If nothing else, college teaches you how to crunch like a pro."

He turned to her. She looked back to him.

"You're... three dimensional," he observed.

She nodded. Blot was, in fact, in her full "natural" form. Her hair still roiled up as if in a perpetual upward breeze, but rather than an imp-shaped void with stark white eyes, she had the full complement of shades of gray.

"So I'm asleep then?" Alan said.

"Yes," she tipped her head back and shut her eyes.

"And this is a dream."

"Sure is."

He whistled. "I must have been exhausted. Everything after the last few pictures is kind of a blur."

"Well, we got back in to drop off the evidence back in the boxes, no problem. They might not all be in the same boxes they started in, though."

He squinted, then shrugged. "We'll just assume the specific boxes weren't important. They probably were, but I'm too mentally exhausted to worry anymore."

"I like that policy. That's a good policy," Blot said. "Anyway, after that we headed home."

"Mmm..." Alan said. "It's going to be hell going through all that stuff."

"I flicked through a bunch of it before... well, I flicked through a bunch of it, let's leave it at that." Blot said, scooching a bit closer to him without opening her eyes. "I'm sure there's a lot more to learn, but here's what I think is the most important. There will be two more attacks before the Ghoul moves. There's no timing associated with them, besides that there will always be three total and always within a four-week period. But they *also* will be within a certain distance of a... let's call it a lair. There was a list of the old ones."

Alan's eyes focused on the far wall of his apartment, which was slowly developing a window. He wasn't sure if he was the one conjuring it into the dream or she was.

"It's always isolated. Usually underground."

125

Photographs fizzled into being outside the window, then subtly shifted to actual views of the depicted locations. The basement of a laundromat. An old subway station. The attic of a church.

"The police couldn't find anything else in common with them. They assumed they were preexisting hideouts of the killers. But the *police* aren't *shades*," she said.

"Something stand out to you?"

She took a deep breath. When she spoke, the words rippled into being in the air in front of them. They began as jagged runes, her own language, then gradually shifted into English.

"'When the days are growing longer, and the places to hide are few. When the light of the foe fills you with fear. Always remember, the foes do not know us, but the world they shape does. There are always dark places for a clever shade to hide. There are always evil figures, with blood more deserving of a place on the ground than flowing in their veins. To call upon the others, to open the way, search for the places the foes have marked for you.'"

A map fluttered into being outside the window. Burning embers marked certain points. One by one, elements upon the map took on a similar glow, matching their description.

"'Where the burning light appears, there will be a ribbon of water. Where the burning light vanishes, a field of green. There you will find The Balance of Shadows. Look for the place where the byways mark the beginning. If the third falls before the bald-faced moon, the others may hear you. If they do not, the place is not right, but there are many places.'"

With these final words, the streets surrounding each of the hideouts took on a glow. They weren't always the nearest streets, and they weren't always in the same orientation, but they always formed the same general shape. Something like a crude rendering of a comb. One street was angled, four more led down from it, and the hideout was on the intersection of the second shortest street and the angled one.

He looked to her. Her eyes were still shut, but her lips were curled into a satisfied grin.

"You figured all that out?"

"It's a nursery rhyme from back home, 'The Balance of Shadows.'" She coughed. "It rhymes in my language. See, that's what they say it'll take to summon other shades, if you're afraid you'll never find your way home again. It's in the middle of a big long story, an epic, about a shade who learned to summon an eclipse at will."

She pointed at the shape.

"That's the first letter of our alphabet. Once I noticed there was a river to the east of every lair, it was staring right at me."

"Oh... So it's the shade equivalent of *X* marks the spot."

"Unless I misunderstand your language, it's like the shade equivalent of *A* marks the spot."

"So we have to find a place like this in Philadelphia. A river to the east, a park or something to the west, and this shape in the streets. It shouldn't be *that* hard."

"Harder than you think. You people sure like your parks and diagonal streets."

"If we get a map of the city and lay out a grid—"

"Um, Alan. I hate to interrupt you, but it's starting to get a little bright out and even with the tint, the shadow of the steering wheel is getting down into a position that's awkward for me."

"Steering wheel... Are we driving right now?!"

A blaring horn jolted Alan awake. He found himself still in the driver's seat of the car. It was well past dawn, and they were in fact sitting in the midst of morning rush hour. The car jerkily rolled forward on its own as Blot did her best to pilot the vehicle while essentially peering over his shoulder. He took control and pulled back to the center of the lane he'd been wandering out of.

"What the hell were you thinking?" Alan asked. "How long have I been asleep?"

"About an hour." She glanced at the clock in the dashboard. "Almost two."

"You drove for that long by yourself?!" he said.

"Not by myself. You were coaching me through it. I guess you don't remember. Sometimes dreams seem to slip away from you."

"That was so dangerous!"

"You needed sleep. You couldn't keep your eyes open. You driving would have been more dangerous."

"We could have pulled over and let me get some sleep without a creature with no experience driving trying to drive through an entire state."

"But then we would have been a whole state farther from home right now."

He blinked his bloodshot eyes. "I'm not going to argue with you. I'm going to get off at the next rest stop. I'm going to get coffee. And we're going to get home."

"I entirely approve of that plan."

He signaled a lane change and wiped some more sleep from his eyes. "Nursery rhyme..." he said.

"Yes."

"He's killing people because of a nursery rhyme."

"We all know it. It would make sense for one or more of us to end up doing it."

"You've got a nursery rhyme that teaches you to kill people."

"You heard the rhyme. It doesn't technically say to kill anyone. It says, vaguely, that some people deserve to die. And it says that bit about 'the third' falling. You could certainly interpret that as the third foe falling. You could probably interpret it as the third of the month. Who knows where a desperate mind goes? Places of safety and calm are few and far between for us. It isn't hard to imagine someone snapping and looking for any way to get the rest of us to help."

Alan's eyes drifted aside. "This is a killer..." He squirmed a bit. "I don't want to feel sympathy for a killer. I don't want to think of him as frightened and searching for help."

Blot shrugged. "No one's as bad as you think. No one's as good as you think. It turns out we've both been told the same lie from different ends, that evil is a thing that exists, and that it'll be an easy thing to spot."

"The leader of the shades is called Stigma. Todd's shade is called Rive. Heck, *Blot* isn't exactly a friendly name. You take hosts without permission and condemn them to death when you find a better host. There's a heck of a lot of indications of evil there."

"I'm not going to defend what we were taught to do. But what we are is what we are. And those words are *your* words. They don't mean the same thing where I come from."

"Then why are so many of them evil-sounding words?"

"Your last name is Fontaine. Back home we have a word that sounds like that. Fon-hayne. It means pickax. Am I supposed to assume you're a miner? Maybe the name thing is an attempt to intimidate your people, maybe it's a coincidence. Maybe someone on this side remembered how scary we were during one of our earlier visits and associated our names with bad things. Maybe it's little slices of all those reasons. I don't know. The point is, with the exception of people giving the orders back home, none of us really knew the truth. We're not here gleefully tearing you people apart because it is our nature to do it. We are doing what we were taught to do in defense of our world. That doesn't make us evil. That makes us pawns. By the darkness, that makes us *victims*."

"What do you think we could do to you that would justify all this?"

"Look around you! You've found ways to shove us around, make us helpless. You're one step away from figuring out the light that burns, like the disciplinarians back home. And if we can come through to your world, you can come through to ours. It wouldn't take much for you to flood through and end us. We were taught that it was your goal, and that the only way to defend our people was to take charge here and prevent you from doing it. Not evil. Defending our people, with the tools we have, because we were lied to."

He considered the words. "I can't think about this right now. A tired mind can't metabolize philosophy." He shook his head. "You said that whole thing rhymes in your language?"

"Very nicely. There's a song that goes with it, too. My grandmother used to sing it to me."

"I always, sort of... I don't now. I guess I realized you must have had your own language. I've seen some of the writing. But you speak English so well."

"We knew where the gateway tree would be. There aren't so many languages it would have been. There's this one, Il y a celui qui semble chic avec les sons R drôles, Tánon Kí:ken Énhskat. So they taught us those three. Then I just had to figure out which one you were speaking and pick up the nuances. It's easy when there are dreams and a soul-bonded link to speed things along."

"Wait, wait, wait. I think that was French in there, and what was the third one?"

She shrugged. "They just called it 'the oldest one.'"

"So you speak French?"

"Pas très bien. La langue est le genre de chose qui nécessite de la pratique."

He couldn't help but smile. "How am I still learning things about you?"

"I'm many layered. Like a parfait." She snapped her fingers. "I should make a parfait next!"

Too many hours later, Alan was pulling into his parking structure. An inadvisable amount of caffeine, saturated fat, and sugar had gotten him through the car ride home, but it had not served him well on a physical or psychological level. He'd bounced back and forth between desperately distracting himself from the situation at hand and trying to solve the many, many problems it presented. Blot, for her part, was more than willing to engage in either case. One moment she was flexing her recently acquired mastery of capacitive touchscreens to try to track down a lair in Philadelphia that fit the criteria. The next she was helping him understand the lyrics to a song on the radio.

Now that they'd arrived at home, it was time to summarize to himself the key points so that his fried brain would have a fighting chance of remembering them well enough to act on them.

"We can't tell the cops what we figured out, because it's from stolen information and based on an otherworldly nursery rhyme, so it's still going to have to be us..." he muttered.

"You'll want to keep your voice lower. People overhearing that might get the wrong idea," Blot advised.

"We're going to have to still handle this ourselves. There's no telling how much time before the next killing, just that there will be two before the next full moon. When's the next full moon? Did we look that up? I'll look that up..." He tugged his phone from his pocket and started poking through it.

"*Excuse* me," snapped a woman.

He looked up to find he'd nearly bumped into his neighbor, Ms. Levitt. From her reaction, you'd think he had sprayed her with goat's blood.

"I'm very sorry," he mumbled. "Didn't see you there."

"Apology not accepted," she said.

There was the sense from her tone and body language that she'd been saving this up for a while, desperate for anything she could perceive as a slight to justify it.

"You are so horribly self-centered. Always thinking about yourself. I try not to stick my nose into your business. Into *anyone's* business, but with all the coming and going, and all the things you've got going through all hours of the night, it's time someone gave you the talking to that you deserve."

"I'm sorry, Ms. Levitt, but I really have to go. I have to—"

"Don't act like whatever you've got going on is more important than what I have to say to you! Do you have any idea the sort of problems you cause? Hmm? You may have straightened out that wrong address thing, but it went on for *far* too long, and then there's the thefts that have been happening. You don't seem to care, which, if you ask me, seems awfully suspicious, almost as though you're involved in—"

"Just walk away," Blot said. "We've got better things to do."

She continued, blocking Alan's way as he tried to step past. "And that strange woman who came and said she was your friend. At least I think she was a woman. I didn't ask, but—"

"Quiet!" Alan snapped. "My god, woman, there is a serial killer on the loose. I have to find him before he kills again, and you're talking to me like I'm an eight-year-old who spilled his cereal on your carpet while you were babysitting. Do you have any idea the day I've had? No! You couldn't possibly, because no one has ever had a day like the day I've had, and the same goes for the day before and the day before. My life is a constant cavalcade of inexplicable nonsense, and I can't just set it aside to listen to you lecture me, *again*, about the inexcusable crime of *having an apartment near yours*. If I don't find a way to handle the tornado of insanity that is consuming me, then people will *die*. So excuse me, I have to go decode a nursery rhyme about killing enemies to summon help, okay?"

She looked upon him with eyes wide and lip quivering. For only the second time since he'd known her, she was actually rendered speechless.

He huffed a breath and stomped his way toward the elevator to the main building. After a few steps, he turned back and stabbed his finger at her car.

"And learn how to park! The car goes between the lines, not straddling it!" He turned and marched on.

"... Hello, police?" he heard her whisper as he walked away. "I've been accosted by my neighbor. Yes, I know his name..."

Alan stepped into the elevator and sniffed. "This'll end well, I'm sure."

A half hour later, Alan was sitting in his apartment, calmly explaining what had happened to a pair of police officers.

"... It had been a long ride back from the country and I was at my wits' end," he said.

The officer was unfortunately not among the handful he'd encountered in his two station shifts. Not that he would have felt good about his familiarity letting him off easy. But at this point any sort of a break would be welcome. And as uncomfortable as it might have been for him, it was worse for Blot. Rather than have to answer a half hour of very reasonable additional questions, he'd taken advantage of the few minutes it took the police to arrive to remove the various shades from the lights. He already knew from his limited experience that the police tended to indulge their curiosity in situations such as this. So while Alan was sitting and answering questions, Blot was pinned to the ground beside him impatiently awaiting an end to the whole endeavor.

"Let me see here..." The policeman flipped through his notes. "A ten-hour round trip in a twenty-four hour period *is* liable to test your patience. Why would you do that just for some pictures?"

"I'm a photographer. Everything I do is just for some pictures."

"Can I see them?" he said.

"Ha!" Blot proclaimed. "I told you!"

Alan nodded and pulled a second camera from his bag. On Blot's suggestion, he'd preloaded it with some shots from a prior trip to the country. He'd even gone so far as to fudge the metadata so it looked like he'd taken them early that morning. The cop flicked through the previews on the camera, then handed it back.

"They look like regular photos to me. Like the sort of thing you could just take at a park."

Alan shrugged. "When you make your living at it, you start doing crazy things to get that extra bit of... something."

"Yeah, I guess." He handed the camera back. "It doesn't seem like there was any criminal intent. And this is the seventeenth call from Ms. Levitt this month, so it shouldn't have come as any surprise that it might have been an oversensitive interpretation of events. Frankly, I'm giving her a ticket for that parking job. But do us all a favor and make some room for sleep next time you do one of these so you don't snap at your neighbors. I can't blame her for thinking you might have been on something. You look like hell."

"Right, sir. Sorry, sir."

They stood and Alan opened the door for him.

"Oh! Finished already?" came a familiar voice.

Alan leaned out after the officer to find Jessie, in full uniform, trotting up the hallway.

"Yeah, it was nothing major. Typical call," the officer said.

"That's fine. This is a semipersonal follow-up," Jessie said, stepping aside. "Hi, Alan. Can I come in?"

"Say no. There's work to do," Blot insisted.

"Yeah, come on in," Alan said with somewhat less enthusiasm than normal.

Blot grumbled. Jessie stepped inside, and he shut the door behind her.

"Wow. It's bright in here," she observed.

"Yeah..." Alan pulled open the drawer on the end table to fetch the fabric shades to start draping over his lamps. "I figured it'd streamline the questioning if I didn't have the mood lighting in place."

"Making plans to get the cops out of your apartment faster. That's not suspicious at all," she joked.

He nodded numbly and continued installing the shades.

"I've got to say, I didn't expect there to be any truth to it when I heard you'd lost your cool. I don't think I've ever seen you scream at anyone. But you really told off the neighbor lady, huh?"

"It's been a rough couple of days."

"Oh, I know it."

He finished prepping the living room's lights and flopped down on the love seat. Blot slipped over to cast herself on the seat beside him, but almost immediately had to swap to the wall behind him when Jessie sat beside Alan instead.

"Just make yourself at home, why don't you?" Blot said.

"Oof... You really do look like death warmed over," Jessie said.

"Road trip for photos," Alan said, lacking the motivation to completely rehash the carefully prepared cover story.

"Yeah. Let's talk about that," she said.

He rubbed his eyes. "Okay..."

"You know you've been working crazy hours. You know you will continue working crazy hours. And yet you planned this trip."

"Sometimes, when the notion strikes..."

"And we have done a *lot* of talking in the last couple of days. At no point did you mention you were planning this."

"Wasn't really a plan."

"See, I've never known you to be impulsive."

Blot slid up to the ceiling and gazed down at them. "I don't like the direction this is heading. She's making way too many observations."

"It's just... been a rough couple of days," Alan repeated. He did not have the intellectual energy to play keep-away any longer.

"Alan, you're teetering. I don't like to see it," Jessie said.

"Sorry."

"Don't apologize. But do take action. Do you still have the card I gave you for my therapist?"

He mechanically reached for his wallet and fumbled for it. "This is her, right?" he said, blinking blearily at a business card.

"Yes. I've got an appointment with her later today. I'm thinking we might be able to sub you in. I think you need it more than me."

"I have a lot to do, Jessie."

"Oh, I know, which is why I'm suggesting you fix this leak in your sanity before the whole apartment floods with crazy."

"I appreciate the concern. But I really don't need it. There's so much to do and—"

Jessie gently took him by the elbow and stood him up.

"What are you doing?"

"Is your bedroom decent?" she asked.

"I don't know. I can't remember the last time I was in there," he said, with far less humor than he would have liked.

"Okay, bathroom then."

"Why is she taking you to the bathroom?" Blot asked. "Is this a human thing I don't know about?"

She maneuvered him through the bathroom door and stood him in front of the mirror.

"Look at that guy," she said.

"... Oof..."

Alan almost didn't recognize the man staring back at him. The bags under his eyes had a purple tinge. His eyelids had a pronounced red rim. The wild mane of hair on his head hadn't seen a comb or brush in too long. At some point his semistrategic amount of stubble had turned into a neglected beard.

"Is that a guy who looks like he's handling things as well as he needs to?" she asked.

"I just need sleep," he said, not quite convincing himself.

"What sort of sleep do you think you'll get tonight if you put your head down with whatever did this to you running around in it?"

He couldn't keep himself from shuddering in response. "You sure this lady is going to let me in on no notice?"

Jessie leaned in and smiled at him in the mirror. "I can be very persuasive." She brushed off his shoulder. "So here's what I want you to do. Take a shower. Maybe try for a nap. Get something to eat. I'll swing by and pick you up at about seven. Appointment's at seven thirty. I've got to get back to work." She gave him a slap to the shoulder and tousled his hair. "See you then!"

She let herself out, leaving Alan to stare into the mirror for a few minutes more. Blot slid up along the wall behind him, visible in the mirror.

"Jessie shares a disquieting number of traits with your mother," Blot observed. "As long as you are going to let a stranger pass judgments on the workings of your mind, I would suggest you bring that up."

"Noted."

CHAPTER 6

Alan shifted uncomfortably in the waiting room of Jessie's therapist. It was like most waiting rooms he'd been in. A little too small, a little too air-conditioned, and ominous in a way that a room with an old TV and old magazines really shouldn't be able to achieve. He was alone, as it wouldn't have been very appropriate for Jessie to sit in on his session, so she'd headed out for some errands, leaving him to squirm in expectation of his analysis. Worse, a voice in his mind wouldn't stop bugging him about the fact that in a situation like this, he absolutely should not be wasting precious time in an office having his brain picked apart.

That voice belonged to Blot.

"We could be out there finding the Metro Ghoul right now," she said. "It's only a matter of time before one of those white-suits shows up and checks your progress, and you're going to have to tell them you spent an hour of your day lying to a doctor."

"Why do you assume I'll be lying?" he whispered.

"Because the truth will get you put back in a cell for observation. Three days is enough, thank you very much."

"Alan Fontaine?" called a voice from within. "You can come in now."

140

He stood and straightened his shirt. Alan was from the school of thought that one should dress in one's Sunday best when going to the doctor. This seemed doubly appropriate when going to a therapist. There were few times in one's life when it was more important to appear well put together.

The inside of her office wasn't precisely as he'd pictured it. There was no couch. There was a desk, but the therapist wasn't sitting behind it. She was seated in one of two chairs that occupied the middle ground between easy chair and dining room chair. They were cushioned, but there was no threat of someone dozing off in them. The lighting was low. Not as low as his apartment's light, but low enough for Blot to have freedom of movement.

Dr. Ling was an older woman. Somewhere in her midfifties if he had to guess. She radiated "doctor" in everything from her wardrobe to her demeanor. Oddly, he found the presence of a clipboard made him feel better about the whole situation.

"Have a seat," she said. "Jessie's said a lot about you."

"Has she?" Alan said, attempting to hide the concern in his expression.

"Relax," she said. "Good things."

Blot slid up behind the doctor and glanced at the note she made on the clipboard.

"It's just a number," Blot said. "There's three initials and a number. Seven. What does that mean?" Blot said.

Alan shut his eyes and tried to pull himself back to the train of thought he'd been on a moment ago. "I didn't think a therapist's office was a place to talk about good things."

"We talk about whatever you would like to talk about."

"In all the movies, it's all 'tell me about your childhood.'"

"Would you like to talk about your childhood?"

"Do you think I should?"

"You're coming off as desperate," Blot said.

He glanced quickly in her direction, then back at the doctor. She made a note. Blot glanced at it.

"And distracted, apparently. Stop being so distracted," Blot said.

Frustration flickered across his expression.

"How about you tell me about this new job? Jessie says becoming a forensic photographer has been an aim of yours for some time?"

"Uh, yeah. I guess I've been working on it for a while. It just felt more important than what I'd been doing..."

For nearly an hour, Alan felt like he was sparring with Dr. Ling. At some point, at Alan's nonverbal urging, Blot had stopped spying on her less than obvious note-taking. Instead, she wandered the walls, critiquing the decorations and attempting to find things worth stealing or spying on. This left Alan to attempt to anticipate exactly what line of reasoning the doctor was heading down and cut off any "this guy is crazy" answers before they could come tumbling out of his mouth.

Intellectually, he knew that this was precisely the wrong way to be handling this situation. At any other time in his life, he might not have *welcomed* therapy, but he would have tried to extract the emotional nutrition it was intended to provide. But he just couldn't afford the beginning of a long stretch of emotional healing right now. No matter how badly he needed it, there were more important things to do.

The doctor glanced at her watch and set her clipboard down. "We're getting toward the end of the session, but I think we can safely start wrapping up."

"Um... Okay. What's the verdict, Doc?"

"I can share my assessment if you like, but only if you are comfortable."

"My policy has always been that it's better to have answers than to not have answers."

"And it's *never* gotten you in trouble before," Blot mocked.

She took a breath. "I think you're evasive. Everyone has their concerns about privacy and fear of being judged, but you have one of the more pronounced cases I've encountered, in recent years at least."

"But am I crazy?"

"'Crazy' is an obsolete term. It's like 'hysterical.' You throw it at a thing to dismiss it rather than addressing it. But let's look at the questions, shall we? Is your current behavior problematic or destructive? I would say, simply looking at the physical toll that it's taken on you, the answer to that question is yes. So now we ask if that behavior is within your control. If it is, then you can take steps to correct it, and you will when you decide the time has come. My job would be to help you come to that decision. If it is not in your control, then you need help. It's clear that you carry the weight of the world on your shoulders. You are afraid of disappointing those who rely upon you. You are afraid of failing those who need your help. Not an uncommon problem, but one that is going to add stress to your life. So that's something I'd like to see you work on."

"Yeah, I'd like to see me work on that too."

"It's important for you to realize that more of this is in your direct control than you think. Obviously, you can't simply choose to stop feeling obligated to solve the world's problems, but the more you are aware that minor failures won't mean major disasters, the better."

"Yeah, if that was..." He stopped.

Dr. Ling folded her hands and waited expectantly.

"True?" she speculated, when he failed to finish the sentence. "I know it can feel like the world depends upon us, but even the most powerful men and women in the country don't act alone. Sometimes that's a relief."

"You should probably wrap this up and get out of here. That was almost a bad slip," Blot said.

Alan felt his jaw tighten. "How do you know?" he said.

"How do I know you aren't the pillar holding up the sky?" she said. "Because no one person is. The world doesn't work that way."

"But what if it *did* work that way?"

"We should really leave, Alan," Blot said.

Alan continued. "What would happen if someone the world *did* depend upon walked in this door? Would you be giving the same advice? 'Don't worry about it? What's the worst that could happen?' How would you treat someone actually fighting to save lives?"

"Your friend Jessie is a police officer. Lives certainly depend upon her from time to time. And my advice is the same. Do your best, but it doesn't help anyone to grind yourself to powder worrying about things beyond your control." The doctor flipped up her clipboard and marked something down.

"We should go," Blot said, peering over her shoulder. "She just wrote down 'delusional' with a question mark. You're going to get us locked up again."

"In a minute!" Alan snapped aside to Blot. "The point is, 'don't stress out' is great advice to someone worrying for no reason, but that's *terrible* advice for someone with something legitimately on the line. Maybe I can't just relax. Maybe I'm supposed to be stressed."

"Alan," Blot said.

"*In a minute,*" he snapped again. "All I want to know is, if all this stress *was* justified, then what? What would be your advice then?"

The doctor stared evenly at him, waiting to see if there was more to the outburst. When none came, she simply smiled. "I would have the same advice that I have for you now. Speak to the receptionist and schedule another appointment. I think there's progress to be made."

For once, Alan was able to resist the urge to drown his sorrows in diner food. He persuaded Jessie to bring him back to his apartment for dinner.

"You sure you don't want help?" Jessie said, sitting at one of the two kitchen tables. "I don't remember you being *super* great at cooking."

"Being a bachelor for a while has made a dent in that," Alan said.

"Are we cooking for her? Are we really cooking for her?" Blot asked, eyes trained on Jessie. "The kitchen is my place, Alan."

"If you're not on board with my cooking, are you sure you want to stay for dinner?"

Jessie shrugged. "There's nothing good on TV tonight, and you're fresh off your first therapy session. Figured you could use the company."

"Fine..." Blot said. "She's getting chicken then. The grilled chicken, not the breaded chicken. We have lemon juice left, right? Check if we have lemon juice."

Alan pulled open the refrigerator. "You okay with lemon chicken?" he said.

"Sure. Really, I should be cooking more often. It seems like the leftovers never last. Like six times in the last couple of weeks I was out of something I didn't remember finishing. It's what you get when you snack in front of the TV."

He started to shut the refrigerator, but Jessie leaned back and caught the door.

"Is that homemade pie?" she said.

"Uh, yeah. But it's kind of an experiment."

"Experimental pie? You are a man of unexpected depths," she said. "Can I have a slice?"

"If you're sure..." he said. He pulled it out for her and set out a plate and utensils.

It was all Blot could do to keep from physically helping with the cooking. Instead, she peppered him with instructions. "Remember to hammer that out a little. And what vegetable are you making? Peas? Keep an eye on the time so the peas get done at the same time..."

"You've been notably taciturn regarding today's session," Jessie said, returning the remainder of the pie to the fridge.

"She thinks I'm crazy."

"Everyone's crazy, Alan. A therapist's just getting you closer to the regular amount."

"I got a little snippy in there," he said.

"Oh, gosh. Perish the thought. You should have heard me in there when I first got started."

"You also talked to me out loud. Twice," Blot said.

Alan froze.

"Pepper that chicken before you put it in the pan," Blot said.

"Something wrong?"

"Just... beating myself up about something."

"Plenty of people in the world to do that besides you, Alan." She took a bite of pie. "... This pie has coffee in it."

Blot turned to watch her. Jessie was chewing slowly, face complex.

"Yeah. Like I said. Experimental."

"I like it," she said, scooping up some more. "It feels exotic."

Blot huffed. "So she's got better taste than you."

"Do you need a drink?"

"What am I, a lightweight?" she said.

Blot narrowed her eyes. "Much better taste than you."

Alan turned back to the meal prep.

"Oh!" Jessie said, her mouth already filled with the next bite. "Did you hear about the break-in up in Boston?"

"Just keep cooking, just keep cooking," Blot said quickly.

Alan tried to avoid accidentally flipping the frying pan off the stove with his shaking hands.

"Break-in?"

"Yeah. It's the weirdest thing. Hang on. There's video." She started to dig out her phone. "Apparently an officer was bugged by the fact that some windows were open in a room that no one had used for a while, so he decided to review footage from the surveillance to see who went in and left it open. There was a big gap in the recording, though. Inexplicable. But when he checked the footage from the *other* room with the open window..."

Alan's heart leaped into his throat.

"We didn't block the camera in the other room!" Blot squealed. "How could I be so stupid? We were in and out and I didn't even check where the camera was!"

She started to stalk along the walls, fingers curling angrily as if to strangle the air.

"This is what they saw," Jessie said, standing to stick her phone in front of his face.

A near-black video on an ad-laden site that probably got half its videos from Cox Media and their competitors revealed a barely visible form stumbling out from behind a shelf to fiddle with the windows. There was no earthly way anyone would ever be able to tell it was Alan. And thanks to the angle of the camera, it was impossible to see the nature of their arrival in the room. It was just a man suddenly in, and then not in, the room.

"Crazy, right?" Jessie said, plopping back down and loading up some more pie. "That's the only footage. All night, no other cameras caught any shot of the guy, interior or exterior."

"Spooky," Alan said, his throat a little dry.

"So they figured, hey, it must be a glitch. You know, a shot from another day that somehow didn't get overwritten or something."

"Right. That makes sense."

"Good, yes. I love you humans and your need to find explanations you feel are plausible. Flip that cutlet," Blot said.

Alan did as the master chef instructed.

"But they dug deeper and they found another anomaly. The footage was blocked a few hours later. Just for a minute or two."

"Sounds like they need to upgrade their surveillance system," he said.

"Security in general, because after they determined there was something up with that room, they gave it a once-over and a couple of boxes had been monkeyed with. All the dust was missing from them."

"Dust? Really?!" Blot said. "If your police are going to be noticing things like dust, I'm really going to have to be more mindful of details."

"Wanna guess which boxes were messed with?" Jessie said.

"No clue," Alan lied.

"The Metro Ghoul case files. Every single box, and only those boxes. You should *hear* the theories people are slinging around about this one. Naturally, people think it's the current copycat trying to keep them from finding him, except unless there have been new developments since I read this article, the evidence is all intact. My favorite theory is that the copycat is trying to get *better* at copying."

"Nuts," he said.

"Start the peas, Alan," Blot said.

After a passable lemon chicken, Jessie having an inexplicable second piece of pie, and a *lot* of mediocre attempts to appear calm and collected, Alan was relieved when Jessie headed home. The moment she shut the door, Blot started dictating.

"It's fine. It's fine," Blot said. "They can't prove it was you, there's no evidence. We just need to be more careful."

Alan leaned on the door.

"We got the information we needed. We've got a whole day before your next shift with the police. That's plenty of time to find the new lair. And the... and we haven't gotten any visits from people looking for more updates."

"I think she's onto us," Alan said.

"What? No she isn't."

"Why did she bring that up?"

"Because it's a major case and you both work with or for the police. She's not really suspicious, and she's certainly not onto us."

"She knows."

"She doesn't know. And if you keep acting like she does, you're going to slip, and then she *will* know. Now focus. We need maps. If we don't get out to at least one potential lair tonight, it's very likely the Ghoul will pick a new victim before we can do anything about it."

He took a deep breath and let it out. "Fine. I'll get the laptop open. Draw that shape out for me. I'm still a little fried. Remembering things isn't a strength at the moment. But how hard could it be to find a likely place between a river and a park?"

The search for the lair went on for nearly three hours. There were two major rivers and well over fifty things that could be considered "green fields" in the greater Philadelphia area. Drawing straight lines between them and searching for something that a twisted imagination would identify as a shade rune would have been an exercise in tedium for a well-rested mind. For the sleep-deprived Alan, it was an exercise in frustration. Blot did her best to help, but two people working on the same laptop wasn't a recipe for efficiency. In the end it was still Alan who spotted the most likely locations. They were all reasonably near the motel where the first murder had taken place, quite near the Delaware River, and just east of this park or that field. Now it was just a matter of visiting them and hoping for the best, or the worst, depending on one's point of view.

"What are the chances we are going to be able to find him?" Alan asked.

"A lot better if you keep quiet," Blot said.

Her eyes were shut, such that her entire form was little more than, ostensibly, a proper shadow. Albeit one in the wrong shape. This was the third neighborhood they'd visited. Blot had confidently disregarded the first two almost immediately. This one warranted closer inspection.

"I don't know if it's the Ghoul," she said quietly. "But there is definitely something... *shady* about this place. It's not in any one place. It's sort of... *everywhere*. It's deep. 'Stained,' I think I heard you say once." Her eyes opened. "I'm not going to be able to pinpoint them."

"I guess I'll keep my eyes peeled then," he said.

"It's not going to be any easier for *you*," Blot said. "If you remember, I was able to hide from you for a while, and we're linked."

"I never had a hard time with Dun and his crew."

"They weren't trying to hide from you. They were trying to intimidate you."

"How do we know the Ghoul will be trying to hide?"

"I guess we don't. But it's certainly no secret that we're out there now. The word has spread that we're a threat to shades. And unlike every single other member of my kind, apparently, I can't hide myself mystically. They'll know exactly where we are, and we'll only know vaguely where they are."

Alan drummed his fingers on the steering wheel and looked through his tinted window. During the day, he had to admit, it was sort of nice having it take the edge off the glare around him. But at night, it made looking out his side and rear windows difficult. Even without a clear view, though, he knew that this wasn't a part of Philadelphia that he would have willingly lingered in if not for the task at hand. He'd managed to convince himself neighborhoods like this were exaggerations. They were the sort of places that people from the suburbs and rural counties believed all cities were. Shifty people with the glaring body language of someone trying to hide their actions from would-be authority figures and snitches were in ready supply. A man who may as well have answered a casting call for a drug dealer lingered on a street corner past the next intersection. Staggering drunks that reminded Alan just a little too much of Todd teetered along the sidewalk. For fifteen minutes, he crept along at low speed, dodged propositions from sex workers, and politely assured pushers that he wouldn't be picking up any heroin today, thank you very much.

He really didn't know what he was looking for. But it couldn't have been more clear when he found it. A young woman turned a corner and made her way up the street. She was dressed in what may as well have been a uniform for the other prostitutes he'd had to rebuff. High heels, a dress a bit tighter and shorter than public opinion and weather deemed appropriate. But she wasn't, for lack of a better term, "advertising" in quite the same way. Quite the opposite. Her head was down. Her gaze darted away from anything that might pass for eye contact. She was trying to make herself smaller, shouting with her body language to be left alone. And she looked tired. It was a bone-deep weariness tinged with edginess. It was a look he'd seen in an intern named Lenny after a few weeks of hosting a shade of his own. It was a look he'd seen in a dozen inmates when attempting to stop a plan to make the prison into a stronghold. It was a look that peered back at him from the mirror these days.

Alan took note of her outfit. He shifted his gaze to her large purse. He rolled down the window a crack for a clearer view. "I think it's her," he said.

Blot looked out the window. "She could be. The sensation clinging to this place isn't any stronger or weaker now than it was a minute ago. But why her?"

"Look at her bag," he said.

She slid a bit closer. "There's black stuff on the bottom."

"Roofing tar, you think?" he said.

"Hmm... It's as good a guess as any. But what do we do about it?"

"I'm going to follow her," Alan said. "Keep your eyes open a bit more than usual."

"Oh, trust me. I'll be watching your back. This is personal, now. If I'm going to be the only shade who can't hide from other shades, then I'm going to make sure that the other shades know they can't hide from *me*. And that means getting us through this unharmed."

Alan shut his window. "Good to know you're doing this for all the right reasons, Blot."

Alan's in-vehicle pursuit of the suspect lasted for all of five minutes. Once he turned a corner to continue following her, the woman stepped not so subtly into an alleyway. Alan stowed his car and said a silent prayer to the patron saint of vehicular theft that it wouldn't be broken into. He then armed himself with his usual one-two punch of a large flashlight and a small can of pepper spray. He also grabbed the smaller of his cameras, as it felt like failure of survival instinct to walk through this particular neighborhood with several thousand dollars of electronics and optics around his neck.

"We're getting closer to the center of it," Blot whispered to him. "If there is an official lair, it's not far from here."

He nodded. This was no surprise. The alley was dark. Branching off the angled street that formed the top of the "rune" from Blot's rhyme meant that the streetlights didn't cut more than a few feet into it. The soft crackle of broken glass underfoot drew his eyes upward, where he found the light above the back door of one of the storefronts had been broken. A scattering of other broken lights and carefully covered windows formed a trail of breadcrumbs that led, ultimately, to a barred grating in the alleyway. It covered a recessed window peeking out of the foundation of one of the buildings. The door was boarded up, but the greasy mud of the alley-way was heavily disturbed with familiar high-heeled footprints. The woman, however, was nowhere to be seen.

Alan glanced down to Blot. Her eyes were shut. Her form wasn't even hers. She was barely there at all, mixed into the dense darkness of the alley. The feathered, half-seen edge traced out his own form. She was hiding, just as she had been in their earliest days together. Somehow that simple sight, his shadow as it had been instead of how he knew it to be, sent an icy stab of anxiety through him. It was like walking through a forest and suddenly finding the wildlife has gone silent around you. The way small, frightened creatures act when there is a predator near.

He felt alone. There were moments, more of them than he would care to admit to Blot, that he longed for solitude. But right now it was a terrifying thought. Alan crouched down to investigate the grating. He raised his camera.

"You need to go," warned a nervous female voice.

Alan sprang to his feet and threw himself against the wall. It didn't matter where the voice had come from. He'd scrutinized every inch of the alley as he'd walked through it; there was nowhere for someone to come from except the shadows, which meant he now had his answer regarding the nature of this woman.

He swept his eyes through the darkness and locked on to her. She didn't look angry or threatening. She looked frightened. But even that didn't tell the whole story. She wasn't cowering away from Alan. He wasn't the thing to be frightened of.

"You were at the motel," Alan said.

He gripped his camera tight and tried to visually separate her shadow from the darkness. Unlike his own, even the feathered, hazy edge of darkness upon darkness of her shadow was difficult to make out. It was an ill-defined blob of black curling off from her body.

"Please, sir," she said, clutching her purse tighter. "Just please go."

"I know what you are. I know what's happening to you. And I know what you did."

She shook her head. "It's not me. And *I* didn't do anything. Please just go."

A new sound rattled from underneath her. The wall behind her, half-seen in the darkness, trembled with a stone-on-stone screech. And slowly the shadow resolved into a figure. But it wasn't the twisted, stretched combat form he desperately hoped Blot was preparing to take on right now. It wasn't the small, impish form like the type he knew to be her true self. This was something else. It was cast along the ground, yet somehow seemed even lower. The eyes appeared peering up at him, small and unsettlingly round. And the limbs... this thing didn't even attempt to adhere to a humanoid form. Its arms and legs were ill-defined and shifting. Numerous. Like something between a squid and a crab, scuttling fluidly along.

Alan raised the camera in one hand and tightened his grip around his flashlight. "Blot, what the hell is that?" he said sharply.

"I don't know what it is," she said, eyes open and stance wide and wary. "It *feels* like something from my world..."

The woman's eyes widened, and she backed against the wall. "You've got one too!" she said. "Oh god, how many are there? What's happening?"

"It's doing something," Blot said. "Even now it feels like a blurry smear, not something sharp and real." She growled. "Tell me what you're doing!" she shouted. "Distract him, Alan. Break his concentration."

It was simple enough to do. Indeed, at this point it was the only tool at Alan's disposal. He tipped up his flashlight and clicked it on. Almost immediately, he wished he hadn't. The woman flinched at the light. Her shade did far more than flinch. The light threw it against the brick wall behind her. Its form didn't make any more sense when sharply defined. Even pinned by the intensity of the flashlight, the many limbs were shifting and shuddering, sweeping past each other in ways that made it impossible to say if there were six of them or twenty. Its head, if it had one, was somewhere in the center of the splat of a shape, identified only by its unblinking eyes.

There was nothing in its eyes or its motion that suggested wisdom or intelligence. It felt like a wild animal. And he'd just cornered it.

"That's it," Blot said. "I felt the effect flicker. It takes concentration to keep it up. And it's already back in place."

Alan snapped a few quick photos while the pinned creature dispassionately surveyed them with its perfectly round eyes. Each flash of the camera caused it to splay and shift its limbs against the wall, and each time Blot's expression became more fascinated.

"I get little doses of what I should be feeling. But they're wrong. He feels... heavy."

"Heavy? What do you mean heavy?"

"Like he's carrying things. A lot of things."

"You can feel that just by being near him?"

"Our senses are better than yours. It's one of many, many ways we're better than you."

The woman took a step forward, fear now colored with desperation and confusion. "W-why does yours talk to you? Can she reason with mine?" she begged. "I'll do anything. Just get it to stop!"

"Blot?" Alan said.

"Right. Reason." Blot eyed the shifting form. "I am not certain this thing will be receptive to reason."

"It's worth a try, because I can't stand here with a flashlight on it forever."

"Fine." She cleared her throat.

The next sounds she uttered were foreign. Unfamiliar. The language she uttered sounded... angular, if such a word could be applied to sound. There was a sharpness to the words, a precision he wasn't certain he could imitate without months of practice. This was Blot's native language. And it was almost haunting to hear it spoken in a familiar voice.

Her words *did* have an impact. The creature, still pinned to the wall by the light, tipped its head. Or at least, it rotated its eyes. The limbs became stationary for a moment. A rolling, rattling sound was uttered from the misshapen form in reply, oozing forth from a mouth that split a patch of shadow beneath the eyes into a half-moon of jagged teeth.

"What did it say?" Alan asked.

"Nothing. It was nonsense," Blot said. "Or a *terrible* accent."

The sound rolled out again. Already-sharp words took on an additional edge.

"That sounds like anger, Blot," Alan said.

"This isn't good. Just go. Just go!" the woman cried.

"We have to find out how it's hiding from us!" Blot started to shift herself, taking on her combat form. "Listen, you feral ghoul, I'm not leaving here without answers."

Again the shifting form froze. A new sound shuddered forth from its form. A long steel-on-stone grind. At the tip of each of the many limbs splayed on the wall, stone crackled and flaked away. Gleaming points caught the light of the flashlight.

"Go, go, go!" the woman said, crouching down. "Not another one!"

The limbs flailed and snapped. The air twinkled. Alan's body performed an involuntary motion somewhere between a flinch and a dodge. Blades of various sizes and descriptions perforated the wall behind him. Some dug deep into the mortar between bricks. Others clanged and clattered to the ground. And one particularly well-placed blade smashed the flashlight out of his hand, casting the alley in darkness once more.

Alan's photographic reflexes were far more finely trained than his self-defense mechanism, and he managed to snap a burst of photos before Blot yanked him desperately into the shadows. The strobe of light treated him to a half-dozen limbs snapping out of the wall and snaring the woman casting the shadow. She was roughly drawn into the darkness, then a second fusillade of hurled blades dug deep into the section of wall formerly blocked by Alan's body and currently occupied by his shadow. He had a split second to come to terms with the odd, cold sensation of a blade penetrating his silhouetted form, to say nothing of the dim realization that if Blot had taken a moment longer to act, the knife would be lodged in his liver.

Drawn into the shadows as he was, Alan could differentiate the form of their attacker as it bounced madly between walls. Blot followed, struggling to keep up.

"He's so fast!" she growled.

Both shadowy figures spilled out onto the street and were struck by the streetlights. Caught in the same current, they streaked along at the same speed. The feral thing abandoned the darkness first. Blot released Alan, dumping him back into reality. The thing's hapless young host stumbled along ahead of him. Neither of them had reentered three dimensions gracefully, but the woman's high heels proved far less suited to the task of a foot pursuit.

"We need a plan!" Alan said. "I don't know what to do!"

"We should have thought about that before we tried reasoning with it. I knew that was a bad idea," Blot said.

Alan caught up with the woman and grasped her arm. "Listen. I can help you, I just need—" he urged.

"Stay back!" she screeched.

She pulled free from his grip and kicked him to the ground. Knives whistled through the air where he had been, then inky black limbs tipped with rusted blades arced up out of the ground and attempted to skewer him. Blot's own vicious form asserted itself and swatted the blades away. The woman made a break for it and disappeared into another alleyway. Alan followed but skidded to a stop at the edge of the alley. Another trio of knives twirled past where a less cautious pursuer would have been.

"How many knives does that thing *have*?" he said.

"I told you it felt heavy."

She flicked a hand up. His backup flashlight appeared in her grip.

"Keep the thing lit. I'll try to keep the knives out of you."

"I don't like the word 'try' in this context," he said.

He listened for the gasping, terrified breath of the woman, then blindly pointed the flashlight around the corner and charged in. The blast of light didn't have nearly the effect he would have liked, as a barrage of blades launched toward him before he'd taken three steps into the darkness of this new alleyway. True to her word, and in a tribute to her skills, Blot swiped a shadowy hand up into reality and "caught" the blades, allowing them to vanish harmlessly into two dimensions rather than strike him.

The feral thing launched another trio of blades, then another. But expert teamwork between flashlight and shadow kept Alan safe. Finally, the pathetic tinkle of what looked to be a razor blade tumbling to the ground at Alan's feet seemed to signal the end of the many-legged creature's ammunition.

"Good," Blot said, rising up into her full vicious battle form. "Now let's see how things go when you're not trying to skewer my host. Get close, Alan. Try to keep the light on him, but off me."

The thing squirmed in the light, claws fruitlessly carving at the cinder-block wall of a convenience store. Blot loomed over him, her own claws flexing.

"Now listen close. If you won't listen in our language, listen in this one. What you're doing is going to get you killed. We are here to get answers. If we get them, and you stop killing, then this whole thing will be over and—"

Three limbs snapped out of the circle of the light and caught Blot by the arm. She dug the claws of her other hand into the wall, and a sort of tug-of-war began. The light was in Alan's hand. It couldn't possibly be casting Blot, so no amount of tugging and pulling from the feral could pull her more than a few inches into the flashlight's glow. But it nevertheless tried, snapping more and more of its limbs to the task.

"What do I do?" Alan said, holding the flashlight steady.

"I'll handle this. Just... keep the light on him."

Alan watched the pair struggle, then turned his eyes to the cowering woman in the glow of the flashlight. She was trembling, eyes shut and hands over her ears.

"You have to go. You *have* to go..." she muttered again and again.

"Listen!" Alan said, trying to snap her out of it. "You have to help me. When did this happen? What is this?"

"It's been years," she wailed. "I thought I was crazy. I tried to pretend it wasn't there. But then... then it... it *killed* him..."

"Years. But the rest of the shades didn't show up until just a few months ago."

"That thing has been in my dreams and in my shadow for years... Ever since I found that body."

"Body?"

"It was dead. It was dead already. And then... I swear it wasn't me! I swear I didn't do it!"

"Calm down," Alan said.

"That thing... that *thing*..."

"Alan, back away," Blot said. "Slowly."

His eyes snapped up to her. Her free hand had carved three long furrows into the wall. She wasn't being dragged into the light, but the thing gripping her *was* being drawn *out* of the light somehow. Alan took some steps back.

"Listen to me, I swear I can help you, but I need to be able to find you again. What's your name?"

The woman trembled, her eyes streaming tears as she watched the shadows struggle with one another.

"He's stronger than me," Blot said, extreme effort in her voice.

"What are we going to do?" Alan asked, taking a step back.

"I'm going to shake him free and we're going to regroup. So give it some space and get ready to run."

He took a few steps back. The thing held firm, causing Blot to stretch just a bit farther from Alan.

"Let go of me. I swear, I will tear you off your host if you don't let go of me right now."

The thing growled and pulled sharply back. Blot squealed and Alan felt a wave of numbness as the connection between them was tested. He dashed closer again to ease the separation and keep Blot from being torn free.

As he moved closer and the angle of the flashlight changed, the feral thing was projected up along the wall. His eyes flicked aside, and the maw of the thing reappeared, contorting into a grin. Two limbs snapped up and struck the window now just within range. The glass shattered, but as pieces fell free, none of them reached the ground.

"No, no, no," the woman shouted.

Three more of the uncountable limbs flicked toward the light. Shards of glass streaked out. Alan dropped to the ground to avoid being struck. The flashlight survived the move, but failed to keep the thing pinned.

He felt it drag at Blot, and again the connection between them was strained.

"I will *not* be the weakest shade in this world. I refuse!" Blot growled, struggling against the thing as more and more of its limbs coiled around her.

Alan tried to train the light on the woman again, but her shade dragged her through the darkness as she squealed.

"Please! No! I'm Marsha! I'm Marsha Gr—"

She was roughly tugged into the darkness, reduced to a silent shadow before she could finish. Any attempt to shine the light upon him now would push him away and probably tear Blot free in the process.

One of Blot's hands extended. "If it'll ever work... let it work now," she muttered.

The fingers of her hand opened, and shining in the black palm was the silver amulet. She clicked it open and clutched it tight. Blot's eyes narrowed and her lips tightened as she attempted to draw upon the strength within the shard. Slowly, the trembling of effort as she resisted the grip of the feral subsided. His eyes locked on the amulet.

"Shard..." he uttered.

The word was the first genuine evidence of intelligence they'd witnessed from the creature.

"Oh, no!" Blot said, tightening her grip until the amulet vanished again. "If it comes down to unlocking the power or losing it, I'll take my chances against you without the locket."

The feral released Blot and drifted deeper into the alleyway. He lingered for a moment, then lashed several limbs up to the wall. Alan stood firm, hand on the flashlight but still unwilling to turn it on, lest they lose the creature. The limbs traced out a sequence of shapes. They were not carved into the stone itself, but instead hung as extensions of his shadowy form. The eyes turned to Blot.

"Gardener," he said. "Before the next moon."

There was a flurry of limbs. Each of the limbs dug into the wall. They traced out arcs that lingered as the runes did, then ended each arc with its own fresh rune. The circle traced out by the ring or arcs rippled blue and black. The thing fell back into it, dragging the girl with it. The sudden yank was enough to dislodge a piece of jewelry from her wrist.

It wasn't like anything Alan had seen before. It didn't just slip into the shadows. It vanished entirely. And not long after, the rippling circle faded as well.

"What... what just happened?" he said.

He turned to Blot. She was watching the runes the feral had rendered as they slowly faded away.

"Did you get them? Do you remember them?" Alan said.

"I remember them. But... they don't make sense. It was my language, but it wasn't. It wasn't a spell either."

"What's the gardener?"

"How should I know?!" Blot snapped. "And I don't know what just happened with that circle, either. For a minute it felt... it felt like *home*. It wasn't home. That wasn't our world, it went to. But it felt like it."

Alan crouched down and picked up the dislodged bit of jewelry. It was a charm bracelet, festooned with assorted trinkets of various shapes, sizes, and patterns. He pocketed it. Blot shook her head.

"Let's get out of here. That thing is more than we can handle now. I need to recover. And we need to figure out what all this means. I need coffee and you need sleep. We'll discuss it tonight in your dreams."

Alan nodded, his eyes drifting down to the pulverized glass embedded in the wall beside him. "Yeah. I'm pretty sure I'm not going to be able to avoid getting another run-through of this whole thing tonight."

Chapter 7

Alan gazed up at the mysterious black shapes traced on the wall. He'd collapsed as soon as he'd gotten home. Since then, he'd been reliving various hunks of the day in his dream, falling into and out of lucidity and being nudged back into it by Blot.

"I just don't know what it means…" Blot said, gazing at the shapes.

Her voice jostled him back into an awareness that he had control over his surroundings. He shook himself a bit, then willed the sketched-out set of symbols a bit lower on the wall so he didn't have to crane his neck to look at them.

"They look just like regular runes to me," Alan said. "To the degree that *any* runes look regular."

"Some of them *are* regular. This one here is definitely punctuation. But it's in the middle instead of the end." She crossed her arms. "I think this is an old form of the language. But even that doesn't explain everything."

She tapped her foot and leaned back, lounging in midair as she casually disregarded physics.

"How long do you figure the… I guess we'll call it the Ghoul?" Alan started.

"It's as good a name as any."

"How long do you suppose he's been here? The woman said she'd encountered him years ago, but from what you've been saying about what you were taught about our world, you folks haven't had a major trip over here since before electricity."

"If he's been hopping between hosts, he could have survived in your world for any number of years."

He scratched his head. "I'd been sort of assuming the Metro Ghoul was just a series of shades all doing the same ritual. Now I'm starting to think it's the *same* shade doing the same ritual."

"Could be either," Blot said. "But please remember that as nice as it would be to stop the serial killer, the thing we need to do to make our white-suited overlords happy is figure out how the Ghoul is hiding from them."

"Either way, we'll need to find him again."

"And *this* is the only clue we've got," Blot said.

A soft clicking sound echoed around them, seeming to come from everywhere and nowhere. Alan narrowed his eyes and looked about. "What's that sound?"

"It's probably your mind about to throw the Ghoul at us again," Blot said, hopping to her feet again and widening her stance.

"Again?"

"Yeah. You've technically been having a prolonged nightmare," she said. "We usually only get a few minutes of talking before the Ghoul or Todd attacks you. It was even *me* once. We'll have to have a word about that, by the way."

"Why don't I remember this?"

"Because I've been doing my best to keep things from getting too unpleasant for you." Blot tipped her head. "Step back."

She placed a little hand on his chest and gave him a light shove, then held up a hand. A fraction of a second later, two empty white eyes appeared in the darkness, and an inky, flailing mass of limbs launched toward Alan with a monstrous screech. He tensed, raising his arms. The sound died away as suddenly as it started. Nothing struck him.

He opened his eyes and found Blot standing with her palm planted firmly between the eyes of the thing, which was now statue-still and lifeless. She huffed a breath and stepped back. The Ghoul hung in the air, inert. Without its horrid, unnatural motion, the thing was almost beautiful. It was a piece of strangely organic modern art, the sort of thing a Lovecraft aficionado would dream up and fashion out of modeling clay and fishing line.

The lighting in the dream swelled slightly. It didn't provide any additional detail for the figure. Indeed, there *wasn't* any more detail. Just as was the case when Blot pulled herself from the darkness, light didn't reflect from the form. Even in three dimensions, it only ever felt like it was *pretending* to be a three-dimensional object. As remarkable and eerily lovely as the shape was, though, he couldn't help but tremble at the sight of it.

"This thing really scarred you, huh," Blot said, stepping back from its form and placing a steadying hand on his shoulder.

"It is a jagged hole in reality that launches knives at me. I'm just glad it didn't scar me in the literal physical sense," he said, his voice failing to buy in to the humor his words were attempting to sell.

Blot turned to him. Her expression had an uncharacteristic amount of empathy.

"Listen, Alan. I know... I know that I don't always act the way you'd want a partner in this whole maddening plot to act. But you need to understand that I am very much dedicated to keeping you alive. Not just because it'll keep me alive. At this point, I could bail on you in a minute. I've got the strength for it."

"That's not very comforting," Alan said.

"Being comforting is a new concept for me, okay?" She brushed some imaginary dust off his imaginary body. "The point is, you're one of the good ones. You've been a little twisted by an unrealistically black-and-white depiction of good and evil, but there's a lot of that going around. I was taught that family and all that was meaningless. The only important thing was what our leaders instructed us to do. The Mission Is All. But that's not true."

She pointed back and forth between them. "This? Whatever this is? It's more than... well, it's more than *nothing*. You are important to me. Yeah, you're the guy who buys me coffee and lets me watch TV and bake pies. But you're more than that. I call you my host. And you've referred to my kind as parasites..."

"That was out of line," he said.

"No it wasn't. It was accurate. I don't have to *like* that it was accurate, but it was accurate. What bothers me more than the word is the fact that I'm not just that. Not to you. We're friends. You're maybe the first real friend I've ever had. I would have had no right to expect such a thing from you, and I still think you're a little crazy for giving it to me. But now I've got your friendship. You've got *my* friendship. And by the void, I actually care what happens to you. So I know it isn't the magic wand that'll whisk this fear away, but remember that I'm right there with you."

She marched up to the frozen Ghoul. "This thing is scary, sure. But it's alone. Sure, it's attached to that woman. But they clearly weren't working together. So we'll always have the edge. You'll protect me, I'll protect you. As for this thing? It'll protect her because it has to, but she clearly doesn't know what's going on. She won't even know to protect it out of self-preservation."

Alan nodded slowly.

"Feel better?" she asked.

"For someone who's not used to comforting people, you're doing a pretty good job."

"I'm a quick learner."

He turned back to the monstrous shape and felt only a tiny flutter of the same fear. In fact, it was a gentle enough flare that he had enough of his wits left to realize something else. "The woman..." he said.

The darkness from which the Ghoul had emerged swirled away like mist in the wind, revealing the cowering young woman.

"What about her? We didn't even learn her full name."

"I wouldn't be surprised if the Ghoul doesn't know it. The way it's just dragging her around, it doesn't have to ask permission. It doesn't seem terribly verbal. And she clearly doesn't understand what's going on. I wonder why she hasn't gone for help. I think she's a prostitute. We as a society haven't been terribly dedicated to solving their problems," Alan said.

"Ah. So shades aren't alone in our crass disregard for each other's well-being."

"I've got to see if I got her in any of the pictures," he said. "I was so focused on warding off the Ghoul that I didn't think to focus on her. If not, maybe you could sketch her."

"Why?"

"So the police could find her."

"What good will it do? You saw what happened to us when *we* went after her. Do you think the police would have a better time? And even if they did, she'd be out of whatever cell they put her in as soon as the lights were out."

"Yeah but..."

Blot raised her eyebrows and waited. "But?"

He grappled with the options available and finally slumped. "I guess you're right. All we have right now is those symbols. And a long-overdue update to the white-suits."

Blot flinched at their mention, then shut her eyes and leaned back. "Wow..." she said.

"What?"

"Every time you mention needing to talk to them, they show up. I think I've even made it happen once or twice, which raises questions I know they'll never answer. But there's no knock at the door. No one standing in your room waiting for you. Not even a ringing phone. Apparently the inside of your head is the one place they can't hear us."

"That's a relief. But let me get up. The sooner we talk to them, the sooner we can get this whole thing over with."

Alan took a shower. They had some caffeine afterward, all the while carefully avoiding any mention of the white-suits, and took their time to assemble their thoughts. Then, when the time was right, Alan said the words.

"I guess we should have a word with the white-suits."

Right on cue, there were three sharp knocks on the front door.

"You know, it takes three tries to get Beetlejuice to show up," Alan muttered.

"Who?" Blot asked.

"Never mind."

He opened the door, where Angel was waiting in their white jump-suit.

"This one. So presumably Stigma is still out there keeping the twins busy," Blot said.

"Hello, Alan." Angel looked vaguely in the direction of the shadow. "Hello, Blot. I don't suppose you've got any updates for me."

"Angel, it has been established you're spying on us. No need to be coy. You wanted an update, we've got one for you," Alan said.

"I see. May I come in?"

"By all means," he said, stepping aside.

They paced through the doorway and sat in his easy chair.

"As a matter of fact, we were aware that you must have made some progress, as we very briefly lost sight of you," Angel explained.

"You did?" Alan said.

"That's interesting," Blot said. "That means whatever the Ghoul is doing, it affects an area, not just himself."

"So what have you learned?" Angel asked.

"We found the Ghoul. It is indeed a shade, and its host is a prostitute. I can show you where the lair was."

"Was?"

"We had a rather significant confrontation that really did not go well. If it hasn't pulled up its roots and found a new place to hide, I'd be very surprised."

"I wouldn't," Blot said. "From its point of view, it got away without a scratch and it still has two more kills before the full moon."

Alan looked to Blot, then back to Angel.

"She was talking, I assume?" Angel said. "I pride myself on my manners, and not interrupting a person I cannot properly see or hear complicates matters."

"Blot suspects the Ghoul might stick around until it's finished the ritual."

"Ritual?"

"Were you not paying attention to us when we discovered that?" Alan said.

"That was in a dream too," Blot said.

"Oh... I'm having difficulty remembering what was a dream and what was real. That's a *great* sign... Angel, we figured out the Metro Ghoul has been trying to perform a ritual described in an old shade nursery rhyme. It's supposed to bring help or something. The point is, it involves three kills before a full moon."

"I see. While this is fascinating, you'll recall that our assignment for you was to determine the means by which they have been evading our gaze."

"It wasn't very forthcoming on that point. We ended up with nothing but a bracelet from the woman it was linked to and a phrase or something that it traced out for us."

"May I see the bracelet?" Angel asked.

Alan handed over the jewelry. Angel looked it over.

"Not terribly distinctive," they said, handing it back. "And the message?"

"Blot couldn't read it. Do you think you will be able to?"

"The shades aren't known for being comprehensive in the education of their lower level operatives. We, on the other hand, have been following their activities for quite some time. There is a chance, at least."

"Um..."

Blot flourished her hands. A pad and pen appeared in thin air, and she carefully jotted down a sequence of symbols. It didn't appear to be the full message, but Alan made certain not to mention that little observation. Blot tore the sheet free and offered it up.

"I am pleased to find that you are no longer as frightened of me as you once were, Blot," Angel said.

"Tell them I was never afraid of them," Blot said.

"She was never afraid of you," Alan said.

"Ah. My apologies, then." They flicked the page and looked it over. "Impeccable penmanship. You are certain this was copied correctly?"

"Yes," Alan said without checking.

Angel stroked their chin and eyed the page a bit more critically. They snapped their fingers. "Ah! I see the problem. You say you can't read this?"

"Neither of us could."

"Fascinating. I don't know why, but I would have thought the incomplete education would have only extended to modern developments. Typically, externally reinforced ignorance is specifically intended to keep underclasses buried in the past. You see, these are shade runes, but they are *quite* old. Older than my present understanding of them. I'll just take this back—"

Blot surged up from the darkness and snatched the page out of their hand.

"No, you won't take it back," she snapped. "If you want our help, you keep us in the loop with what you find out just like we do with what we find out."

She eased into the darkness, page in hand. Angel leaned back in the chair and surveyed the place where Blot had been. Blot slid aside such that Angel was gazing at empty floor.

"That is reasonable. If you can decipher similar messages without checking with us, you can more swiftly establish communication and perhaps acquire the information we seek."

"Wow... I expected more of a fight on that one," Blot said.

"The issue is that the information I require to help you decipher this is too sensitive to leave my laboratory." They smiled. "I don't suppose you'd like to come with me?"

"You want us to come into Schrödinger's apartment?" Alan said. "Is that... allowed? It seems like that's the sort of thing that would require a memory wipe or something like that afterward."

"Naturally, I'll need you to keep your hands to yourselves."

"Sure we will..." Blot said deviously.

"It is for your own protection, of course. I have taken pains to protect everything in my laboratory with wards similar to those on my pad, so if Blot were to *mistakenly* attempt to take something from the laboratory, it would result in a brief, painful, and automatic punitive measure."

"We'll see about that," Blot said, somewhat less confidently.

"Very well then," Alan said. "We agree."

"Splendid! Right this way!"

"A few ground rules, if you do not mind," Angel said. "As a gesture of good will, I will present them as requests, rather than orders. That said, if you do not agree, I will have to order you instead."

"So the illusion of trust and hospitality," Alan said.

"Human nature being what it is, it is the best I can offer. I have tremendous insight into human nature, you realize."

"Because you are a human. Yes. You've mentioned," Alan said. "What are the rules?"

"In addition to the aforementioned request that you keep your hands to yourselves, I ask that you also remain nearby. My laboratory is deceivingly large, and portions of it can be dangerous to minds and bodies unprepared for it."

"Just like your average human."

Angel placed a hand on their hip. "Alan, I must again point out that you have a sentient shadow and have made repeated jaunts as a two-dimensional specter, and yet I do not question *your* humanity."

"Fair point. What else?"

"I request that you remain aware of your personal possessions and do not leave any of them behind."

"Airplane rules. Got it," Alan said.

"Please refrain from speculating about the purpose and nature of any unidentified books, artifacts, or periphery. If you must know something, ask. Do not, however, expect an answer."

"Okay..."

"And that should be all. I hope I have been clear?" Angel said.

"Crystal," said Alan.

"Excellent, then let us proceed."

Angel jangled some keys and unlocked the door. When they opened it, it revealed the bizarre, physics-defying grand library that they'd caught glimpses of whenever Angel slipped away. Angel held the door open. Alan marched past, sliding Blot along with him.

Angel shut the door. They fitted a key into the deadbolt and locked it. When they removed the key, the door faded from view. The realization that he was now trapped here only slightly tempered Alan's raw wonder of the place.

It was enormous. Sprawling in a way that the view through the door barely hinted at. Endless rows of bookshelves lined six tiers of balconies. Warm, gentle light came from flickering candelabras. The floors, walls, and pillars were a cool, ivory-colored stone polished to a high gloss. Shelves and other furniture were some manner of blond-colored wood, seemingly without a finish but worn and faded wherever it might come into contact with hands.

Notably absent were windows and doors. The distant walls were simply more of the same: white, seamless, and pristine from the floor to the vaulted ceilings.

"Don't like it..." Blot said. "It feels bright."

Alan didn't question the odd statement. The place wasn't really any brighter than his apartment. Candles simply didn't cast enough light to really be problematic in their brightness. But he found himself squinting nonetheless, like his body knew something about this place that his eyes didn't.

"This way, please," Angel said. "It would be best if we handle this quickly. I am confident that Gabriel and Dina would agree that a visit is necessary. Though, I am not confident that they would be pleased to learn we lingered."

Angel stepped quickly to the stairs and navigated to the next level. The bookshelves visible from below didn't tell half the story of what the tier had to display. Long, low tables along the far wall were covered with artifacts arranged with museum-level care. Mounted, labeled specimens. Pieces of skeleton labeled with years and locations. Folded white clothing of countless styles. Dried and pressed flowers. Racks of vials with lengthy scientific labels. As random as it all seemed, the thing that seemed most out of place was, of course, the place that Angel was leading them.

"Prior to this assignment I did all my work out of a more remote location, so I've had to reclaim a bit of space here for the coarser work associated with my role," they explained.

Just ahead was a workbench that was at once too crude for its surroundings and too ornate for a proper workshop. It looked as though whoever had made Louis XIV's bedroom set had been asked to stock a carpenter's shop. Stout legs carved with gold-leafed filigree and tipped with claw-and-ball feet held up an angled work surface cluttered with jeweler's tools.

"This is the place I would like you to stay," Angel said. "It won't take a moment."

Angel walked briskly toward a nearby stairwell. Alan turned to the workbench.

"Steal something," Blot said.

"No. Angel said to keep our hands to ourselves."

"They were probably talking to me. I'll bet they didn't make any wards against humans."

He eyed the doodads on the table. Most of the equipment was unremarkable. There were small hammers and anvils, pliers of various sizes, and antique soldering irons. Six pieces of jewelry in various states of completion were carefully laid out. All of them were silver, and looked vaguely like they belonged in a set with the locket Angel had provided.

"If you don't try to steal one, I will," Blot said.

"I think that's a bad idea."

"Nothing ventured, nothing gained," Blot said.

She rose up from the shadows, struggling a bit more than usual. After a moment to gird herself, she reached a dainty black hand out and poked one of the half-made pendants. Something like a golden arc of electricity jumped from the pendant to her finger, and she snapped back into two dimensions with a pained yelp.

"You can't honestly have expected anything else to happen," Alan said.

"Now you try," she said.

"No!"

"Come on, Alan! I want to see if I'm right. It didn't hurt that much."

He gritted his teeth, squinted his eyes, and slowly extended a finger, fully expecting a shock of his own. It never came. He poked the same silver ring she'd attempted to grab with no repercussions.

"That's strange. I wonder—*ow!*"

An attempt to touch a second piece of jewelry jolted him painfully.

"Ah-hah!" Blot said. "It's a single zap per item. They were trusting no one would be willing to risk another zap!"

"I'm not taking any of these." He sucked his finger. "And you shouldn't either."

"No, of course not. None of those. They're right in the open. But if there's something really enticing, and I figure out how to do it without them seeing, I'm fully willing to take a zap."

Footsteps signaled Angel's return. They appeared at the base of the steps with a large three-ring binder that simply did not belong in a place this fancy.

"This is a bit of personal research," Angel said, plopping it down on a clear part of the workbench. "I have copied it from the main tome and added my own insight."

They flipped through the binder, revealing pages neatly arranged within. Each page was hand-lettered with a sort of artful precision not seen since monks stopped illuminating manuscripts. The paper was thick and oddly textured, possibly vellum.

"Let's see your page again, please," Angel said.

Blot flicked it into reality and handed it to Alan. He handed it over.

"Now listen closely, Blot. And watch, if you are able. I am going to attempt to demonstrate the difference between this older dialect and the one my records indicate should be your native tongue."

"How do you know so much about shades?" Alan asked.

"We are skilled observers. Now look, here. This indicates that the following few symbols are intended to be interpreted as numbers, not letters..."

Angel was an efficient teacher, though it helped that the message was so short.

"I think I see... My grandmother used to write a bit like this..." Blot said, nodding through the last bit of instruction. "It's not *so* different from what I'm used to, if you look at it the right way."

"So that means that the message that the Ghoul left for you is... thirty-nine, end of sentence. Then without a word separation before or between, the following sequence of numbers. Ninety-five, thirty, forty. And finally, the sentence 'Left of The Way of the Burning Light.'" Angel glanced between their notes and the message. "That appears to be accurate. A code, perhaps?"

"Beats me. Blot?" Alan said.

"It's nonsense," Blot said.

"Nothing," Alan relayed.

"Ah. Unfortunate, but we have at least learned the dialect that the Ghoul speaks. That isn't without value. If nothing else, it implies that it arrived here... in the year 1886 at the very latest."

"Really?" Alan said. "He's been here that long?"

"Naturally, we cannot be certain based on a single message. It could simply be an old message, or an intentional attempt to deceive. But until we have information to the contrary, I suspect it is a very old shade. Which means there may be a handful of shades who have perfected this technique long ago and have seen fit to teach the newest batch... Something to consider." They shut the binder. "You did well to find this information, but I must impress upon you the importance of finding the Ghoul again and uncovering its means of stealth."

"Keep them talking," Blot said.

Alan tried to keep from giving Blot a hard look. "Let me ask you this. If we find the Ghoul and we work out how it's hiding, are you going to stop it from killing again?"

"*I* will not stop it from doing anything," Angel said. "I am forbidden to interfere."

"Except for the times that you already did."

Angel crossed their arms and dictated with the speed and precision of an infomercial disclaimer. "The Shard of Shadow was never intended to be released into general circulation, and for reasons you are not entitled to know, returning it to the Dawn was rendered inadvisable. We can keep an eye on you, and we wish to keep an eye on the shard, so giving it to you and keeping it secret from others was the most neutral course of action. As for Trent Street, must we go over that again?"

"Ouch!" Blot blurted. "Keep them going."

"So you are just going to let the Ghoul kill people, even when you can stop it?" Alan said.

"We aren't shepherds of the human race... Any more than any *other* human is a shepherd of the human race. If we squander our resources preventing a handful of murders, we may not have the capacity to correct larger threats that no one else would be able to."

"Okay, we can go now," Blot said.

Alan tightened his fist and made a mental note to find out just what Blot had been up to.

"You may, of course, take whatever actions you see fit to stop the Ghoul yourself," Angel continued. "We merely require that you uncover the means of stealth first. Doing so should make it much easier for you to pursue vigilante justice."

"It isn't vigilante justice. I work for the police now," Alan said.

"Unless there has been a significant change to the rules and ethics associated with law enforcement, I doubt your specific level of authority is sufficient to justify apprehension, let alone execution, which may well be necessary to stop this scourge with any finality. You don't even have a badge."

"... I have a lanyard," Alan offered.

Angel gave him a pat on the shoulder that managed to miss being condescending by mere inches. "Then I hope justice will be served. Let us return you to your apartment. The hour is late and you could use a few more hours of sleep."

Their host led the way down toward the stairs. Alan glanced at a collection of goods.

"Why do you have this stuff?" he asked.

"We all have our areas of interest."

"You're interested in skeletons and flowers?"

"My interests are many and varied. Constructing a proper ward is far more art than science."

"Considering it is magic, I would say that it's not science at all."

"There is more science in magic than you realize. But the point is, a proper ward draws upon forces present within a world. Those forces are in everything. They come from the very elements that form a world, both in the periodic table sense and the earth, fire, wind, water, ether sense."

"You threw the fifth one in there."

"There are actually eight, but that isn't relevant to the conversation. The point is, I must study things of every type and form in order to divine the proper ways to influence the world with the maximum effect and the minimum interference."

They continued down the steps. "I really wish I could share more with you," Angel said. "I think it would fascinate you, and as one who seeks to find structure and composition in scenery, you might even have the proper skills to put it to use. It all comes down to seeing shapes both in what we have and what we need. Negative and positive space, but in a context where space is defined not by objects in a viewfinder, but... well, that takes us to a level of specificity that I'd best avoid."

Angel jangled the keys in front of the space where the door had once been. "When this is all over, you might consider working with us in a more direct and formal way."

"Wait... People can do that?" he said.

"Of course," Angel turned the key in midair, and the door imposed itself on reality. "We're only human after all."

Alan stepped out of the grand library that was Angel's laboratory and into the drab hallway of his apartment building.

"I look forward to your further discoveries," they said.

Angel gave him another pleasant pat on the shoulder before shutting the door. Alan made a point to watch the apartment number fade from view. It returned to a sign labeling a utility room. Bit by bit, he could feel whole sections of his recollection from within the laboratory vanish. No matter how tightly he gripped the images in his mind, he couldn't help but have them slip away. Within moments, he was left with only fragments. He knew he'd been inside. He knew it was a huge place with books. He remembered their conversation and the nature of the message, and he knew that there were now great empty gulfs in his memory.

He turned and stepped toward his door, but paused. Ms. Levitt's door was open a sliver, straining against its chain lock so that she could eye him suspiciously.

"Hey, Ms. Levitt," he said wearily. "Just... dealing with some utility... stuff."

"Have you learned nothing about coming up with lies?" Blot asked. "Specificity. You give exactly the level of detail that would be necessary to explain why someone would be doing something and—"

The door thumped shut.

"... And I guess some people will ignore it and think what they want to think regardless," she concluded.

"Yeah."

Alan slipped into his apartment. Maybe it was a side effect of Angel forcibly removing memories, but it felt like he had a wet blanket over his head. He hadn't had a proper night's sleep in ages, and waking up in the middle of the night for this little rendezvous hadn't helped. He trudged to his bed and, within minutes, was sound asleep.

The dream started to resolve around him. Bright sun. Green grass. It was the land in Upstate New York. Not as it was when he'd last seen it, but as it was when he was a child. In truth, there wasn't that much of a difference. It was a bit less overgrown, but a disused piece of land didn't change as much as a city might as the years turned into decades. Nonetheless, it was certainly the land of his youth. It was in the way it felt. He felt lighter in spirit, not yet burdened by things as epic as a battle with otherworldly entities or as mundane as saving receipts for tax season. He just felt free.

No plot asserted itself as he tromped through ankle-high grass and breathed the fresh air. He just explored. In time—or at least what passed for time in dreams—he came upon a familiar hill topped with a familiar tree. Leafless and stern, its two main branches reached toward the blue sky. Seated in the crook was the impish companion that invaded so many of his dreams these days. She was dressed, as always, in her flowing rags. She clutched an ancient-looking writing slate in one hand and a stylus in the other.

At the first sight of her, recollection of the events of his life started to flow in. His mood soured. Dark clouds rolled over the sun, casting the whole field into a gloomy gray.

"Sorry," Blot said, kicking her feet.

"Sorry for what?" Alan asked.

"When you fell asleep, I was all set to get back to business, since this is the one and only place we can actually get some privacy from prying eyes. But... I don't know... it just seemed like you needed some of this. It doesn't feel great to know that if I so much as show my face in your dreams, you fall into a pit of despair. I kind of miss the early days when I could just be a part of the dream and watch you do your thing."

He rubbed his eyes. "Don't worry about it. It is what it is. What exactly are we going to get to work on? We didn't learn much except that the message the Ghoul left was nonsense, and it's probably been here for a long time."

"It isn't necessarily nonsense," Blot said, hopping down to the ground.

"Because you didn't show the whole message," Alan observed.

"Right. Based on what Angel showed us, I figured out the rest. I'll be honest, it doesn't make much more sense, but that's what I figured we could work on."

She rubbed her hands together and flicked her wrist. A checkered bit of cloth unfurled from her hand as though she'd somehow concealed it in her palm. It settled down over a rectangular shape that, after a few helpful flickers of Alan's mental image, turned out to be the top of a picnic table. She set the tablet down and smoothed it out, the motion of her hands converting it to a roll of paper.

"Get some rocks, would you?" Blot said.

Alan nodded and kicked around in the grass until he found some smooth stones. He tossed them to her, and she pinned down the corners of the bit of paper.

"You've really got to teach me how to work a dream like you do," Alan said.

"You've just got to stop thinking so hard about it and just let it happen," Blot said. "Shaping dreams is basically the same thing shades do to shape ourselves. It just takes a little less effort for dreams. You just set expectations for reality, and eventually reality has to oblige. At least the parts of reality you're in direct control over."

He sat on the opposite side of the picnic table and peered over her sheet of paper. It had the full message, which turned out to be: *39 Full Stop 954030 Left of the Way of the Burning Light Pause 75 Full Stop 434666 The Way of the Cooling Darkness.*

"I don't suppose this has any profound meaning to you," Alan said.

"Not most of it. Except there are some poems from when I was little that used some of these words. They're pretty obvious if you think about it." She pointed. "'The Way of the Cooling Darkness' is where the sun sets. And the 'Way of the Burning Light' is where the sun rises."

"Okay, yeah. That makes sense. What's with this 'Full Stop' and 'Pause' stuff?"

"That's what you'd have to do if you were saying it out loud."

"Like punctuation?"

"Weren't you paying attention to Angel?"

"I was a little busy trying to avoid dwelling on the fact that I might technically have been paying a visit to heaven."

She sneered. "Please. That wasn't heaven. But anyway, yeah. I guess it's like punctuation. Except we don't have the same sort of punctuation as you. And the Ghoul was using it wrong, because the monster didn't make any room between it and the stuff around it."

"Let's not assume the Ghoul didn't know what it was doing. I need a pencil."

"Well?" she said. "Make one."

"Oh, right." He held out his hand.

After a few seconds of trying to conjure a pencil into his grip, he thought about what Blot had suggested. Instead, he tried to imagine a void that only a pencil could fill. The dream reality made a quick revision, and he was holding the classic Dixon Ticonderoga that he'd bluffed his way through so many standardized tests with.

"Oh, wow. That does work," he said.

"Told you."

"The way I figure it, let's assume it knew who it was talking to. A younger shade and a semiclueless human. And the only way this makes sense to me is for 'Full Stop' to just be a period. And I guess the 'Pause' would be a comma?"

"While you're at it, change 'The Way of the Cooling Darkness.'"

"West? And 'The Way of the Burning Light' would be east?"

"Yeah."

39.954030 Left of East, 75.434666 West

Alan tipped his head to the side.

"You know... Assuming 'Left of East' is actually..." He held out his hands. "North, then this is looking like latitude and longitude."

"Map stuff?" Blot said.

"Yes. How likely is it that an ancient specter would use an even more ancient language to deliver information from a modern GPS?"

"As likely as anything else. So where is that?"

"I don't know. I don't speak GPS. But I think it's nearby. I think we're around forty."

"How would I check? With your phone? With the map thing?"

"Yes."

"I'm on it!"

She shut her eyes. At the very edge of hearing, Alan became vaguely aware of some thumping and clacking. It caused the overcast field around him to waver and tremble like someone was tapping on the glass of his personal aquarium.

Blot's eyes opened. "It's super close. Less than an hour away. In some woods west of the city."

"So a serial killer has given us a location in the woods."

"Yes. What do you suppose it is?"

"The beginning of a bad slasher movie."

"I don't think we are going to find the Ghoul there. It doesn't fit any part of the 'ritual' it's been trying to do."

Alan sighed. "We're going to have to go there, aren't we?"

"We don't really have anything else to go on, besides heading back to the same neighborhood and hoping it will go differently for some reason."

"Fine... We're going during the day, though."

"I won't be able to help as much during the day."

"And the Ghoul won't be able to *do* as much during the day." He sighed. "Plus, maybe if we're lucky, it won't have had time to restock on knives."

"It'll be fine. How about you just try having a proper lucid dream for once? Get some real sleep. I'll leave you to it while I try to get things ready."

She hopped up and trotted around behind the tree, vanishing from the dream. The clouds overhead lingered. He squinted at them until they sheepishly parted.

"Okay. Let's see what we can do with this."

Chapter 8

A lan jerked awake to the sound of a cell phone notification. He knew he hadn't set an alarm. Today wasn't an on-call day for the police station, and he'd yet to throw his name back in the mix for Cox Media. Barring any more nightmares, he should have been able to squeak out something resembling a full night's sleep.

He fought his eyes open to find his cell phone dangling in front of his face.

"Sorry," Blot said. "This is the third time he called, and the messages haven't been pleasant."

Alan tried to pull together enough of his wits to not sound like a drunk when he finally answered. "Mr. Cox?" he said thickly.

"Fontaine! Where the hell are you? Why didn't you answer?"

"I told you to take me off the rotation... Didn't I?"

"I don't care if you did or you didn't. The essay part of your art-sy-fartsy photo-essay about the prison finally took root somewhere. One of those hipster guys who was such a darling at Sundance last year is looking to do a behind-the-scenes for his next movie, and we're going to be doing some of the on-location stuff for Philly."

"I'm sure other people can handle taking photos like that. Why do you need me?"

"I don't. Marie-Anna said she wanted you. She's doing the video part."

"Why does *she* want me?"

"Doesn't matter. The point is, you've got two hours to get down there and do some preliminaries."

"Is this really the best—"

"Two hours! Check your email for the address. And contact Marie-Anna to let her know where you'll meet her."

Cox hung up. Alan looked blearily at the phone until he could remember how to check the time. It was six a.m. He'd had a grand total of three hours of uninterrupted, non-nightmare-riddled sleep.

"You're going to do it, aren't you?" Blot said.

He kicked his feet out of bed and heaved himself into a wobbly standing position.

"The more money I can bank, the more I can focus on the nonmoney stuff later. And besides. If the boss's girlfriend wants me on the job, who am I to argue?"

"This is stupid, Alan. You need to rest at some point."

"It's a behind-the-scenes photo shoot. I just have to squeak out three or four good shots, because they never use more than that in the finished product. It'll be autopilot."

"For once you're doing this to yourself, you realize," Blot said. "This isn't 'I have to do it' or 'Blot's making me do it' or 'The white-suits are making me do it.' It's not the shades or the Dawn..."

"I have too many people telling me to do things..." he muttered.

"This is you. So don't come crying to me when you get in a fight with the Ghoul and you just nod off because you spent a couple of hours taking pictures of people taking pictures when you could have been sleeping."

Alan mumbled something incoherent and trudged off to the bathroom.

"You don't look so good," Marie-Anna said.

Alan stepped out of his car and checked his camera rig. "The side hustle's been picking up," he said. "I didn't expect to be working today."

"You didn't?" she said, handing him his laminated backstage badge. "Remmy didn't mention that. Are you going to be able to do this? You look like death."

"Compared to what I've been up to lately, this will be a walk in the park." He looped the badge over his neck. "It seems like these days I draw all my authority from little pieces of plastic-covered cardboard."

"I'll be doing interview stuff and video. I'll point you to photo opportunities. I want it candid but well framed. We're shooting for completely natural reactions, but as polished as a staged shot."

Alan nodded sluggishly. His brain started to translate her request into the proper settings. A nice Bokeh effect in the background. Try to catch flashes of enthusiasm, genuine laughs, those moments of thought between question and answer.

His fingers moved of their own accord, tweaking and massaging settings to the proper levels. "Why'd you want me?" Alan asked.

"A good reason and a bad reason," Marie-Anna said. "Which one do you want?"

"Can we end with the good one?"

"The bad reason is Cox trusts you with me," she said.

It took a few seconds for the statement to trickle through Alan's sleep-deprived brain.

"He's not *that* type, is he? The kind of guy who doesn't trust his girl with another guy? ... And does that mean he thinks I'm gay?"

"No and... I don't know, maybe?" she said. "I would've broken up with him ages ago if I thought he didn't trust me. I get enough of that from my dad. And if you think he thinks you're just trustworthy across the board, let's not forget that time you stole my credentials for the art show. But you're here because he trusts you to be able to pull off what I need you to pull off. Believe it or not, he's protective of my career. He wants me to have the best equipment, the best jobs. The best partner. Which brings me to the good news. You're the best photographer we've got, and I want you on my project."

"I'm touched, Marie-Anna."

"Yeah, well, judging from the bags under your eyes, you're going to slide a few notches closer to mediocre, so let's hope you can pull it together enough to not embarrass me. I've been wanting to produce this kind of content for years. Come on. The guy's over here."

"Over there! Photo op!" Blot said.

Alan turned and snapped a burst of pictures. In retrospect, it was indeed a poor decision to take this job, even if the boss would have given him a hard time about it. Having Blot as a second set of eyes was the only thing that had saved him from delivering nothing but shots taken a half-second too late to be worth taking. Even with her head on a swivel for him, this wasn't his best work.

"Okay! Ha ha! I'm sure we'll see you come awards season," Marie-Anna joked with the director. "And don't forget to put me in the credits!"

Alan snapped a few shots of the joking exchange, then nodded to Marie-Anna as she approached.

"Let's see them," she said quietly.

He handed over the camera, and she clicked through the pictures.

"Eh... Good, good... Decent... That one's perfect. That one's good... Okay, good enough. I think you pulled it together for me, Fontaine. Still did better than Dennis or Bill would have done, so getting you out here was the right call. Thanks for not screwing me over. Why don't you give me the SD card so I can turn these in and you can get some sleep?"

He nodded and popped the card out to hand over. "Hang on. I have the case for it," he muttered.

A bit of fishing in his pocket unearthed the errant bit of plastic as well as some spare change and the charm bracelet. He handed her the case.

"What, do you have a daughter or something I don't know about?" she said, taking the case and clicking the card into it.

"Hmm? No. I found it," he said.

Marie-Anna took it from his hand and held it up. "Oh... shame. Some cheerleader is going to be bummed she lost her bracelet."

"What makes you think it's from a cheerleader?" Alan said.

"I guess I don't *know* it is, but if these beads here aren't supposed to be school colors, I don't know what they are. And that weird cat-head charm looks like a mascot to me." She handed it back. "Anyway, get some sleep." She paced away, leaving Alan to stare at the bracelet.

"Why didn't you notice that, Alan?" Blot said.

"You didn't notice it either," he hissed at her.

"I don't come from this world. You can't expect me to have the same social context as you. Presumably *you* went to school."

"I'm not at my best, okay?"

"You'd better let me keep that bracelet," Blot said. "We don't need you accidentally showing off any more clues."

Alan made it home, but only just. Lack of sleep and constant stress had taken their toll on him. The abundance of shadow sliding in the last few days hadn't done him any favors either. Though there were lives on the line, his performance with Marie-Anna illustrated if he didn't get some sleep, two of the lives likely to be lost were his own and Blot's.

Blot was cast on the wall above the headboard, listening to the slow rhythm of his breathing. A few weeks earlier he'd installed a pair of shelves above the headboard for her, which were presently home to her mug of coffee and Alan's phone on a charger. It was her intention to use the phone to continue researching and problem-solving. The laptop was easier to use. There was work to be done, but right now, her mind was on other things.

Her white eyes gazed down upon Alan's sleeping form. It had been months since she'd selected him as her host. At the time, she hadn't had a choice. Her training had a lot to say about him. He was a poor host by shade standards. He was no more capable of combat than any other average human. Neither he nor his family had any significant influence. Worst of all, he had no aspirations toward such things. She could take time to ease him toward directions that were valuable to her, but she'd been taught that in cases like his, the best choice would be to abandon him for a better host.

It was just one of the many ways in which her training had been revealed to be, if not outright evil from the point of view of humans, at least contrary to what she'd *believed* it was for. Her time with Alan had seen her through to more than one victory. They were victories against foes far more capable than either she or Alan. She didn't think there was anything special about him, and she knew there wasn't anything special about her. The only difference between them and their foes was that she and Alan worked together. Not toward any of the goals they had set forth for her, but for her own goals. They were compromising, collaborating. And it had only happened because she had stuck with him.

Perhaps that was the point of that little twist of training. Perhaps her teachers knew that, given the time, any of her kind might form more powerful partnerships with their hosts to serve their own ends if they tried. And that would take precious resources away from the goals of her superiors. And thus they instructed shades to abandon hosts that could not be bent to their whims.

Alan shuddered again, rattling Blot from her train of thought. More and more these days, she found herself treading unfamiliar territory for her, and dangerous territory according to those like Dun. She was thinking about what she had done, and what she was doing, to her host. Alan hadn't had a proper night of sleep in weeks. The horrors they'd faced had started to work their way into his dreams. And though Blot had certainly not been the driving force in confronting the likes of Todd and Rive, there was no doubt that had he never met her, Alan would never have had to face them.

He twitched in his sleep. His eyes fluttered. Another few moments and whatever was stalking in his mind would shake him awake. It was time for her to do something.

She shut her eyes and slid herself along the link between them. The mists of darkness parted, and she found herself in the police station. It was flickering and dim. Most of the lights had been smashed. Muffled voices murmured in concern and fear. The meaty slap of huge feet thumping down on the cheap tiles drew her attention to a nearby hallway.

Blot hurried around to find Alan and Jessie backing against the wall, retreating from the absolutely massive form of the Ghoul. Alan's mind had taken the liberty of embellishing reality somewhat. The feral shade wasn't a shifting mote of black as it was in reality. Now there were dashes of blood red and midnight blue. Drops of some horrid, ichorous substance oozed off the monster.

Jessie fired her weapon fruitlessly at the Ghoul as it advanced. Blot stared at the imaginary version of the woman. Unlike the monster, Alan's mind had conjured her up with remarkable accuracy. It betrayed just how much of his mind was consumed by her these days. For a moment, Blot recalled another small but important part of her training, one that insisted relationships like that should be eased away when working with a host. Blot was supposed to ensure that *she* was the most important thing in the life of her host. Though she had dismissed that bit of training just as surely as she'd dismissed most of the rest, she still found herself recoiling at the idea of sharing his mind with her. The only difference was that her own reasons were quite selfish. She didn't want to share him.

Blot shook the thoughts away and turned her attention to the shadow that was cast from Alan whenever the lights overhead flickered. White eyes peered out of it, Alan's recreation of Blot herself. That was new. Normally, when Blot didn't assert herself into the dream, even when something "shady" happened, Alan remembered himself as he was, with his natural shadow. Now she was with him. On one side, Jessie. On the other side, Blot.

The dream slowed to a crawl. Alan's fears stretched a moment out into an eternity. She watched as the muzzle of Jessie's gun flashed one last time before the gun clicked empty. She watched as Alan stepped forward, one hand held in front of Jessie to shield her. The other stretched in front of his own shadow to shield his recreation of her. Blot felt a flutter of warmth at the gesture, at the thought that he would seek to protect her, even when at the whims of his subconscious.

She didn't want to just pop up and pull him from the dream into a lucid state. That might mean that his body was still resting, but it robbed him of the equally valuable rest for the mind. Without asserting herself, though, she couldn't change the dream. That required his permission. But he *could* play a role in it.

Blot slid behind him and took her rightful position, replacing his false image of her. She felt herself slip into the same slow, drawn-out nightmare moment. With a slow flick of her fingers, she teased out a military-looking cylinder with a jangling pin and thrust it into the hand Alan used to shield her.

His head turned. His eyes locked on to the grenade she had provided. She could physically feel the tone of the dream change as he recognized it for what it was, a flash-bang. He pulled the pin in the weapon and heaved it into the writhing mass of limbs stalking toward him. A booming thump shook the fabric of the dream, and a blinding flash left them briefly in a void of white. When the station returned, the walls were splattered with the same goop that had been weeping from the Ghoul. The black creature was gone, simply marked as "destroyed" in the dream with little concern for what might have become of him.

Alan turned to Blot. "Are you okay?" he asked.

"Fine. I'm fine," Blot said.

He turned to Jessie. "Are you hurt?"

"No. No. You did it, Alan! You killed it!" Jessie said.

"Yeah... Yeah, I guess we did."

He marched forward to investigate the residue left behind. The feeling of relief and victory was felt as something akin to a change in temperature, the room cooling off after broiling in fear and anxiety. Blot slid over to the dream version of Jessie and grinned.

"He asked me first," she jabbed, before vanishing from the dream to let Alan rest properly.

CHAPTER 9

Alan left the house that afternoon with a somewhat clearer head, his full complement of light- and chemical-based weaponry, and three hours of sunlight left. The coordinates they'd translated had taken them to the twisting roads of a state park. With the sun still in the sky, his mental image of a Camp Crystal Lake–style horror-movie setting fell well short of reality. There were hiking trails. There were picnic tables. Overall, it was downright wholesome.

"I feel like fate is lulling me into a false sense of security," Alan said warily.

He parked his car and double-checked he had his camera and flashlight where he could reach them.

"I like this place," Blot said. "Lots of shade."

"There is that. Plenty of hard shadows for the Ghoul to hide in, too."

"And for us to hide in, let's not forget."

"Are you feeling anything? Any insight into what we're going to be walking into?"

She slid up the trunk of a nearby tree and shut her eyes. "Hmm... I... no. Nothing... Nothing obvious, anyway."

He poked at the map app on the phone. "It's not super easy to get a raw latitude and longitude out of this thing, but I think we've got a couple hundred yards to go. Eyes open. Ears open. Whatever shade-specific sense organs you've got, open."

"Oh, trust me, if we encounter anything, I'll know about it before you do."

He hiked through the forest. It was mostly pine trees. The shade kept it a good deal cooler than he would have expected. Even with the exertion of trudging through the undergrowth, the dreary late winter weather had him fighting off a chill.

As the coordinates on his phone ticked closer to the position the Ghoul had given them, the cool air took on a downright frigid bite.

"You feeling anything yet?" he asked.

"Still no," she said.

"I'm getting that someone-just-walked-over-my-grave feeling."

"Maybe it's just your nerves. Stand still for a second. With your back against this tree."

He did as he was told. She stretched up the shady trunk and peered ahead.

"It's this direction, right?" she said.

"I think so."

"Then I think I know where we're heading. Bear left a little."

He stepped away from the tree and adjusted his path. He barely made it five steps before he spotted what she was indicating.

Amid the pines was a single bit of standing deadwood. He didn't have an eye for plant species, but there was no doubt that whatever type of tree this was, it was a match for the one back on the family land. He could almost imagine it was the same exact tree, except the years hadn't been quite so kind. Its two main branches were a bit stubby, having lost more of their secondary branches to weather and time.

"It's like a gateway tree," Blot said. "But weaker."

"Weaker?"

"I don't know what other terms I can put it in. A gateway tree can open a path to our world if it's properly aligned with an eclipse, but it needs to have some life to it. Not actual life, obviously, because they're usually dead. But... oomph."

"So the Ghoul sent us to what *would* have been a gateway tree if it were a little more powerful."

"So it would seem."

"And we're of the opinion that the Ghoul is probably looking for a way to get help from others like it, based on the ritual."

"I'm way ahead of you. You think *it* thinks this is where they'd show up." She curled around the tree. "And it didn't give us the coordinates until it saw the shard."

She held out her hand and let the locket drop down. If there was a change to the tree, it wasn't one visible to the senses available to Alan. Blot's dark figure slid along the tree, locket clinking and bouncing against it.

"Anything?" he asked.

"Does it look like anything is happening?" she said. "Maybe it needs to be open..."

She clicked the locket open, revealing the shard. The faint, half-seen glow of the fragment of stone fell upon the tree. Alan felt a distant intensity from the mystic focus. Again, Blot ran the shadowy fingers of her free hand over the stout trunk of the tree and circled around it. When she was through with her investigation, she pulled back to Alan's side. The locket twisted in the breeze beside him.

"Nothing," she muttered.

"This *does* rely upon a serial killer's actions being driven by some sort of logic or reason," he observed. "Not exactly a safe assumption."

He stepped up to the tree and leaned a bit closer, checking for some sort of markings she might have missed.

"It can't be a coincidence. The Ghoul gives us this message, which would have taken some modern technical savvy to get. And the coordinates point to a tree with an uncanny resemblance to the one *I* crawled out of and *you* slept in front of during an eclipse that brought us together."

"Maybe we're just reaching. Looking for patterns where there are none. I mean, look at these creases here from where the bark was," he said, pointing at the tree. "It looks like a letter *Y*, but so does *anything* that splits from one line into two." Alan reached out to scratch at the shape. "It's probably on there because..." His fingers brushed the surface of the tree. Rather than flaking off the offending shape, the whole surface of the tree bowed inward under the pressure of his touch.

He took a step back, eyes wide and heart fluttering.

"Do that again," Blot said.

Alan squinted and turned his head aside, pressing gingerly at the tree.

"It's not going to bite you," Blot said.

"You don't know that. This tree is already doing something I've never seen a tree do. Biting is not outside the realm of possibility."

He leaned harder. The tree continued to distort under his touch. The sight and sensation didn't make sense. The tree still felt solid. If he didn't see it moving, he would have believed it wasn't deforming at all. And the way it looked as he did it didn't meet expectations for reality either. It didn't look like a flexible surface bowing to force. It looked like the pinching, uniform distortion of a lens being held in front of an image. He pressed still harder, but even with his full weight upon it, he couldn't produce anything more than the bizarre dimple in reality.

Blot's fingers crept up along the tree, adding her strength to the shove. It bowed inward slightly more. Then she curled her arm along Alan's until her fingers overlapped his.

There was a new sensation now. The tree felt thin, somehow, like there was scarcely a sheet of paper separating him from some sort of opening beyond.

"It takes both of us..." Blot said. "Here, put the locket on."

"We don't know what's on the other side of this thing," he said.

"And we're going to find out."

She hooked the locket over his neck. A fresh flutter of mystic intensity rushed through him. It saturated his body, but his brain couldn't quite make sense of it. Like light beyond the spectrum his eyes could see, but extending to all his senses. A temperature he couldn't feel. A scent he couldn't quite place.

While he was still grappling with it, he felt Blot rise up behind him.

"Here we go!" she announced.

She gave him a firm shove, and Alan stumbled forward. He threw up his hands to steady himself. When they struck the tree, it distorted like a rubber sheet. After a moment of resistance, he burst through it. Any tension holding him back vanished. The surface of the tree rippled along his body, tickling against his skin like a permeable membrane.

Without the support of the tree, Alan went pitching forward. His hands struck something new, something hard and smooth. Then, as he stumbled forward off-balance, his face struck it too.

"Ow!" He recoiled and rubbed his nose.

"What happened?" she asked.

"There's a wall right on the other side."

"Oh... Fine. Back against the tree and deep breath."

"Wait, wait, wait!" he said.

"What?"

"What's our plan?"

"I pull you into the shadows, and get around the wall."

"And then what?"

"That's about as far as we can get without knowing what's on the other side."

He nodded. "Okay... Okay, so just promise me we'll take it slow and we'll keep track of the way out in case we have to get away in a hurry."

"Oh, if it comes down to cowardice, you can trust me to come through brilliantly." She paused. "Brilliantly... is that another of those 'light is good, dark is bad' things?" She waved it off. "Doesn't matter. Come on! Let's see what's on the other side."

Once he was able to scrape up enough nerve to do so, he turned his back to the tree.

"Extra deep this time," she said. "We don't know how far we're going to have to go."

He drew in a breath. Normally at times like this, he would shut his eyes. The transition from reality to the shadows was challenging for a mind unaccustomed to having to choose between two and three dimensions. But this time he wanted every bit of information available. He saw the black forms of Blot's hands emerge on either side. One hand held tight against his chest. The other gripped the dangling locket. They pulled tight. He hit the tree and continued. It warped against his body. He snapped through, and his back struck the wall and once again continued. The cold of the shadows claimed him.

Alan knew there couldn't have been more than an inch between the tree's surface and the wall beyond. He shouldn't have been able to focus on it. But distance meant little when he was in this form. He found himself staring at a much healthier tree. Dark gray craggy bark had a dusting of lighter gray moss. It started to streak along his vision as Blot dragged him along the wall. This view shifted as they curled around a corner. Now the way ahead was clear, his view revealing a sprawling forest. Though it had been afternoon before they entered the tree, here it was the depths of night. Thick clouds reduced the light of what must have been a very bright moon to a dull glow, barely enough for them to discern the shapes of trees a few yards away.

Blot released him. He surged back to three dimensions and stumbled forward.

"Mmm..." Blot said, rising up beside him in three dimensions. "Do you feel that?"

"Feel what?" he said.

"This place feels so... *lively*," she said. "I've never had such an easy time pulling myself up."

Alan took a moment to assess what he was feeling. "Lively" was not the word he would have used to describe this dark place. He felt off-balance.

Disoriented. A few experimental steps left him with the wobbly feeling of walking on a floor you're not sure will support you.

"I don't feel right... We're not... this isn't *your* world, is it?" he said.

"No. No, no, no," she said. "This is still very much your world. But it feels more like home than anywhere else in your world that I've been. It feels... I don't know... like an embassy. A little bit of our soil set up in your world. It feels... it feels like whatever was on the other side of the hole that thing opened in the wall."

"That thing isn't here, is it?"

"I don't feel it here. Not a hint of it."

He looked about. While in the shadows with her, he'd been able to see the shapes of things a bit closer to the way she did. With his physical eyes, things were even harder to navigate. What he'd thought was a wall blocking the way through the tree turned out to be a pillar or obelisk. It was a stark white color, so pristine and white it almost hurt his eyes to look upon it surrounded by such darkness. Barely visible lines separated the individual blocks that created it. He ran his finger over it, but the workmanship was of such quality that he couldn't even feel the separations. It stood nearly as tall as the tree, tapering subtly as it rose skyward, ending in a flare and filigree. It wouldn't have looked out of place supporting the awning of the First National Bank. There wasn't another such pillar in sight.

"At least we'll be able to find our way back here easily enough. But I can barely see anything else." He reached back to the holster for his flashlight.

"Don't," Blot said, touching his hand. "I'll keep my eyes open for you, but if this *is* a place for shades, that would be very bad manners. Like me busting down the door of your parents' house in combat form."

"Right. Okay. That's fair." He hesitantly took his hand away from the light. "So, how far does this place go?"

"I don't know." She looked to him, her white eyes sparkling with excitement. "Let's find out."

They moved with caution. Within minutes, it was clear that whatever this place was, it was enormous. Blot led the way. She hadn't gone so far as to adopt her combat form, but emotions were running high for her. On one hand, she was flush with excitement. On the other, she treated every flutter of a leaf as a potential threat.

"It's weird having you out like this for so long. Almost like a dream, only with a little less shading."

"It's effortless here. Honestly, I almost feel like I could separate from you and not lose myself here."

"Let's not try that, okay?" Alan said.

"Relax. It's just an observation."

He pointed. "What's that over there?"

She turned and looked where he pointed. It wasn't so much something as the lack of something. A short distance away, the underbrush smoothed out in a way that didn't seem natural. They headed in that direction. Slate slabs formed a walkway ahead. Just beyond them, cocooned in ivy and other climbing vines, was a gate.

"Signs of civilization." Alan groped for his camera. "I should be taking pictures, but I'm not sure what the exposure settings should be for an ethereal nether-realm." He raised his camera.

"No flash," she said.

"I know, I know."

He snapped a picture and checked the result. The glow from the screen felt uncomfortably bright in this place, but he squinted at it and made a few strategic adjustments to settings. Three more samples finally got him something blurry but recognizable.

"My hands are usually steady enough that I wouldn't need a tripod, even in low light. I guess exploring some hunk of the afterlife is enough to give me the jitters."

"The afterlife?" Blot said. "So, what? You'd believe this is a trip to hell to go with your supposed trip to heaven?"

"I guess not. I would expect more fire if this were hell."

"Not everything is a part of your mythology. If it were, wouldn't Angel's lab have had... what do you have in your heaven? Clouds? Harps?"

"There might have been a harp. There might have been clouds. I can barely remember what it was like in there."

"The point is, either your imagery is wrong, or we're not taking jaunts to one particular religion's vision of the different flavors of the great beyond."

Further philosophical discussion was interrupted by a rattle in the darkness. In less time than it took for Alan to turn to the source, Blot darted in front of him and lurched up into her twisted, vicious form. One clawed hand held him back. They swept their eyes over the scene for anything that might have made the noise. The only thing that stood out was a row of small clay pots standing along the edge of the slate walkway. Blot poked one of them with a claw. Then another.

As her claw approached the third, it rattled on its own. A streamer of black launched from behind it and curled through the air. Complex curls and loops traced through after it, following its path. The leading edge had the faintest hint of animal features, a curving beak, perhaps, and flailing claws.

"Back, back, back!" Blot said, throwing her body in front of Alan's.

The thing bounced and bobbed between branches and walkway slabs. It ducked behind pots and curled around tree trunks. Finally, it launched with full speed toward a small garden gnome guarding the path just at the edge of Alan's visibility. It curled tightly around it and vanished, though its arrival to the gnome was enough to leave it rattling in a slow circle.

"What the hell was that?" Alan said.

"I looked like a rikt," she said.

"What's a rikt?"

"They're creatures from back home." Blot started to ease back to her proper shape. "Carrion eaters. Like... squirrels."

"I don't think squirrels eat carrion," Alan said.

"Fine, then they're like"—she snapped her fingers—"they're like."

A pair of voices helpfully offered a suggestion. "Crows."

Again, Blot surged up to her so recently abandoned combat form. She grasped Alan roughly and held him back. The figure approaching from the trees didn't look very threatening, but looks these days were dangerously deceiving.

Their visitor, or perhaps their host, was a dark-skinned woman. She was old. If it wasn't so unkind-sounding, Alan would have gone with the word "decrepit." He would not have been surprised to learn her age was brushing triple digits, but she moved spryly. Her clothes were worn but well-kept, the sort of outfit too messy to wear day to day but with too much life left to throw away. Work clothes. Heavy canvas pants. An old plaid button-down shirt with rolled-up sleeves. Both in shades of gray. She had heavy leather work gloves and leaned on a rake as a wizard might lean on a staff. Though it was near pitch-black here, she wore a floppy wide-brim hat. A somewhat more youthful shadow mimicked her posture. It lacked her height and had a wide-hipped, impish build a bit plumper than Blot's. And, of course, it had piercing white eyes. She marched up to the garden gnome.

"They certainly think like a crow," the elderly woman and her shadow said in unison. "Mischievous. Clever. And this place is lousy with them."

She stooped to reach for the gnome. The telltale stiffness of arthritis stopped her short of reaching it, but her shadow continued down to pluck it up and guide it to her hand. She grinned and gave it a shake. A serpentine shadow unfurled and thumped to the ground, clinging to the gnome's shadow just as any other denizen of Blot's world might. It released a croaking cluck and popped into a somewhat better-defined shape, this one more akin to a particularly lean and broad-beaked rooster with the tiniest dash of blue coloring the feathered fringe of its silhouette. Seeing color mixed into the pure black of shadow was almost more unsettling than anything else about the creature.

It strutted around, head turned to keep a single wide eye trained on Alan and Blot. Alan steadied his hands enough to snap a decent photo.

"Who are you? What is this place?" Alan asked.

"I'm..." She shut her eyes and furrowed her wrinkled brow. "Forgive me, it's been a spell since I've had to answer that question in the singular. You can call me Gladys. This is Mote, stretching out on the ground here."

The shadow briefly abandoned mimicking her position to offer a pleasant wave.

"Together, we're the gardener. And that'd make this the garden."

"The gardener... The Ghoul mentioned you. It sent us to find you," Blot said.

"Yes. I imagine it would." Their hosts pointed to the locket about Alan's neck. "And you, my boy, have got an eye for accessories. The Ghoul has standing orders to send any shade with a shard to me. No sense us standing here, jabbering in the wilderness. Come. I'll dust off a chair for you."

Blot and Alan looked to each other. Tellingly, Blot kept up the combat form as they followed the gardener down the path.

"The Ghoul... Metropolitan Ghoul?" Gladys said.

"Metro Ghoul," Alan said hoarsely.

"Ah. Folks do like to shorten up words these days. Always in such a gosh-darn rush all the time."

Of all the things about the situation, for some reason the most un-nerving for Alan was how perfectly the gardener and her shade harmonized. Both voices were female. One was youthful and the other ancient. But they melded so perfectly it sounded like a single voice with some very curious harmonics. He was inclined to call her by her name, but he instantly understood why others wouldn't. It felt like one was leaving half of the duo out, and calling them separate names felt equally strange, as they certainly acted as one.

She continued. "If you've come here calling it that, I suppose it's been misbehaving again."

"It murdered a man," Alan said.

"Did the man have it coming to him?" Gladys said.

"That's not really for us to decide. He—"

"Yes. He was a real jerk, if the police record was to be believed," Blot said.

"Those are the ones it picks. Who's it got as a host this time?" the gardener asked.

"A prostitute, I think," Alan said.

The gardener nodded. "Suits it. Suits it. It's always someone like that. The kind of person who'll take some licks and have everyone else look the other way." She sighed. "Only it doesn't look the other way."

"Does it work for you?" Alan asked.

"Not much of an employee type, that one. I'm its teacher. And anyone who gets a lesson agrees to do some jobs for me and keep their nose clean."

"It's been doing a rotten job of that last one," Blot said.

Again Gladys sighed. "Lasted longer than last time. Here we are."

A house emerged from the darkness ahead of them. It wasn't a turn of phrase. As they approached, what first seemed to be little more than dense shadow parted to reveal a small but comfortable cottage that had been enrobed by the darkness. Alan and Blot stopped at the door as she stepped inside.

"Got you rattled, have I?" Gladys said without a glance in their direction. "That's fine. We can sit on the stoop. Just don't go running off."

She stepped through the door, leaving Alan and Blot alone. Blot had been gradually easing back to her proper form. She turned to face Alan.

"What do we think?" she whispered.

"I think the gardener is managing to be the spookiest thing in the spookiest few months of my life, and that's saying something," he said. "What's with the duet with the shadow?"

Blot scratched her head. "That's a new one. Rumor had it there were shades who could pull a sort of 'puppet-master' thing with their hosts, but I never met one, and even the rumors never claimed more control than a hand or an arm. This looks more like teamwork."

"Does she feel powerful to you? I'm not getting the same vibe I got from Dun or Rive or any of them."

"If she's got it, she's not flaunting it."

The gardener returned with a pair of chairs. They were full-size dining room chairs, the kind of bulky heirloom furniture that populates the parlor in your great aunt's house that no one's allowed to go in. She didn't seem to have any difficulty carrying them, though from the look of the shadow, she wasn't the one doing most of the lifting.

"It'd be easier to answer if you asked me instead of each other," she said, setting the chairs down.

She took a seat. Alan slid the seat a few inches farther away and sat as well. Blot allowed herself to slide back to two dimensions and sat in the shadow of Alan's chair.

"What exactly—" Alan began.

"Before we get to it, I want to go over a few things, just so we know where we stand." Gladys pointed to the locket. "You got that bit of jewelry from the Glints, didn't you."

"The Glints?" Alan said.

"Sharp dressers. Plenty of white. Won't mind their own darn business."

"Glints!" Blot said. "We've been calling them white-suits. That is, when Alan isn't getting them confused with angels."

"If the Glints are angels, I'm not too keen on meeting my maker," Gladys said. "Not that I was rip-raring to do it regardless. Point is, you don't walk around with a bit of kit like that without working with them."

Alan tugged at the locket. "Actually, I think they gave this thing to us as damage control. They didn't seem terribly fond of the idea of a Shard of Shadow showing up."

"Hah. No, they wouldn't."

"What are they, if not angels?" Alan asked.

"What am I? What are you? What is anything? They're just a type of thing. Interested in... well, I'm sure they gave you the whole speech. Balance and that. Not to be trusted. Never trust anyone who thinks they get to decide what's balanced. Just means they're the ones with their thumbs on the scale. They've got some worthwhile know-how, but you don't last as long as we have in this world by trusting a Glint."

"... What if we _were_ working for them?"

"It'd mean you had bad judgment or no way around it. Can't say either would surprise me. You're young, and a fella with a shade isn't liable to end up spoiled for choice most days. But some folks I work with would be liable to look at you with a good deal more concern knowing you're associated with them."

"What sort of people?"

She snapped her fingers. "I ought to be setting out snacks or something. Sorry. I don't do much eating these days and even less entertaining."

She stood and paced into the cottage again. Alan and Blot glanced at each other.

"I didn't expect investigating the mysterious message from the Metro Ghoul to feel so much like visiting my grandmother," Alan said.

"She reminds me of my grandmother, too," Blot said. "The shade, not the human."

"They're acting and speaking exactly the same."

"Yeah, but my grandmother was a shade."

The gardener returned with a pair of mason jars and some glass dishes and spoons. They were more than a handful, but her shadow helpfully handled the jars while she handled the rest. One jar was filled with pickled carrots. The other with pickled beets. She spooned out a plateful of each. A sharp, sweet smell of sugar and vinegar filled the air.

"Where were we?" Gladys asked.

"You work with some people who don't trust Glints."

"Right, right. Of course, they wouldn't. The kind of people I've got in mind have got themselves all wound up on the idea of keeping an eye on the Glints."

"There are people who keep an eye on the Glints?" Blot said excitedly.

"There are people walking around with the ability to spy on just about anyone and tell them what to do and just have them do it. Sounds like someone you wouldn't want wandering around all willy-nilly."

"But how do they do it? And who are they?" Blot said.

"We should get back to talking about the Ghoul, we don't—" Alan began.

"Drinks," Gladys said, vanishing back into the house.

Alan twitched. "Spooky is giving way to irritating..." he said.

The gardener's patience-taxing hospitality eventually provided, to Blot's delight, a pot of coffee.

"Coffee..." Alan said. "Is it a standard thing that shades are coffee fiends?"

"I've never met a right-thinking adult who didn't like coffee," Gladys said. "Now, what were we talking about?"

"The people who watch the Glints," Blot said. "I—"

"Oh! Sugar? Cream?"

"Black is fine!" Alan said quickly, before she could vanish again.

"Okay then. The folks who watch the Glints," Gladys said. "What of them?"

"How do they do it? Who are they?"

She raised her hands. "Not my secrets to give. I get more than my share of help from the Dusk, and I don't need them giving me the cold shoulder."

"... The Dusk," Alan said. "The people who combat the shades are the Dawn, and the ones who combat the Glints are called the Dusk."

"Don't go complaining to me about it, I didn't name them," Gladys said. "Point is, they're out there, and they wouldn't be so keen on you for working for the white-suited devils."

"What do they know about the Glints?" Blot asked. "I went through a fair bit of training back home, and I didn't learn a *thing* about the Glints. I didn't even know they were called that."

"Oh, I know. Information like that wouldn't get back to where you come from. They'd sooner lose one of their own than let that kind of information slip."

"But why?"

"I'm flattered you think I have all the answers. I *don't* have them. Not all of them."

"You've clearly got more than we do," Alan said.

Gladys sighed. "This is mostly piecing bits together and figuring, mind you. Alan, take your flashlight there and shine it on the pinwheel."

He hesitated. "Are you sure? Blot said it would be rude."

"So long as you don't go pointing it at anyone who'll get shoved around by it, it'll be fine."

Alan slipped the flashlight free and clicked it on. They all squinted at the intense light that poured out. Three pots rattled and wobbled as rikts they'd not realized were there scattered to avoid the light.

"All right. So here's what I've worked out. That flashlight? That's where the Glints come from. That shadow, that's where the shades come from. And that pinwheel, with the shadow on the back and the light on the front? That's where you and me come from, Alan. See how the shadow's much bigger than the flashlight? Now imagine if the shadow had folks like Mote and Blot roaming around in it. That's liable to make you nervous, there being so many of them and not so many of you. Nervous enough to make darn sure they don't figure out where you came from, and make double sure that pinwheel that separates the two of you stays nice and solid so they've got somewhere else to wander around, rather than come to you. Probably it'd be worth making sure they had something to keep them busy, too."

"So they're afraid of us?" Blot said.

"Could be," Gladys said.

"And they seek 'balance' because it keeps the battle between shades and humans going, and keeps it from turning into a battle between shades and Glints?"

"That's what I worked out. Could be baloney. Who knows? But I'm doing all the jabbering here, and the Glints being a part of this makes it tricky. So before we dig any more holes, just what are you doing for them?"

"They have offered us protection in the past and are now threatening to take it back if we don't help them," Blot said. "It is more extortion than employment."

"Protection from who?"

"The rest of the shades aren't very fond of us," Alan said.

The gardener sipped her coffee. "So you're the traitor. Blot, right? And Alan?"

"You know about that?"

She grinned. "Funny you don't know about the Dusk, because they sure know about you. Guess they haven't seen clear to introduce themselves yet. Not formally anyway. But you've met one. And I've met them all. They keep me informed. You don't stay alive as long as I have by not knowing what's going on in the world, either."

"How *did* you stay alive so long?" Blot asked.

She sipped again. "Hiding. You hide from the Glints, you hide from the Dawn, and you try not to associate with any shades with their heads still full up with all the drivel they taught back at your home."

"There are other shades who aren't dedicated to the fighting?" Blot said.

Gladys lowered her head and glared at Blot, as if glancing over the top of glasses that weren't there.

"Do you think you're the only shade who decided overthrowing a whole world that couldn't care less about you was more trouble than it's worth? Plenty of us have taken the cowards way to a long, relatively happy life. Not a hard decision when the alternative is getting hunted down by the Dawn or 'balanced' by the Glints."

"So the Glints kill shades?" Alan said.

"What the Glints mostly do is justify whatever actions they want to justify. Plenty of people die to keep things on an even keel by their measure. I don't know how much of it is direct. I don't really want to find out. Best to let them keep themselves occupied. So long as things are rolling along the way they expect, they're happy. Hence all the hiding. What have they got you doing?"

Alan and Blot paused and looked at each other. A brief and unpleasant moment of realization rolled through Alan. Frequently to his detriment, it had been his policy to tell the truth early and often. As his involvement with this scheme rolled forward, that policy had weakened bit by bit at the urging of Blot. But now he didn't need urging. His first instinct was to lie.

"What happens if you don't like what you hear?" Alan asked.

"Unless you start trying to tear me apart, not a whole lot. Part of keeping your head down is leaving people in one piece," the gardener said.

Blot "stood" from the shadow of the chair and tried very hard not to appear as though she was getting ready to make a break for it.

"Go ahead. Tell her," Blot said.

"The Glints say the shades they've been watching have figured out how to hide themselves."

"I'm aware. I can see why they did it, but they're playing with fire with that one. That's liable to get the Glints *really* agitated if you don't do it subtly enough. You spend a couple millennia being nosy, you're going to pitch a fit if you can't spy properly."

"They sent us after the Ghoul to try to find out how he's hiding, so they can start hunting the others again. They figured we'd be able to track the Ghoul, and they'd be able to track us."

Gladys nodded. "Except they can't track you if you're getting close to the Ghoul, right? And they certainly can't track you anywhere near my front door."

"That first part seems right. And you'd know better than us about the second part," Blot said.

"If they wanted you to figure out how the newcomers are doing it, they sent you after the wrong shade. The Ghoul's picked up tricks that even *I* haven't got the hang of. It's still the only one I've met who could pull off a shadow portal."

"A shadow portal?" Alan asked.

"Quick way from just about anyplace dark to a place like this. Don't distract me, boy." Gladys swirled the coffee in her cup and watched the rippling surface. "This is just like the Glints, to pull a thing like this. Misdirection. If you want to bring one side down, you do it by pulling the other side up. That's the problem with trying to balance things. You're always working on the other side of the problem."

"I realize if they wanted us to uncover how Stigma is hiding, they should have sent us after Stigma, but—"

The gardener whistled. "It's Stigma, is it? That one's been talking big for some time. He finally came through. Stands to reason why things are turning out different this time."

"You didn't know Stigma was in it?" Blot said.

"Specific things like names don't always make their way here, except when it's the Dusk doing the talking, and they don't worry much about the shades who're still towing the company line. I've got to learn about that stuff in other ways, and names don't enter into it. Let's not let ourselves wander off. You left a 'but' hanging out when you were talking."

"Right, right," Alan said. "Why exactly do you say they did wrong by sending me after the Ghoul?"

"The Ghoul can hide. It's more a little like the way I like to teach folks to do it, but it's not the way Stigma and his crew have started doing it. At least, not from what I've heard."

"There's more than one way to hide and I don't know *any* of them?!" Blot snapped.

"Should have stuck with them just a little longer," the gardener said.

"So how is it done?" Alan asked.

Gladys gave him a disappointed look. "You really don't expect me to lay all that out for you, do you? I've been honing this to a good sharp point for a dog's age, and my life gets worse just as soon as it stops working. I wouldn't give you my secrets if you were Stigma. I sure wouldn't give you my secrets knowing you're working for the Glints, willingly or not."

"We have no love for the Glints," Blot said. "What we've got from them, and what they're threatening to pull away, are distraction wards to keep enemies from killing us and Alan's family. If you could teach us to hide, we could ditch them."

"That's a fine thing to hear," Gladys said. "Might even be true. But it's also just what I'd say if I was trying to find out what I was after to make my bosses happy."

"Can you at least tell us what's different about how they hide and how you hide?" Alan asked.

"Stigma's crew, near as I can tell, is using Dawn techniques to hide themselves."

"Really? How did he get his hands on Dawn techniques?" Alan asked.

"That's none of my concern. It just helps me out, because my own recipe is a healthy batch of my own work with a dose of Glint magic."

"How did you get Glint magic?" Blot asked.

"That's none of *your* concern. I just wish I could have a bit more. Maybe something fresher."

Blot's eyes brightened and she cocked a grin. "Really..." she said.

She rose up out of the shadows, once again imposing herself on reality. With slow, artful motions, she held out one hand. A perfect magician's flourish fanned out a stack of paper strips.

The gardener squinted, then fished in the pocket of her shirt to fetch a very thick pair of glasses. She slipped them on and gazed at the visible symbols.

"That's a ward. That's a Glint ward," the gardener said.

"That's a *stack* of Glint wards," Blot said, folding them into her palm and vanishing them. "Or, since you've just said you would like to have some new Glint magic to look over, I'd call that a stack of *currency*."

Gladys removed her glasses and, for the first time since they'd met her, moved fully independently of her shadow. They gave each other a pointed, knowing glance, then synchronized again and looked back to Blot.

"I think I'm going to like you. You want to deal? Let's deal. But I think I have some things the two of you might be a bit more interested in than just what your Glint masters sent you for."

"I'll take whatever I can get," Blot said. "What have you got?"

"Seems to me, a properly curious sort might wonder how I learn what I need to know. The things the Dusk can't bring themselves to care about, things like that. I don't get out much after all."

"Okay, I'll bite. Who are your other informants?"

"Follow me."

Gladys, rake in hand, led the way along a new path, which trailed behind the cottage. Unlike the slate step stones that led to the cottage itself, this one was formed by nothing more than the passage of time and countless trips back and forth.

"This place goes on forever," Alan said, looking about.

They'd been walking for five minutes at least. Though the gardener was spry, she wasn't setting a strenuous pace. Regardless, it underscored the fact that this, whatever it was, was not the hiking trail that had led them to the tree that served as the gate to this place. By now, they would have had to spill across to a familiar path, but the forest simply kept going.

"It goes on as far as it needs to," Gladys said.

"What is it? It feels much more shade than human," Blot said.

"It only feels that way because you haven't been home in a while. It's closer to half and half. This is what you would call an echo." She tipped the rake to knock a stone out of the path. "It would probably be better to call it a shadow, but honestly, with shades that's a term that is already pulling more weight than it should have to. You make it the same way you make a shadow, though. Enough light on one side and you end up with a dark copy on the other that can be an awful lot bigger without really amounting to much of anything. Plus it can move around even if the original shape doesn't."

"I'm not sure that's how I'd describe a shadow," Alan said.

"That's how I'd describe this place," she said. "Here. This is what we came to see."

Emerging from among the trees was a curious sight. These days curious sights were pretty much the only ones Alan ever got to see. This one, at least, was closer to surreal than horrifying. It was a field filled with crudely made scarecrows. Crosses fashioned from lashed sticks were hung with ragged flannel not unlike Gladys's. Some had pants dangling like banners below. Others had shoes sitting at the base. Heads were burlap sacks stuffed with something dry and stiff, with faces stitched on with thick twine.

"Boy. You must really be dedicated to keeping the crows away from your garden," Alan said.

One of the scarecrows rattled.

"They never did keep crows away. And they *attract* the rikts around," the gardener said. "Get out of there, you!"

She swept her rake at the ground beside the offending scarecrow. It rattled again, then a familiar blue-tinged streamer darted from it. The rikt bounced between different scarecrows, rattling them like bouncers in a pinball table, then curled around the shadow of the rake itself. Once it reached the tines, it resolved into a more defined shape again.

"You want to show off for the guests, do you?" she said. "You're making me wish I hadn't tinkered with you lot."

She fished in another pocket and found a wad of waxed paper. Unfolding it revealed a bit of meat trimmings, the sort of cut you'd toss to the dog if you had one, or in the trash if you didn't. It was all gristle and fat. She tossed it toward a stake driven into the ground just off the side of the path. The rikt crowed excitedly and leaped from the rake with enough force to nearly wrench it from her hand. Midleap, the trailing edge of its black form snapped from the rake to the stake, and the creature started to shred at the shadow of the meat.

Alan's stomach turned a bit at the spectacle of meat twitching, tearing, and vanishing seemingly on its own.

"Is that your pet or something?"

"'Pet' implies some sort of obedience," the gardener said. "They aren't what I'd call trained. But they're not without their use. Enough about that little scamp. We came here for these."

She led the way a bit farther into the field of scarecrows. While the first few were unremarkable, past the second row their shadows started to show a not wholly unexpected bit of detail. They were human shadows, or at least shadows more humanoid than the effigies casting them. Some stood. Others huddled. Most swayed and wavered. There were men, women, and even a few children.

Alan looked to Blot. She was looking upon the shadows with equal interest. Rather than vague fascination, she had a far more troubled look on her face.

"Are these shades?" Alan asked.

"If they were shades, they'd tell you as much," Gladys said. "Do you see any white eyes staring back at you?"

"Then what are they?" Alan asked.

"What do they look like?" the gardener asked.

"They look like shadows."

"There you are, then."

"But shades *are* shadows."

"Shades are shades, Alan," Blot said quietly. "Shadows are what we replace."

"But... are these human shadows? The ones the shades tear free?" he said.

"That they are," Gladys said. "Shouldn't have taken so many guesses."

She marched out among them. Some turned to regard her. Others seemed oblivious to her presence.

"For a long while, there wasn't much in the way of new blood here, so to speak. Once enough time passes since an eclipse and the Dawn has had their chance to whittle away at whatever came through. Plenty of newcomers these days, though."

"But how? Do they just come here?" Alan asked, crouching to look over the shadow of a young man.

"That would make my life a good deal easier, but no. That's why I've been tinkering with the rikts. Now and again I send them out there to track down any stragglers that seem like they've got some fight in them and bring them back here. I've got to send a few at a time, because like I said, 'training' is a generous word for what I've managed with them, and sometimes it takes them a while to come back."

"Why not send them all at once?" Alan asked.

230

"With a bunch of fresh shades about, I've got to take it slow. You don't want to see a rikt that's spotted a weakened shade with no host."

"Why do you bring the shadows here?"

The gardener looked at him curiously. "Wouldn't you? Seems the respectful thing to do. This used to be part of a person. That person might not even be around anymore. Seems only right to find a place for them. Make them comfortable for as long as they're going to stick around. I like the gossip, too."

She flipped the rake and tugged at some weeds weaving up out of the ground at the base of the nearest scarecrow. "They're not chatty, so much. Different ones remember different things. But they remember a good bit about who took them. The feel of them, anyway. And they share it."

"How?"

"We haven't got the time, Alan," Gladys said. "It's not something that you can learn from a textbook. There's finesse to it. A little different for everyone. But I have a chat with each one, then give them a place to stay until they go."

"They go?"

"They last different amounts of time. Some of them are gone in days. Others linger for years, maybe longer than the human they were torn from. But they all either fade away or pull free and wander off eventually."

"Why did you bring us here?" Blot snapped. "What's this got to do with us?"

The gardener laughed. "Nervous I'm making an offer to him and not to you?"

"I'm nervous that's what *he's* going to think you're doing. The Glints already hinted about a 'cure' that got him insultingly intrigued," Blot said.

"Relax. This isn't that. Well... it is, but the cure I've got in mind is a little different," she said.

"One that kills humans but not shades?" Blot said.

It was a relief to Alan that she asked the question with wariness rather than enthusiasm.

"I don't know if the word's changed, but the way I learned it, a cure was about saving lives, not costing them." She stooped and set about weeding a bit more carefully. "In order for a shade to live in this world, it needs a host. And in order to take a host, they've got to tear a shadow away, essentially condemning the human to either a life linked to the shade or death when the shade moves on. And it is the *shade* who gets to decide. It's an inherently unfair, unbalanced situation. Maybe that's another reason the Glints are so obsessed with balance. But I think there is a solution."

She started to stand up. Alan rushed in to lend a hand, but before he could do so, her shadow pitched in, easing her up to her feet before falling back into synchronization.

"I used to think the solution was just getting rid of the need for a human as a host. But that's got its own problems. Not the least of which is that I couldn't figure out how to do it for anything more complex than a rikt."

"Those things don't need hosts?" Alan said.

"Not a living one. It only needs something with a distinct shadow as an anchor. It can last a few minutes between them. That's not a lot, but it's enough. The whole world is a bunch of shadowy stepping stones for that critter now. But I *did* figure out how to get the dislodged human shadows to stick around. It's just possible it would work to stick a human's shadow back onto its original body. Just three problems."

"That would kill the shade."

The gardener waved her hand. "No, no, no. The shade would just need a new host."

"But then *that* human would need the cure," Alan said.

"Are you two going to keep chattering, or are you going to let me finish?" Gladys asked. "It's very simple. Pull off the shadow of the human, set it aside, pair it with a shade. If they don't get along, find a new host, stick the shadow back on, and try again. Most shades and humans aren't going to work out. But I'm a fine example of a good pair. And you two seem to get along."

"Mostly," Blot and Alan said.

"So it'd take some work, but we *could* match shades and hosts that'd work, at least as well as any other relationship, and if things fall apart, try again. But like I said, three problems. We need the human *and* the shadow to try it, we need a lot of the right sort of power to even try..."

"The right sort of power?" Alan asked.

"Shards of Shadow," Blot guessed.

"That's right. Three of them, at least. And fresh ones. Untouched by human hands."

"Why?"

"They aren't meant to be used by humans." She tipped her head. "No, that isn't fair. A human has a harder time using them efficiently. If it's been touched by a human, it's probably been drained. The shards take time to recover. Three or four fresh ones, if used properly, should be enough to keep on top of things. Then it's just a matter of finding the right twist of Glint magic to make it all work consistently."

"Why Glint magic?" Alan asked.

The gardener shook her head. "Something about shade and Glint magic coming together. It's like—"

"Oil and water?" Alan said.

"*Fire* and water?" Blot said.

"Dynamite and a match," the gardener said. "A little bit of each, mix them together, and you get a lot of bang out of it." She clapped some soil away from her hands and huffed. "So, the cards are all on the table. Now let's ante. What I'm after is Glint magic, shards, and a matched set of human and shadow. What I'm willing to offer is information and maybe a couple of tricks."

"What we want is to know how... let's say how *Stigma* is hiding himself, in a way that we can inform the Glints," Alan said.

"By the heavens, you don't start with that!" Blot said. "We want a way to hide from the Glints. And to hide others."

"Let's head back. This'll take another pot of coffee, I think," the gardener said.

"Or three," Blot amended.

Haggling, it turned out, was one of the other skills Blot excelled at. For nearly forty minutes, she'd gone back and forth, talking up the content of the wards and the relative accessibility of the Shards of Shadow. Alan bit his tongue rather than be the good boy he was raised to be and point out that they had no clue how to get even one more shard, let alone three.

The first thing that the gardener was willing to part with was technically the only thing they'd been sent to get, which was the mystic mechanism by which Stigma and his crew were hiding themselves. That had taken three of the stolen Glint wards. Knowledge of how to perform what Gladys insisted was a far superior method, the method she was using and the Ghoul likely used a version of, was proving far more costly.

"Seven more wards. That's all I have," Blot said. "How else are you going to get more of these?"

"You are here to inform upon shades to the Glints. I won't give you the tools to teach them how to find *us*. I have no problem giving away my assessment of the secrets of the others. Unless things have gotten better since I came over, the shades didn't come here with plans regarding the Glints, so wiping out the means to hide from them doesn't leave them any less prepared than when they started."

"If you teach us, then we won't have to talk to the Glints at all."

"You'll forgive me if I don't trust you. I've known you for all of an hour, and I've known far too many shades to suspect you can keep your word. You're welcome to use the Dawn method. It's working well enough for Stigma and the others."

"That won't work. The Glints know all about Alan's life. They'll be able to find us, and once they do, we'll have to give them the method, and then they'll defeat it and it won't work for us anymore. We need one to keep, *and* one that works. That way we can seem like we are playing along, then when the time is right, poof!"

"Oh, I know it. But you could hand me a whole Glint spell book and it wouldn't be enough to persuade me to let you leave here with the proper technique to shield yourself from discovery. There's too much to lose. If you want something else, ask for something else."

"There isn't anything else I want!" Blot said.

"What about the Ghoul?" Alan asked. "The Glints may only want it because they think it will lead them to the way to find the others, but it's still a killer."

"How many has it killed. Just the one?"

"*Just* one?" Alan said. "Isn't that enough?"

"It's too many, but it's not all it'll do. There's bound to be—"

"We know, we know. Two more at least before the next full moon," Blot said.

"Clever pair, you two..."

"We want help stopping it."

The gardener leaned back in her chair. "It won't do to have it running around... But helping you find it is the same as helping you find me. I can't do it."

"Can you hold on to it? You can stick human shadows to those scarecrows. Is there any way for you to keep the Ghoul here, like a prison? A prison for shades has worked once before."

"Oh, certainly. The handful of us still lingering here have to police ourselves. There are other places better suited to hold it than this, but if you tear it free, I can lock it down. But that's nothing for me, that's for you."

"But if we find the woman's shadow, if we bring them here."

"Oh! Interesting... So you track down her shadow, if it still exists. Then bring me the girl and her shadow... If you'll lend me the use of your shard, it might have power enough to give the cure a try. And *that's* useful for me."

She mulled it over. "You're not giving yourself an easy job, you know. The shadows aren't liable to be hanging out where you can find them. They scurry off. Head to a place where the human they were attached to felt safe. Or just a place that loomed large in their mind. It isn't always a place that's obvious."

"You let us worry about that. What do you say?"

"It'd go a long way to proving you could be trusted. It'd go a long way to proving you are useful. And it'd potentially get us a big leap closer to finding a way to give shades and humans a fighting chance to get along with each other. ... I'll tell you what. I'll send a rikt along with you, to help you find her shadow. They can usually get a decent whiff of where a shadow's gone if you can take them to a place where the human who lost the shadow has spent some time. Bring the shadow back, and I think maybe we'll have more business to do in the future."

Alan turned to Blot. "What do you think?"

Blot's look in return was dirtier than he would have liked. "I guess I'm game," she said finally.

"Grand," Gladys said. "Though, I've got to warn you. If the Ghoul's working its way through its ritual, you're not likely to have an easy time of it trying to capture him."

Alan stood. "Not having an easy time of it is effectively the only part of this whole experience that I've become accustomed to."

"Very well then. The wards?" she said.

Blot produced them and handed them over. The gardener donned her glasses. She looked over the pages, a grin widening as she did.

"Excellent, wonderful." She folded them neatly. "Strange as it may seem, even after all these years, I've never much developed the tongue for the shade dialects, so lean forward a bit and listen close, would you?"

Blot did as she was told. The next words were the first to be spoken exclusively in the more youthful voice. A complex and downright beautiful sequence of arcane-sounding syllables flowed from the gardener shade's mouth.

"Of course..." Blot said with a nod. "It seems so obvious in retrospect."

"Fetch me a rock, would you?" the gardener said.

Alan stood and paced a short distance away. Among the grass, he found a stone small enough to comfortably fit in his palm. He held it out to her, but she was too busy reading over the wards again. Her shadow plucked the stone from his hand. One finger lengthened into a claw and easily carved a simple but precise shape into the stone's surface.

Gladys produced a clucking sound with her tongue.

The pots and branches along the path started rattling and thumping as rikts dolphin-dived their way from anchor to anchor. The blue-tinged one fought its way to the front of the pack and squawked happily as it drew near. Its black streamer of a body struck the stone hard enough to knock it from the gardener's hand. Blot plucked it up from the ground. The creature made a contented roosting sound while entirely hidden in the shadow of the stone.

"I said it before, but it won't listen to you very much." Gladys pointed at Alan. "It won't listen to you at *all*. It's sort of wishy-washy on things that don't have shadows. But it's excellent at finding loose shadows, and it'll always come back to the stone if it doesn't have something more interesting to do. Of course, if it finds something *too* interesting, it might not come back at all. I'm still waiting on three or four of them to come back before I risk sending another batch."

"What do we do if we find the girl's shadow?"

"That'll cling to the stone as well, though it'll make it a bit crowded for the rikt, so it'll probably wander off at that point. It'll come back here eventually. Most likely." The gardener stood and stretched. "I'm getting tired. Time to hit the sack, I think. Good luck to you. Run along."

A few minutes later, Alan and Blot stood at the base of the white column.

"I'm not entirely certain this went the way we intended," Alan said.

"I'm not entirely certain you should have volunteered to go hunting for a shadow that might not even exist," Blot said. "It isn't as though we don't already have enough on our plates. But it *did* get the door open for further dealings. So good job, I suppose. And it got us this!"

She tossed the stone up in the air and caught it. The rikt tumbled down and bounced on the ground before popping back into its "proper" form, though as was the standard, a ribbon of black still ran from the creature to the rock like a leash.

"Hold the rock, would you?" she said.

"Can't you just vanish it like everything else?"

"It's got a shade-creature attached to it, Alan. That'd be weird."

She handed it to him. The rikt hopped up to be cast along his arm like a perch. If he focused, he could vaguely feel phantom talons gripping at him. It was a tingly, itchy sensation.

"Yeah. Heaven forbid this whole situation starts to get weird," he said.

"Turn around," she said.

"Why?"

"Because I have to apply the stealth thing the gardener taught me."

"You *have* to?"

"One, I don't want us to just pop into visibility right outside the gardener's door. That'd be a little obvious. It's bad enough that we probably disappeared for them once we stepped in. Two, if we've got work to do that'll lead to questions from the Glints, we'll need the stealth to give us time to do it. Three, I'm itching to actually cast a spell for once in my life."

"What do you have to do?"

"I have to trace some runes onto your back. It'll last until I add a final rune to deactivate it."

"It has to be done to *me*?"

"It's based on Dawn magic, which is in a roundabout way based on *our* magic, but with a human twist. They only have humans to work with most of the time. Now hold still. These things can get finicky if they aren't shaped just right."

Alan did as he was told, trying his best not to squirm from the combined sensations of a shadowy finger tracing a shape on his back and a set of unseen talon's working their way up his arm to perch on his head.

He didn't need to ask her when she was through. It was made clear by the wave of tingling chill that washed over him.

"There. That should do it!" she said. "I cast a spell! Too bad it won't do us much good for long. But I should really study it a bit. Maybe if I can figure out how it works, I can get some other spells to work. Or at least I can learn how to see through it enough to get a feel for Dun's squad again."

Blot snatched the rikt rock. The beast hopped happily to her presented arm.

"Easy, boy. Easy," she said, waggling her fingers to keep its attention. "This is going to feel a little strange, but we've got to get you through the tree, okay?"

She gave the feathery silhouette a ruffle, then swished around the pillar. Alan heard the confused cluck of the creature drop to silence. Blot reappeared.

"Okay, quick. Deep breath and let's get out of here."

CHAPTER 10

T he ride home had been a test for Alan's focus. His mind was in a thousand places at once. For one, he was mindful of anything resembling a message or visit from the creatures he now knew as Glints. If he had indeed vanished from their supernatural field of view once he got close enough to the tree, and then *stayed* vanished since then, he could only imagine the sort of agitation and confusion that was building in the white-suited overseers.

There was also the lurking specter of the Ghoul. They *had* just gone where it'd sent them, meaning it knew where they were, so if it was still in a vicious mood, it could easily have been waiting. Todd and Rive remained a threat, as Blot and Alan's ditching of them on the side of the road couldn't have left a good taste in their mouths. Pile on that the additional task of finding a woman's lost shadow, and his mind had very little space left for something trivial like driving safely.

He squinted at the setting sun. "I swear I'm suffering from some sort of supernatural jet lag," he murmured. "We spent an hour in a place where it was overcast and the dead of night, and now it's evening again."

"Look at him!" Blot said gleefully.

Alan glanced aside to find the shadow of the rikt being cast as though it were perched on the headrest. It was pecking and nudging at the handle just above the car door, causing it to flap and click.

"He's curious."

"He's a poltergeist," Alan said.

She made a soft swishing sound with her mouth and held out a hand. The rikt regarded it with a cocked head, then pecked it.

"Ouch!" she said with a gentle laugh. "You rascal."

"Blot, you just giggled."

"So?" she said, waggling her fingers and dodging another peck.

"So I don't think I've ever heard you coo over anything, and the only kind of giggling I'd have expected from you is the kind that trails off of a maniacal cackle."

"We've got to go to a butcher shop and get something for him," she said, disregarding his observation. "For treats. He'll be more obedient if we reward him with treats."

"I don't think it's supposed to be a pet, Blot."

"Oh, let me have this, would you?" she said, her voice with a more familiar edge to it this time. "This is a piece of home, okay? There aren't a whole lot of pieces of my home that I'd be happy to find, but rikts have some happy memories for me. My grandmother used to feed them. Bones and stuff. Whatever didn't make it into the stock. Rikts will eat basically anything that used to be alive. And it's good luck to watch them eat, you know."

"To *watch* them eat?"

"Yeah."

She snuck her fingers close enough to give it a scratch. Again, it regarded her with a vacant, confused look with its wide white eyes. Rather than a peck, it fluffed its feathers, giving its shape a fuzzy, complex texture around its edge.

"I guess it's folklore, but we lived by it," she continued. "See, a rikt mostly eats stuff that dies on its own. So when something's at death's door, rikts start to get very interested. They'd follow and follow and follow. Sometimes they'd help death along if they were very hungry, but mostly they would just follow and watch and wait. We used to say they were, what do you call it... *heralds* of death. Once they take an interest in you, it means *death* took an interest in you. And if they ate something *else* while you were around, it meant death passed you over. Lucky. Grandma said if you kept the rikts fat and happy, you'd live forever."

"I think I have some mints in the glove compartment," Alan said.

Blot popped it open and fished one out. She held it up. In a single peck, the rikt gulped down mint and wrapper. A moment later, a retching hack sent the mint launching back into reality. It slapped wetly against the windshield.

"If it's good luck to watch them eat, what's *that* mean?"

"It means we should probably get some meat sooner than later," Blot said.

Alan took a turn. They were getting close to his neighborhood.

"You know... You talk about your grandmother a lot. You don't talk about your parents. Or siblings or anything like that."

"Nothing much to say. They weren't around for very long."

"What happened to them?"

Blot laughed. "Your guess is as good as mine. Grandma never told the same story twice about it. Sometimes they were on secret missions for Stigma. Sometimes they were off hunting monsters that no one else could kill. Her stories never said they were dead, which means they were dead. Probably doing something embarrassing or pathetic, for her to make up so many stories."

She sighed. "Or maybe Grandma just liked telling stories." She shook her head. "I don't want to talk about it. Let's talk about something else."

Alan remained silent for a moment. He wanted to dig deeper, but talking about the past gave Blot's white eyes a distant, fragile look. Better to leave that be for now.

"We need to decide what we're going to do," he said. "If the goal is to make more progress hunting down the shadow and the Ghoul before the Glints notice us, we probably can't go home."

"That's good thinking. We can't really go to your parents' house either. Angel's been there, after all."

He drummed his fingers on the wheel. "We could go to a hotel... But I really think we need some help. And I can only think of one more person who might help us out."

Blot gave him a hard look. "Jessie..." she said.

"Unless you've got a better idea."

"I guess that's the best we've got. But don't forget we've got jobs to do."

He glanced at the rikt as it started flapping the handle again. "Yeah, I think I'll have some handy reminders."

He pulled to the side of the road and tapped Jessie's contact. Nothing happened. Two more tries convinced him to restart his phone. When it woke back up, he was hit with a barrage of missed calls and notifications.

"Evidently 'the garden' screwed with my cell reception," Alan said. "I missed two calls from Jessie."

He tapped her contact again, and this time the call went through. She answered after barely two rings.

"Alan! Jeez, where have you been?" she said.

"More photo stuff," he said vaguely. "Is something wrong?"

"Not especially, but I just wanted to check in on you. It's not like you not to answer."

"Yeah. Things have been a little... frantic lately. Sorry about that. Just catching up on what I missed. Hey, listen, what are you doing tonight? Can I come by?"

"We should have come up with a good story before we called her," Blot said.

"I, uh, I just need to—" Alan stumbled.

"Yeah! Sure. Come by. You like Greek food? I was planning on ordering tonight. I could have sworn I had leftover steak, but I guess I finished it."

"Oh, uh, sure."

"Great! How far away are you?"

"I'll be there in about five minutes."

"I'll wait until you get here to order. See you soon!"

"See you then." He hung up and glanced at Blot.

"Evidently having good friends means not needing to tell quite so many lies to get along," she said.

"Yet another reason to keep a few of them around," Alan said.

"I guess," Blot allowed. "You should stop at a store and bring something. That's good manners, right?"

"Yeah, I'd say."

"Great! We can buy a treat for Chu-chu."

"Chu-chu?" he said. "We're calling it Chu-chu?"

"I'm calling *him* Chu-chu. I don't care what you call him."

The rikt hopped and caught the shadow of the handle above the door. After dangling from it for a few seconds, it seemed to wriggle out of its full birdlike shape and into a sort of serpentine sprite. It coiled itself into the tiny shadow of the handle and released a couple of contented clucks, unseen in the darkness.

"Is that thing going to behave itself at Jessie's apartment?" he asked.

"I'll make sure he stays entertained," Blot said.

Alan arrived at Jessie's apartment building. Since they'd rekindled their friendship, he'd never actually been to her place. He'd dropped her off, and he'd picked her up, but he'd never been inside. The building itself wasn't too different from his own. Not quite so tall, and without its own parking structure, but otherwise it had the same feel. The sun had almost entirely set by the time he arrived, and the building's entrance was on its east wall. To Blot's delight, as they approached the front door, they were bathed in shadow. To her dismay, however, the inside lobby awaiting them was quite well lit.

"Wait, wait," Blot said, as Alan reached for the door. "Let's feed Chu-chu first. I don't know how he's going to handle bright light, so we should make sure he's content first."

He pulled the carved stone from his pocket. As indicated by the gardener, the rikt did tend to favor the stone. And it was very good at cramming itself down into whatever tiny shadow the stone cast. He shook the stone, as Gladys had. The rikt unfurled and hopped down.

The only thing that seemed to fulfill the rikt's requirements of "dead animal" and Alan's requirements of not leaking blood everywhere turned out to be a bag of the unsettlingly named "jerky nuggets." He opened the bag and glanced around to make sure he wasn't about to be observed feeding a chunk of salty dried beef to thin air. The coast was clear, so he fished out a nugget and held it down.

Chu-chu looked bemused at the piece of meat. Alan looked at the treat's shadow, which he now realized was hanging completely on its own, since Blot wasn't mimicking his position at the moment. He waggled it a few times, but Chu-chu refused to treat it as anything but a curiosity. Then Blot slid up and simply touched the shadow of the food. Immediately, the rikt hungrily gobbled it up.

"I don't think he likes humans," Blot observed. "But he does like jerky."

"Then I guess he's officially your responsibility," he said.

"As if there was any doubt," Blot said. "Give me another. And the rock."

Alan did so. She tossed the rock into an outer pocket of his bag, then dangled the meat over it.

"Inside, Chu-chu. Otherwise it's lots of bright light, and you know you don't want that."

She dropped the meat inside. The rikt popped free and shriveled into its sprite-like serpentine form. It whizzed about a bit, then dove into the pocket with a thump. Alan stepped into the lobby before it could change its mind, pinning it inside the pocket and Blot down to the ground.

A few minutes later, Alan was stepping into Jessie's apartment. Like him, she lived alone. Considering she had a few years on the police force under her belt, being able to afford the place without roommates wasn't quite the same achievement for her as it was for him.

The place was a bit more lived-in than his own as well. It wasn't dirty, but it wasn't quite as orderly as he would have imagined. A coffee table was half-piled with boxes for Blu-rays and console games. A blanket was wadded up on one side of the couch. Basically, the place looked like it was in the midst of a middle-school sleepover. The only thing missing was an open pizza box and a two-liter bottle of Mountain Dew.

"Hey, good to see you," she said. "Left side of the couch is mine. Sorry things are a little messy."

"Don't worry about it. There's clean-up-before-they-visit friends and there's just-be-you friends. Good to know I'm on the second list. That's the fun list."

"Darn right it is." She grabbed a menu off the end table. "Here you go. If you're getting a gyro, get the platter and an extra pita. Same price and twice the goodies."

"Right, right," he said, dropping his bag by the couch and sitting down. "I, uh, I wonder if we could talk about something."

"It'd be kind of awkward if you came all the way over here and then didn't talk about anything. Is it about the new developments in the Metro Ghoul case? I know you're dying to talk about that."

"There are new developments in the case?"

"Yeah, there are," she said, like she was about to share some juicy gossip. "I mean, you know I don't like talking shop outside work, but this one's good." She sat next to him on the couch and leaned over to turn off one of the lights.

Blot slipped up along the wall and gave Alan an uncertain look.

"What's that about?" Blot asked warily.

"Why'd you turn off the light?" he said.

"You've got light-sensitivity problems," she said, picking up a cup of tea from the end table. "And since I don't have any of your moody red shades, it's lights off, right? But anyway, this'll be in the papers tomorrow. It's on the internet already. They struck pay dirt from the stuff you spotted on the roof."

"Oh yeah?"

"Yep. You saw the towel and, what, the footprints? And when they investigated, there were some shards of glass under it. Big ones. Well get this. They were able to pull a print. No match yet, but the blood matched the victim, so it's fairly certain the print belongs to the murderer. We just need one more break. If we can get our hands on the suspect and match the print, that'll be enough to hold them. With any luck, the copycat's going to be stopped before they get a chance to strike a second time."

"Let's hope," Alan said. "I'd hate to see him get any closer to the end of the ritual."

"What did you just say?" Blot said sharply.

"Don't dignify it by calling it a ritual. We're talking about a serial killer," Jessie said, pulling out her phone. "Let me see if I can find the story." She looked down to her phone.

"You can't be slipping up like that. We're not supposed to know it was a ritual," Blot said.

"*Skaw!*" Chu-chu exclaimed from inside his pocket in response to Blot's sharp tone.

"Quiet, Chu-chu," she shushed.

"Squa-squa-squa-*kaw!*" the creature squawked again, this time a shade more agitated.

His pocket rustled and the serpentine form of Chu-chu slid out. It popped back to its rooster-like shape and was cast across his chest as though it were perched on his lap. Alan gave Blot a hard look.

"No, no, no." She made a soft swishing noise. "Not right now. Back to the stone. You'll get another treat!"

The rikt didn't obey. He didn't even acknowledge her. As he was cast across Alan's chest and gave his thigh a phantom itchiness, Chu-chu was perfectly still, his head turned aside to gaze at the far corner of the room.

"Skaw..."

Alan glanced up. He froze.

"Maybe just let him sit there, then," Blot said. "He's not causing any trouble and he..." She glanced up to Alan and saw he too was staring off into the corner. "What's wrong?"

She turned. Chu-chu's stone-still vigilance was not without reason. Something had slipped out of the kitchen. It moved with slow, deliberate shifts. First to the leg of an end table. Then to the base of the lamp. The light cast it across the couch beside Jessie before it finally resolved into a recognizable form. It was a rikt, though even to an untrained eye, one would be hard-pressed to confuse it with the creature Blot had taken as her pet. It was larger, with longer feathers and an overall more scraggly, ancient look.

"Why is there another rikt here?" Blot said quietly.

Alan's eye twitched. He couldn't answer without Jessie hearing. As if it were reading his mind, selecting the action that would most concern Alan, the other rikt gingerly transferred itself from being cast by the pillow on the couch to perching on Jessie's shoulder.

He dug his fingers into the arm of the couch, not sure what to do, but knowing that this couldn't possibly be good. On the surface, the presence of yet another supernatural creature, and an unexplained one at that, made Alan uneasy. Deeper down, a far greater concern gnawed at him. Blot had said that rikts showed up when death was near... and this one had selected Jessie as its roost.

"Shoo! Shoo! Get out of here," Blot hissed at the creature.

It was unimpressed.

Jessie muttered under her breath and scratched her shoulder precisely where the rikt had chosen to perch.

"I've got to look into getting new fabric softener," she mumbled.

"Itchy?" Alan said.

"Yeah. It comes and goes. Sort of a pins-and-needles thing. I hope I don't have a pinched nerve. I *just* got back in the patrol car again." She thumbed through her phone. "I can't find the new story. It's all still that break-in at the Boston records room. I... hey! Here it is again!"

She tapped through to a video and slid over to present the phone to him. The two rikts eyed each other with wary respect, like enemy soldiers daring each other to step across a border.

"Check this out," she said.

He looked at her phone, where a video of the footage he'd seen several times before looped a few times.

"Yeah, I've seen this," Alan said.

"You're doing that thing where you're trying to sound calm, and it makes you sound crazy," Blot whispered.

"But look at the shadow. Someone put eyes on it. Every now and then, I'll see the video with eyes on it, and then when I get to the station and try to show it off, I can't find it anymore. I don't know what sort of weird prank someone's trying to pull, but it's serious creepy pasta stuff."

"Oh... Heh... I didn't notice the eyes," Alan said, shifting his gaze pointedly to Blot.

The shade let the dim light of the room nudge her into her proper place, then shut her eyes and gradually eased herself into Alan's proper silhouette. The only evidence that something was up was the single hand that was reaching up to attempt to snatch Chu-Chu.

"I'm going to have to send an email. This is on a regular news site, for heaven's sake. They can't be sharing doctored videos."

Alan fished into his bag beside him and subtly plucked out a piece of jerky. He tossed it behind the couch. Jessie's rikt eyed it intently, but the less stoic Chu-chu squawked lightly and dove after it.

Jessie's head popped up. "Did you hear something?"

"Like what?"

"Like a bird." She screwed her finger in her ear. "I think there's a nest outside my window or something. Anyway, you came here to talk about something. What's up?"

She pocketed her phone and glanced up to him. Alan fought valiantly to keep from glancing at the rikt that was standing watch on her shoulder.

"I... I came here because I'm... I could use some help."

It occurred to him that he'd come here for a dozen different reasons, none of which was reasonable for someone who didn't know the whole story, and most of which fell under the nebulous heading of "badly needing help." He tried to sift his way through the pile of things for something he could use to introduce the whole mess in something approaching a palatable way. It wasn't easy, because the bulk of his brain power was currently splitting his mind into two separate warring camps, one of which was demanding he tell her about the supernatural creature that was quite literally sinking is claws into her, and the other was worried about the inevitable reappearance of the *other* supernatural creature and how to keep it a secret.

"It's a police thing," he said.

She smirked. "I had a feeling. Listen, if you want to talk about it, talk about it. You know how I feel about work and play overlapping, but this is all new to you. I can't expect you to build up the work-life balance overnight. Especially not while you've been doing the freelance thing for so long."

"The police have, like, records on people. Particularly if they've committed crimes, right?"

"Yeah."

"If I needed to know something about someone, what would be the policy on getting access to those records?"

"The policy would be that you have an actual legal reason to look into that, or the ACLU is going to come after you with torches and pitchforks. I would think that'd be obvious. The cops aren't supposed to just dig into people's business out of curiosity."

"But what if it's to do with an active case?"

"That would be up to the investigators. Which, I should emphasize, you are not."

"Right, right. That makes sense."

"Who, pray tell, were you hoping to run a background check on?"

"I've been thinking a lot about the way the Metro Ghoul does things, and I thought maybe, you know, we could search for people who might fit the pattern for prior copycats."

Jessie's eyes widened. "Gosh, Alan! Are you suggesting we analyze similar crimes and attempt to assemble some sort of a profile? Stop everything! I've got to call the department and tell them about this revolutionary new investigative tactic that is so firmly entrenched in police procedure already that there have been at least five TV shows about it."

She slapped him on the shoulder. "Come on, man. Give us some credit. That stuff is already underway."

"Right, okay. Good. And if we were to want to look into who they were searching for..."

"Let me repeat, this isn't *your* job. For the purposes of this case, you're just a civilian. The police hold back details for crimes still under investigation. For crimes like this one, they hold back other details to try to curtail further copycats. Mostly the finer details of execution. And the finer details of motivation."

"Okay..."

"So what you're asking about, that's on the top of the no-no pile. In the best case, making that sort of information public would lead to vigilantes and other 'concerned citizens' acting on it. In the worst case, it would give a road map to people with delusions of grandeur who want their names in the paper and to feed whatever demons are lurking within them."

"Right, okay. That makes sense."

The rikt on Jessie's shoulder ruffled its feathers and preened a bit. She shivered and scratched a bit more industriously at her shoulder. Alan shut his eyes and tried to make a list of the things he should be working toward. He needed help finding out things about Marsha, the current host of the Ghoul. He needed to ease his way toward asking if he could spend the night, rather than risk going home and encountering Angel. He needed to...

"Do you have a pad or something?" Jessie said. "I want to get the order written down so we can call the Greek joint before they close."

He nodded and reached for his bag. A bit of rummaging unearthed a legal pad, which he pulled free. He was still grappling with how to proceed, so the act of flipping through to a fresh page was largely on autopilot. If he weren't so tired, he might have noticed the book was terribly dusty. If he weren't so distracted, he might have noticed the pages he was flipping through were written in an odd shorthand that he didn't recognize, let alone write in. If he was well rested and in his right mind, he never would have handed that particular pad to a sharp-minded, sharp-eyed officer of the law. And if Blot hadn't been forced to "hide" with her eyes shut, she would have stopped him.

Instead, the sleepy, distracted Alan handed the pad over.

"Jeez, Alan," Jessie said, leaning aside to snag a pen off the end table. "Do you go Dumpster-diving for your stationary? This thing smells like a basement."

"Uh..." Alan said, ignoring pieces of his mind starting to wake up.

Jessie flipped a page down and looked it over. Her expression shifted from bemused to stern.

"Oh, actually, I think I have another pad," Alan said quickly, reaching for it.

Jessie deftly moved it from his reach and flopped it to the first page. Both of their eyes came to rest on the small stamp on the top right corner of the first page. *Exhibit C-107.*

Her eyes narrowed. "Where did you get this, Alan..." she said.

"It's just... I just..." he stammered.

"This is from Boston City Records. Alan, on the day of the break-in in Boston, you were off taking some pictures in the wilderness."

Blot started to subtly reach down for his bag. The motion was hidden from Jessie by the couch, but it was visible in the corner of Alan's eye. She was reaching for the bag of jerky. Alan realized she was planning a diversion that would only cause more trouble.

"No!" he snapped at her.

"But you said you were," Jessie said.

"I... that 'no' wasn't for you. Yes, I was taking photos."

"Do you have anyone to vouch for your whereabouts?"

"No. I was in the woods. Why are you asking me this?"

"Because if I don't, someone else will soon."

"You think I robbed the Boston police station?"

"I think you have no alibi for the night it happened and you have what appears to be one of the court records that would have been in the boxes that were disturbed. If someone gets a search warrant to go through your apartment and computer files, are they going to find something they shouldn't?"

Alan didn't answer. From the look on Jessie's face, there wasn't going to be an answer that would do him any good.

"Alan, I think I've made it clear what I require from a friend at this point. But if I haven't, let me say it now. I need you to know that you can trust me. And I need to know that I can trust you. I'll ask you again, and however much or little you say, I want you to speak the truth. What is happening to you? What is going on?"

Alan sat silently. He couldn't bear to lie to her, but he couldn't bring himself to speak the truth. There were too many dangling threads. Anything he might confess now would cause the whole web of lies he'd spent the last few weeks weaving to unravel. It would endanger him, it would endanger her, and it would endanger Blot. She waited patiently for the longest few seconds of his life. Finally, she spoke.

"Okay then. That's fair." Jessie tightened her lips. "I think it's time for you to go, Alan. You're going to have to think about what comes next. And so am I."

Alan tightened his fists briefly, then leaned on the arm of the couch to sluggishly climb to his feet. Before he could fully stand, he felt the back of his shirt tug sharply down. He flopped back onto the couch.

"Oh, no," Blot said. "I'm not going to have you blaming me for losing a friend because of a heist that was my idea. If this is how it's going to be, this is how it's going to be."

"What was that sound?" Jessie said, head cocked to the side.

Blot opened her eyes and snapped back to shape. She rose up on the wall. Jessie's eyes darted vaguely in her direction. She blinked rapidly, her eyes apparently not quite able to focus on the form rising up. She looked around for something that might be casting the shadow.

Blot slid closer to where the rikt was perched on her shoulder.

"Look, you," she growled at the creature. "You've got your claws into her, and she can see me because of it. The damage is done, so you might as well sink them in nice and deep."

The creature regarded her distrustfully and shuffled a bit closer to Jessie's head. Blot grew impatient and made a motion to snatch the creature from her shoulder. Predictably, rather than give up its perch, it huddled down and clutched tighter before shriveling into its sprite-state and coiling itself invisibly into the shadow of Jessie's shirt.

"*Ow*," Jessie yelped, rubbing at her shoulder and tugging at her shirt to see if she'd been bitten.

When she looked up, her eyes focused on Blot. This time there was no blinking, no uncertainty. After a second or two, her brain finished processing what she was seeing. She scrambled back against the arm of the chair. "What in the hell?!" she squealed.

"Hi, Jessie. Pleased to meet you," Blot said. "Ever since you saw the photo back in the hospital, I figured *something* had happened to you. I guess you picked up a freeloader. That prison must have attracted its share of rikts once the ritual started."

"Wh-what? What's going on?!" she said, her voice an almost silent half gasp as she climbed backward over the arm of the couch.

"A lot, Jessie," Alan said. "More than you could possibly imagine."

Blot picked up Jessie's tea and held it out. "You should probably have a drink. Maybe it'll help you calm down," Blot suggested.

Jessie's response was an incoherent bit of raving. She backed to the far wall of the living room, then retreated to her bedroom to lock the door.

Alan and Blot stared at the door as muffled raving continued from the other side.

"I wish you hadn't done that," Alan said quietly.

"First of all, *I* didn't do that. That other rikt did it, and then *you* did it by handing her that pad. Honestly! It's like you've never had to hide evidence before. But what's done is done. It was that or lose Jessie. I don't like her, but she's your friend, and by the darkness, if you think I'm going to be able to hold your sanity together on my own, you're sorely mistaken."

She glanced back to the door and snapped her fingers. "Do you think she's calling the cops on us? I'll go check." Blot slid toward the door, ready to pop underneath.

"Don't!" Alan said. "Give her a minute."

Blot shrugged. "Fine. But if she tries to call the police, I'm stopping her. Until then, it looks like she has one of those coffee pod machines. I'm helping myself."

After five minutes, the raving had cooled to a soft murmur of self-discussion. After ten minutes, the door clicked open. She silently marched across the room and pulled open a drawer. She fumbled a bit with a box and pulled it open, revealing an old, beat-up pack of cigarettes. She shakily put one in her mouth and lit it.

Jessie took a long, steadying drag from the cigarette and breathed the smoke out. She eyed the cup of coffee that was floating in midair, then looked to where Blot was cast on the wall, sipping at it. She took another puff on the cigarette.

"Tell me everything."

"It might put you in danger."

"Tell me *everything*."

And so he did.

He told her every detail that he could recall. He opened his laptop and showed her the pictures, played the recordings. With the rikt dug in, she could see the eyes on the shadows. She could hear the other voices. He told her about the election, about the prison. He told her about the Dawn, and about the Glints.

Through it, Jessie listened. She was tense, her eyes were wide. But she listened closely, absorbing every word. Eventually, the rikt hiding amid her shadow unfurled itself again. Perhaps it was coincidence, perhaps the creature was being territorial in the presence of Chu-chu, who had happily climbed out from behind the couch again. It may even have been a greater understanding and wisdom than they'd given it credit for, but the elder rikt kept its claws tight and thus kept Jessie's ability to see the shades intact.

"And that's why I need to do this," Alan said. "It doesn't matter how close you get to the Metro Ghoul. You won't catch it. The girl's just a host. For all I know, it's already abandoned her. And if it didn't... I've seen what it can do. I've had a run-in with it. You won't take it until it decides it's done. You just don't have the tools."

Jessie nodded. She dropped the butt of her cigarette into the seltzer can that was serving as her ashtray, then pulled another cigarette from the pack.

"I thought you quit smoking," Alan said.

"Three years ago I quit smoking and I quit drinking. Of the two, I'd prefer a setback with cigarettes." She lit the cigarette. "So what do we do about this?"

"We?" he said.

"You're still my friend, you're still in the middle of this mess, and if what you're saying is true, it seems like you're the only solution we've got."

"I had a feeling we could count on her," Blot said.

Alan glanced in her direction and gave her a dubious look.

"I take it she hasn't always had the best opinion of me?" Jessie said.

"It's nothing personal. Just a privacy and freedom thing. She has to twiddle her thumbs and lay low whenever I'm not alone. And you're the reason I haven't been alone as often as usual."

"I had a *lot* of coffee go cold because of you," Blot said, tipping back the last few drops of her latest cup.

"And she's the reason you get double coffees at the diner."

"Yeah."

"... What happens to all the coffee?"

"I asked the same thing!" Alan said.

"Why are you humans so hung up on body functions? Alan's got every natural and supernatural force in the area tugging his strings, you just found *out* about supernatural forces, and we've all got a serial killer to worry about. Are we really going to stop everything to discuss if the shadow lady goes to the potty?"

"I don't understand shades and Glints and things. I do understand bathroom breaks," Jessie said.

Blot grumbled. "It's all just *substance*, okay? We're two-dimensional, so we can pack it as tight as we want, but when we come out into the open, that substance has to come from *somewhere*. And when we need to heal, that needs to come from somewhere too. That's what happens to what we eat or drink. It becomes part of us, just like it becomes part of you when you eat. The only difference is that we can choose how to store it and how to use it. Happy?" Blot said. "Can we move on?"

"... But what about when you get too much of it?"

"We just shed it."

"Like a dog? Like dog hair?" she said.

"If that's how you want to interpret it."

Jessie puffed again, then stubbed the barely started cigarette out. "Yeah. Fine. Let's move on. Ground rules. I'm not going to break the law for you. And you're not going to break the law. Not again. If we're going to work together on this, we're going to find a way to do it within the bounds of the law. At least for the things that have legal precedent."

Blot grumbled. "Do you know how hard I had to work to get him to start bending the rules, and now I'm going to have to start working on *you*?"

"No one said we can't bend the rules. But no breaking. I'm a police officer. This is the way it's going to have to be. There's no legal precedent for charging a..."

"Shade," Blot said.

"A shade, right. And honestly, I can see why you haven't spread the word. Warning about a threat that most people can't see isn't going to do anything but cause widespread panic. I don't know the solution, but it's not my job to figure it out. As things stand now, as far as I can figure, the woman the Ghoul is attached to is the one guilty of the murder in the eyes of the law. But because she didn't actually do the murder, and the only piece of evidence solidly linking her to the murder scene is a single fingerprint, plus all the other oddities that are going to muddle things... the American legal system isn't set up to cope with the supernatural. This woman is probably going to walk. Minimal jail time at best. So don't worry about her doing the time for the Ghoul's crime. But you say you can cure her?"

"We *might* be able to *restore* her to the way she was before becoming a host," Blot said.

"She's, understandably, sensitive about terminology that treats her like a disease," Alan said.

"But you're a parasite," Jessie said. "You chose a host to support you."

Blot crossed her arms. "Babies do that for nine months, don't they? You don't call *them* parasites."

"Fine. But you're confident you can do it?"

"It's the best option we have."

"And what happens to the Ghoul?"

"Gladys says she'll keep it locked up."

Jessie's jaw tightened. She took a slow, severe breath. "I don't like having to trust someone who is operating literally outside the bounds of the law." She reached for the pack of cigarettes, then curled her fingers angrily and flicked it across the table. "Hide that, would you?" she said.

Blot's hand slid across the table and pushed it into the shadows.

"If you knew you had a hard time resisting them, why did you have a pack in your house?"

"Because it's not really quitting if you don't have access to something. It's just dodging the problem. Anyway, I can reconcile this as a jurisdiction thing. The Ghoul is outside my jurisdiction. We're going to extradite it to the gardener, and we'll deal with the woman. What do you know about her?"

"Plenty," Alan said. "I know what she looks like, I know what she sounds like. And unless the Ghoul has moved—"

"And it won't move until two more kills or a full moon, whichever comes first," Blot added.

"Then we know the neighborhood she hangs out in."

"Shouldn't be hard for your people to find her, right?" Blot said. "So the police can find her while *we* are looking for the shadow."

"We're no strangers to tracking down a suspect based on less information than that. The problem is, there's no way for us to know all that without getting into the supernatural stuff, which won't hold up in a court of law."

"I see the problem," Alan said.

Blot grinned. "So what we need is a plausible lie. Something to bridge the gap between what we know and what we're supposed to know." She rubbed her hands together. "This happens to be an area of expertise for me."

The discussion took a turn toward calculation and deception, as tended to be the case when Blot was in charge of things. Something about having a problem to work on seemed to help Jessie to become if not more comfortable with things, at least better capable of coping with them. At some point Chu-chu got a little rambunctious and had to be calmed down with a handful of their rapidly dwindling stock of jerky. Jessie's rikt briefly abandoned her to snatch some, but it returned to her shoulder just as soon as she'd grabbed some of the meat to bribe it. They ordered, received, and consumed two gyro platters, four pitas, and some baklava before they came to a solution that met the legal and moral requirements set forth by Alan and Jessie.

"Anonymous tips," Jessie said, tearing some remaining pita to blot at stray tzatziki sauce. "They're a staple of crime dramas, but we really don't rely upon them very much in real law enforcement. At least, not in our station. It turns out if you give people the opportunity to 'help' but no possibility of facing the consequences of a lie, you'll get all sorts of bonkers, unhelpful, or outright dangerous 'tips.' But I think I can persuade them to publicize a tip line. It'll take a bit."

"And while you're doing that, we can try to find the woman's shadow," Alan said. "And we'll call with a tip once there's a tip line to call."

"I'll have to coach you through what it'll take to get a tip taken seriously. It's sort of an art to get past the people on phones sometimes. But that can wait until morning. And none of the rest can happen until morning."

She stood and gathered the tins leftover from the meal. "You can't go home, right? Because..." She shut her eyes and conjured the words to mind. "Because the utility closet across from your apartment is home to a creature who claims to be a human but may be an angel—"

"They're not an angel," Blot said under her breath.

"—and they are keeping you under surveillance and might stop you from helping the woman the Ghoul is using as a host."

"That about covers it," Alan said.

"I'd normally need proof for that sort of thing, but right now the shadow of an invisible chicken is eating beef jerky out of my candy dish, so I really don't think my own eyes are any more trustworthy than your word. So... pillows and blankets."

She marched out of the room and returned with a pillow and a comforter with a design featuring one of the less remarkable boy bands of the nineties.

"Here you go. I have work in the morning, but you're welcome to stay. I don't have a spare key, though, so once you're out, you're out until I get home."

She turned to Blot, who was cast along the wall, trying to coax Chu-chu into accepting more scratches.

"Do you need anything for sleep?" she asked.

"I don't sleep."

"Oh... Okay. Well, then, sleep well, Alan. Stay awake well, Blot. I'll see you tomorrow." Jessie marched silently into her bedroom.

"I shouldn't have come here... This was a mistake," Alan said quietly.

"It would have had to happen eventually," Blot said. "It seems like humans aren't nearly as capable of maintaining complex tapestries of deception as shades are. It would have been a problem."

"This is also a problem."

"But it's a you-*and*-Jessie problem, not a you-*versus*-Jessie problem. ... And I was right, by the way."

"About what?"

"I said that if you were to spend the night together, it would be at her place."

He glared at her. "This does not count as spending the night with her."

"Both of you are in the same home, overnight. Technically correct is still correct." Another attempt at patting Chu-chu led to a barely dodged peck. "She's a good friend to you, though."

"At this point, I'd say she is certainly my best friend."

Another attempt got past the rikt's defenses and earned another adorable floof of feathers.

"She asked *me* if I needed anything," Blot said quietly.

"She's a good host."

"Yeah but... I'm your shadow. And from what I've seen of humans, you have a really hard time accepting new things as people. I would have expected her to talk to you about me. But she talked to me. She's a keeper, Alan."

"She's not even mine to keep."

"Well don't drag your feet. The chances of you finding another woman I'd give my blessings to are pretty slim, so don't let this one get away."

"I'll try not to disappoint."

CHAPTER 11

When Alan's eyes opened the next day, a handful of remarkable things had already happened. Perhaps because she was too busy fawning over Chu-chu, Blot remained an extra lurking in the corner of Alan's dreams. For the first time in far too long, he spent an entire night without having to engage his conscious mind while sleeping. His brain was even kind enough to avoid sculpting his recent traumas into nightmares. That was probably more due to profound mental exhaustion than actual mercy.

A second minor miracle came in the fact that Jessie managed to wake up, shower, and head to work without once waking him up. He rubbed the sleep from his eyes and found a note on the coffee table giving him a rundown of toiletries and suggesting Pop-Tarts for breakfast.

As a result of all this, by the time Alan was back in his car, he was feeling more like a functioning human being than he had in weeks. He was rested, showered, and fed. Thanks to Jessie's choice of shampoo, he smelled a little bit like a fruit basket, but all things considered, it was a fine morning. That they'd spent the last hour lingering in the shady alleyway of the motel where the murder had occurred managed to only slightly diminish that fact. They were waiting for the rikt to, for lack of a proper term, catch the scent of a missing shadow. The bright light all around meant they could be reasonably certain no shades would be attacking them without warning. Things felt uncharacteristically optimistic.

Until the phone rang.

"How will we know when Chu-chu has the scent?" Alan said, digging for his phone.

"I would guess he would *go* somewhere."

Alan glanced at the phone. "It's Mom or Dad," he answered. "Hey, Mom."

"Hello, Alan."

He froze. The voice was not his mother's. It wasn't his father's. It was the cool, and mildly disappointed tone of Angel. The white-suited watcher continued.

"I am relieved to hear your voice, as I was concerned something had happened to you. Knowing that you are well, but still beyond my capacity to surveil you, suggests you may be up to something right now."

"Why are you at my parents' house?"

"I think you know the answer to that, Alan."

"You had *better* not be threatening my parents."

Angel sounded pained. "I've done nothing to them. I even brought your mother some nice fresh Jersey tomatoes. She'd indicated a craving for them on my last visit. Gabriel and Dina have been quite clear on the proper course of action should you show the signs of disobedience. At the current stage, I am to remind you of my access to your loved ones. I don't like the idea of hurting them."

"I don't like the idea of you hurting them either. Ask Dun and the rest of his underlings how I feel about that sort of thing," he said. "I thought you wouldn't be able to find the place if you meant them harm."

"Our wards, perhaps unsurprisingly, have specific exceptions for us."

"That's the trouble with relying upon a locksmith to keep your house safe," Blot said. "He's liable to keep a key for himself."

"Alan, I know that the nature of our relationship is not one that could be considered friendly, but I at least had been pleased at how cordial we were able to be. I do not want to do anything unpleasant or untoward. I honestly do not think I have it in me to do anything of that sort. I am new to the field, and I lack the detachment that has made Gabriel and Dina so thoroughly effective."

"So they're the ones who will pull the trigger on my family if you suspect I've been tugging too hard at my leash."

"Yes. Or, more accurately, they are the ones who will decide that your parents are no longer deserving of our protections, leaving them at the mercy of the whims of your other enemies."

"Far be it for you to do your own dirty work," Alan rumbled.

"Don't let it get to that, Alan. Tell me what is happening. Give me something to report to Gabriel and Dina."

"We've found something, but there is more to do."

"Then tell us what you've found."

"We've found how Stigma and the others have been hiding from you."

"Splendid! Then we need only meet for you to deliver it."

"Not yet."

"That is not an answer they will accept, Alan."

"The fact that they won't accept any behavior from me that doesn't necessarily align with their own interests is the very reason I can't have you keeping an eye on me until I finish what I've started."

"Perhaps if you'd share your plans, you might find that we are willing to help, or at least forgo interference. You do know that we don't like to interfere if we don't have to."

"That would feel a lot more sincere if you weren't calling from my parents' house to issue a warning. You'll get the information you sent us to get. I promise you."

"That would feel a lot more sincere if you weren't currently using that very information to avoid us." Angel took a breath. "You will tell me how you are hiding immediately."

Angel spoke with the depth and resonance of one of their irresistible commands. Alan did not feel terribly compelled.

"I suppose that does not work over the phone," Angel said. "Such was my suspicion, but I had to do my due diligence. I am relieved, to be honest. I find I am not fond of that tactic."

"Angel, I just need a little more time."

Angel was silent for a few moments. "For the time being, Gabriel and Dina are focusing intently on Stigma and... others. They have not noticed your apparent deception, nor will they until the next time they visit me for an update. Two days. It is the best I can offer you."

"I'll take it."

"But if you take that time, and Gabriel and Dina arrive and find what you've done, they will be... pragmatic." They delivered the final word as though it was the most vicious of threats.

"Understood," Alan said.

"So be it." Angel's voice took on the muffled sound of someone turning away from the receiver. "Mr. and Mrs. Fontaine, I thank you again for your hospitality. The bacon, lettuce, and tomato sandwich was delicious. I am afraid I have to be going. Would you like to talk to your son?"

After the infuriating sound of Angel politely handing over the phone, his mother spoke.

"You have such nice friends, Alan. A whole bag of tomatoes. And they're so ripe. It's a talent to pick out the ripe ones, you know."

"Mom, is everything okay?" Alan said.

"Sure! Your father broke the fence with the weed whacker, but that's easy to fix."

"Great. Listen, take care. I've got to—"

"Wait! Did you get that call about the land?"

"No. What about the land?"

"There's a new buyer! Or maybe the same buyer is back again. I don't know. But for some reason he's insistent on talking to *you*."

"It's not my land to sell."

"I know but he's very insistent. Maybe he's a youngster and doesn't like talking to the old folks."

"Mom, you're sixty-three. Don't talk like you're in your nineties. But I missed a lot of calls a couple of days ago. I was... busy. And I'll be pretty busy for the next two days. But after that I'm going to come over and we'll figure it out. Take care, though. I have to go."

"Okay. Talk to you soon," she said.

Alan hung up. "We've got a brand new two-day time limit," Alan said. "After that, we lose the stealth and have to cope with Glint interference again."

"Two days is better than no days," Blot said, carefully tipping a trash can up for the rikt.

Chu-chu completely ignored the freshly revealed underside of the trash can, instead diving into it to rummage around. He resurfaced with a chicken bone to gulp down. When he finished, he hopped back down and tipped his head. A low sound, something like an inquisitive crow, churred from his throat. The rikt compacted into the long, curling sprite form and darted off with purpose. It dolphin-dived between this bit of trash and that, leading the way back to the car.

"I think he found something. See? It's good luck when they eat. Let's go!"

***

Getting Chu-chu to lead the way from the safety of a tinted car proved to be a test of Blot's patience and Alan's ability to drive while distracted. Whatever sense it was using to track the shadow seemed not to rely upon anything as direct as scent, so it could still follow the trail while in the car. And indeed, it was quite happy to remain in the car rather than face the light of day. But traffic laws and the need for roads didn't matter quite so much, so its dives toward the window came at inopportune times, and angry crows demanding the car drive through an alley or off an overpass were difficult to calm down again. Worse, the trip seemed to cause it to change its target multiple times. Three separate times they'd come to a point in the city that Chu-chu seemed to indicate was worth investigating, only for them to step out of the car, poke around for a moment or two, then launch off into a new direction.

It took much of the day, but eventually Chu-chu's straight-line instinct started to align with the actual roads. They were headed almost due west, retracing their steps across Philadelphia. This proved irritating for all involved, because as the sun slid toward afternoon, it was shining through the one untinted window.

"We're getting pretty far from the heart of Philly," Alan said, watching the signs on the road as they became increasingly unfamiliar. "Are we sure we're interpreting his directions correctly?"

"Your guess is as good as mine. I can feel a sort of pulse from him. I think it's a taste of however he's tracking the shadow. It's definitely getting stronger. I think that's probably a good sign."

Alan's phone chirped. Blot obligingly pulled the phone from his pocket and entered his passcode.

"It's from Jessie." Blot's tone was notably less irritated than usual when mentioning Jessie. "'The anonymous tip line is open. It is a website. People with tips should be visually detailed. Indicate gender, clothing, etc. Here's the link. I will try to pull overtime so I'm on duty if something worthwhile comes in for investigation.' Well, that's handy. I can do this while you're driving. Let's see…"

The phone chirped again. It was another text message, this one with a photo.

"It says, 'Guess who decided to join me at work today. I think it figured out if it sticks around, it gets treats,'" Blot said.

She turned the phone for Alan to glance at. It was a selfie focused primarily on her shadow, which featured the rikt perched there like a particularly surly parrot.

"I'm going to tell her that hers is a female," Blot said, tapping away at the phone. "And that she could pick a name. You people love dogs, and you wouldn't call your dog 'it.'"

She tapped out the message and sent it, then flipped one of her many stolen Cox Media pads out into reality. She found a page with a particularly artful sketch of the frightened young woman they'd encountered.

"Remind me on colors. Colors are hard for me to remember sometimes."

Though Blot's skill with touchscreens had massively improved in a relatively short amount of time, it still took her quite some time to fight with the phone's keyboard until the proper message was typed. At first, Alan was worried Blot would be too obvious, but then he remembered how seriously she took the art of manipulation. Her strategic flubbing of minor details while nailing the broad strokes of everything from outfit to hair style were nothing short of a masterpiece. It was written in the voice of a person ashamed at potentially having to admit to patronizing a prostitute, which gave an extra little bit of credence to the half-remembered name, "Marsha G-something. Maybe G-R-something."

When she was through, she sent a message to Jessie informing her of the tip. In the meantime, the urgent clucking turned into a constant low crowing. Sussing out precisely what Chu-chu was staring at with his single side-turned eye was difficult.

"There's a big neighborhood here," Blot said. "It might take us a while to narrow things down."

Alan narrowed his eyes. "Do you have Marsha's bracelet?"

Blot summoned it with her usual ease. Alan glanced down, then glanced up.

"It's the school. Marie-Anna was right. Those are the school colors."

They'd made their way a fair distance out into the suburbs, so the school in question was a middle school that was smaller than the first floor of the school Alan went to. The school day had ended long ago. From the looks of it, the building was empty, but there was still enough light to complicate matters. Not only would they be easily visible from any residents of the sleepy little suburb, but both Chu-chu and Blot would have difficulty using their abilities.

He stopped the customary distance from his actual target to disguise his intention as he shut off the engine. "I don't like this," Alan said, leaning into the back seat to find his bag. "The second time using this ski mask, and it's to break in to a school this time."

"It's the third time you're using it. Remember? You broke into the police station twice."

"Thanks, Blot," Alan said, stuffing the mask into his pocket.

Chu-chu was spoiling for the hunt. He'd contorted himself into his sprite form and kept darting through the windshield, only to be pushed back inside by the fading sunlight.

"I feel worse about breaking in to a school for some reason."

"How would you feel about breaking in to a bank? We haven't done that yet, and—"

"Let's just focus on the task at hand. After this I think I'm done planning heists for a while. How are we going to do this?"

"We'll get Chu-chu back on the stone, then you head around the east side of the school, in the shade so I can work. I'll keep an eye out for security cameras, you keep an eye out for witnesses. Don't put that mask on unless there's a camera, because at this time of day, that's a bit obvious..."

For once in this entire ridiculous enterprise, fate seemed to smile on them. The school was separated from the rest of the neighborhood by an assortment of sports fields and parking areas. As such, their biggest threat of observation was from a man sullenly walking a teacup terrier. The school wasn't exactly maximum security, but it did have some external security cameras they could see. Overcoming them required the very complex tactic of waiting for the sun to set far enough for the school's shadow to extend to the small playground to the east of the building. The only thing he had to do until then was not appear to be creeping around a middle school, which would have had unpleasant connotations even if he wasn't planning to break in. A shady bench at a public park turned out to be the best place to sit and observe. Alan made the best of the time by snapping some pictures of the scenery. Chu-chu made the best of the time by running absolutely rampant in the branches of the tree they were sheltering under.

"Oh, that squirrel is a goner," Blot said, gazing up from the ground as the leaves rustled with the motion of their expert tracker.

Alan glanced to the school. "A few more minutes. I never thought I'd get this good at estimating time from the advance of lengthening shadows," he said.

Blot slid up along the tree trunk. "You know... There's something we haven't discussed, and I think it's best to get it over with sooner rather than later."

"Oh?"

"If this works, if we *can* find the shadow, and the gardener *can* reapply it, what does that mean exactly?"

"She said it. It means things don't have to be life or death anymore for shades and humans."

"Right. But I'm not talking about shades and humans. I'm talking about Alan and Blot," she said.

"We don't even know if my shadow is retrievable. I mean, if Chu-chu can track them based upon hanging out in a place where the human who lost the shadow hung out, then you'd think he'd have been hunting for *my* shadow. Come to think of it, we don't know the shadow we're looking for is necessarily inside the school either. It could just be some other human's shadow. How would that work? Could you attach another human's shadow? Would it matter?"

"You lost your shadow hundreds of miles from here. It'd probably be closer to there than here. And that's beside the point. You know what I'm talking about. Talk of a cure has been a sore point between us even when it was just a theory. There is a chance that by tomorrow we'll know for certain if there is such thing as a *former* host. At which point I very much suspect the tone of our partnership is going to change."

"Afraid you're not going to be able to dangle my life over me anymore?" he said. He'd intended the line to have a playfulness, but it came out with a bit more of an edge than he'd expected.

"... A little," she replied. "It's not as though I've given you much more motivation than that to keep me around. You've been a better host than I've been a guest."

"There's a long road between us and that decision."

"Yeah, but what's at the end of it? You seem to flip-flop on wanting to plan everything and 'crossing that bridge when we come to it.' I need to know what we're going to do."

"Obviously, I'd like my old life back. But I don't foresee untangling myself from the tornado of supernatural horrors that it has become. Not anytime soon, anyway. So for the time being, I don't think, even in the presence of a solution, I'm liable to survive for very long without you to watch my back and yank me into the shadows when a barrage of hurled blades is flying at my face. So we're in this for the long haul."

"Uh-huh. And then?"

"And then it'll be a choice, for once."

"But what will that choice *be*?"

"It won't just be my choice to make."

"But what choice would you make?"

"I don't know!"

The branches in the tree rattled extra hard, then the squirrel launched from the tree and went bounding toward the school.

"Huh," Blot said. "I guess the squirrel got away."

Alan squinted at the retreating creature. "Not quite it didn't," he said, jumping to his feet.

While the creature was still alive and well, its shadow had the notable addition of a dangling, fluttering noodle of a creature being dragged along. The rikt, in its sprite form, was hitching a ride directly toward the school.

"That thing is more clever than I've given it credit for," Alan said.

When the squirrel passed into the shadow of the school, and thus the moat of sunlit sidewalk was no longer a concern, the rikt bounded off and started to bob and bounce between bushes, flowers, bike racks, anything that was stable enough to cast a shadow if there was enough light.

"It's going to go right for her shadow, if it's in there," Alan said. "What are the chances it'll actually bring it back to us?"

Blot glanced about. "Probably not as good as if we'd just waited until night and brought it back to Gladys directly. And nice as she seemed, I'm not going to pass up the opportunity to be the one to deliver that shadow. No one's looking. Just get to the school's shadow and take a breath."

Alan tried to balance moving quickly and not drawing any attention to himself. "Do we know if the cameras can see us from where they are?"

"If they can, then we're about to really confuse a security guard."

He squinted at the light of the sun as it vanished behind the roof of the school. As soon as he was in shadow, he felt a sharp tug at his ankles. A half-controlled dive and a tackling hug from behind tugged him into the shadows, and he raced toward Chu-chu and the school.

The door ahead had a nice big glass front, which was no obstacle at all for a shadow, and once they'd slid into the dim interior of the school, they were free to slide to a well-hidden corner and allow Alan to pop back up.

He leaned against a wall decorated with finger paintings and science projects about the solar system while Blot stretched this way and that.

"No cameras inside," she said. "Just stay away from the windows and you won't need that mask."

Alan crept through the hallways of the school. Blot led the way, eyes half shut as she followed some nonphysical sense.

"Chu-chu's downstairs. In the basement. Should I pull you through the vents, or do you want to find some stairs?" Blot asked.

"Let's save our energy," he said. "For all we know, this thing is going to put up a fight. Heaven knows everything *else* has."

The basement was easy enough to access and was a good deal darker than the main level. In other words, it was the perfect place for a shadow, or shadow creature, to hide. There were classrooms, but they were mostly the specialized ones. Art rooms, band rooms, and storage rooms. They moved through the dim hall, scanning for signs of their less than faithful tracker.

"You know, I've been living a lot of nightmares recently. I didn't expect *this* one to come true."

"This isn't your school nightmare," she said. "You're wearing pants."

"No, that's not what I—"

"Wait," Blot said. "I think... I think I understand what the gardener meant about gossip."

"What?"

"I'm feeling... I don't know how to say it. Feelings. Fear, mostly. Anger. Hopelessness. It's not me and it's not you."

A rattle came from behind a door. Alan stepped forward and reached for the handle, then stopped and rummaged in his bag for gloves. "No prints," he muttered to himself.

Blot tried the knob. When it didn't turn, she slid her fingers between the door and the jamb and defeated the latch.

Beyond the door was what seemed to be a recently repurposed room. It had the long, wide steps of an orchestra room, but the only instruments here were in large, dusty boxes.

"The air's thick with emotion, Alan. It almost hurts..." Blot said unsteadily.

"I have a feeling this room got decommissioned for classes for a reason," Alan said.

Even without Blot's metaphysical sensitivity, he could feel a chill in the air that had nothing to do with temperature. It filled him with an awful, grinding sense of foreboding, like the room was holding its breath.

"I should give you the locket. Maybe you'll be able to feel it," she said.

"I don't want to feel it. I've got enough scars in my brain. Just the tension is starting to—"

"*SKAW!*" Chu-chu crowed, his large, round eye becoming visible on the floor as he strutted out from beneath a stack of boxes.

Blot slid around. "The stack's flat against the wall. I think the shadow's back there. Give me the stone."

Alan handed it over.

"Someone's hurt this girl, Alan," Blot said, dragging the stone with her as she edged farther behind the boxes. "Not just when the Ghoul tore her shadow off. I'm getting a lot of bad, and nothing good. And if shadows come back to where they felt safe, the hurt must have lasted a long time if she came all the way back to an old school."

"Is this what ghosts are? Are ghosts just dislodged shadows?" Alan asked. "Because this feels an awful lot like what people say they feel in haunted places."

"Don't ask me to figure out how you people chose to explain the metaphysical. Just get ready if I toss you the rock."

"Why?"

"Because this thing feels like it might bolt."

"And what am I supposed to do about it if she does?" he said.

"Like I said, be ready for me to toss you the rock, and then just throw the rock at the shadow."

"I don't know if I feel comfortable throwing rocks at the terrified shadow of a tortured young woman."

"Would you rather her tangle with Chu-chu?"

The pile of boxes lurched.

"She's moving. Quick!"

A mote of black, barely human shaped, darted out and flitted along the wall. Chu-chu dove after it. The two shapes streaked across the room. Chu-chu hopped from object to object, the walls and ceiling becoming something of a personal obstacle course for the creature. The shadow moved more freely, but with less purpose. Its motion wasn't that of a frightened animal. There wasn't that much logic or intelligence. This thing wasn't just emotional. It was nothing *but* emotion. And it was either unwilling or unable to leave the room.

It was just possible that Alan, Blot, or Chu-chu individually could have cornered and pinned the shadow to the stone. But the rikt was not a team player. It bounded and launched itself in the darkened room, knocking over music stands and overturning boxes like a poltergeist. Not until Alan had the bright idea to turn on his flashlight and use it to corral both Chu-chu and the shadow did things finally take a turn in their favor. A three-pronged attack eventually drove the shadow into the corner, where Blot jabbed the stone into its form.

Any further attempt for the ill-defined shape of the shadow to depart or wander was unsuccessful. It simply shuddered and tugged in place.

"Well…" Blot said, plucking up the stone and whisking to Alan's side. "That was relatively painless."

He surveyed the damage with a sweep of the flashlight. The room looked like it had been ransacked. "We should probably get out of here. I'm not pressing my luck that we haven't set off an alarm or something with all of this. And my inner child is freaking out about causing this much of a ruckus in a school."

When they left the school, the rapid slide toward evening had left them with far more flexibility regarding where they could emerge from the shadows. Blot dragged Alan about halfway to the car before he started to get antsy in the shadows. They emerged hidden behind the restrooms in the park across the way.

Blot tossed Alan the stone.

"Here you go," she said. "Good old shade magic. A stone that can link firmly to a stray shadow, but leaves a shade untouched. I think I'm going to have a lot to learn from Gladys."

Alan held the stone in his hand, looking to the barely visible haze of shadow clinging to it.

It took a stretch of the imagination to resolve the faint outline cast from the stone as a human.

"It's so weak compared with you," Alan said.

"There's no comparison. The only similarity between a human shadow and a shade is that we can both be cast from a human. You assuming that thing would compare with me is like me assuming a photograph would compare to you. Why do you think I don't mind tucking *that* away in the shadows with me but I didn't want to do the same when Chu-chu was hooked to it?"

"Speaking of Chu-chu," Alan said, glancing over his shoulder. "I can't help but notice he's still following us."

Blot grinned and turned.

The rikt was creeping along behind them. It would dive to this object or that, clinging to the shadow and eying them for a moment or two before diving to a closer object.

"I told you he likes us. Gladys is nice and all, but she didn't name him. Help me find a good rock. Maybe if I carve that shape on it, he'll have something nice to cling to and he'll stay close."

"He alternately ignores me and treats me like a perch, Blot," Alan said. "And he's got a bad habit of very visibly slamming into the shadows of little objects. I think keeping him around is going to be problematic."

"He's a very clever creature, though. Give me some time and I'll have him eating out of the palm of your hand."

Alan sighed and kicked at the grass as they approached the street. "Next you'll be saying he followed you home," he said, fetching a likely stone.

CHAPTER 12

A short time later, Alan and Blot were nearly to the police station, where they would hopefully be able to collaborate with Jessie. Night had fallen, and despite Blot's best attempts to carve a matching mark into the stone Alan had found her, Chu-chu had not joined them in the car. He did not run off either. As they drove, his sprite-form was diving and hopping from mailbox to tree to sign, anything that could serve as a temporary perch.

"It's sort of beautiful, isn't it?" Blot said. "The way he moves? Imagine the freedom of moving like that... That's almost how we get to be back home."

"Almost?"

"Yeah. Once we come here, we get a little more malleable. I guess it comes hand in hand with being robbed of a physical body. It's a shame that the gardener hasn't worked out how to give that level of freedom without an anchor to us shades."

"Why do you suppose Chu-chu isn't just taking the direct route?"

"Because he likes me and he wants to stay around me," Blot said. She sighed and pulled out one of her pads. "Feels weird not to be running toward something or away from something."

"It does feel weird. And it feels weirder that it feels weird, because that used to be the default for me."

Blot summoned a pencil as well. She turned to a page that was utterly covered in runes.

"What have you got there?"

"This is what's written on your back. The stealth stuff that was stolen from the Dawn," she said. "I've been picking at it whenever I get a spare moment. Mostly while you were sleeping. Considering the fact that the first order of business for the Glints is going to be to figure out how to crack this, seemed like it'd be good practice to give it a try as well."

"Did you make any progress?"

"Some. Mostly I ruled a bunch out."

"Well, you're almost out of time. We're only about twenty minutes away from the garden."

"Every little bit helps," Blot said. "The Glints are so eager to see how the spell works, it must be pretty simple to defeat. Half the time the structure of it betrays its weaknesses. And there are always weaknesses. They're built right in."

"Wait... You build weaknesses into your spells."

"It's how magic works, Alan. Equal exchange. You can dump endless amounts of magic into something and really overdesign it to try to make it completely flawless, or you include the flaw from the start in exchange for an easier path to the desired goal. I've heard some of your fairy tales and things. You can always break the curse with true love's first kiss or something stupid and random like that. Why do you think a wizard would include that?"

"Because those stories are fiction and they needed a way to make love important in a tangible way."

"Maybe in a story. But in reality it's because if you trade the rare but obtainable as the key to undoing the spell, you can get away with a much simpler structure to the spell."

"Who exactly are you making this trade with?"

"The cosmos. Reality. The powers that be. Darkness. Light. Whatever governs the mysticism intrinsic to the spell." She glanced at him. "This is all very basic magic theory, Alan."

"I guess I missed that elective in college."

She scrutinized the shapes, poking them with the pencil. "The problem is, I already ruled out a trade like that... So if there's a flaw, it's just because of a weakness that's a result of the spell, rather than a weakness that's part of the cause of the spell."

Alan glanced in the back seat. He'd tossed the stone there. Every few moments a bit of motion visible in his rearview mirror would make his heart jump until he realized it was the shadow. "Our passenger is getting more active," he said.

"Mmm?" Blot said. "I suppose she is."

"You said you could feel something from her. Emotions?" he said.

"Yes."

"Are you feeling them now?"

"Not so much."

"I think I am."

"Doesn't surprise me. Metaphysical stuff like that is as much about who you're talking to as what you're saying. Before, she was probably just oozing pent-up emotion, and now she's calling for something."

"Calling for me?"

"Calling for..." She raised her head. "A human who has lost its shadow." Blot turned and glared at the vague shape shifting along the back seat. "That could be a problem."

"We have something putting out a supernatural distress call to every human with a shade. Yes. That sounds like a *big* problem."

"Look at the bright side. Would you know how to track something like that?"

"No."

"Then let's hope the other shades in the area will have equally clueless hosts."

"Gee, thanks."

"Mystically clueless." She sighed. "Like me, at the moment. It's such a short spell. Too short to be ironclad, and *also* too short to hide anything..." She tapped the page a little harder, as if to punish it for being so evasive. "The spell hides the person... The spell hides *us*... So we can't search for the person the spell is cast on..."

"What about the spell?" Alan said.

"That's what I'm trying to figure out."

"No, I mean, why can't you just look for the spell? Half the time you look for anything you're feeling for magic, right? So why not just search for the spell that's hiding them?"

"Because that..." She squinted at the runes, then glanced at Alan. "Okay, let's hope that the other hosts are *more* mystically ignorant than you. If Gladys is right, and this is how the others have been hiding, this could be a serious asset. Active magic is far more visible to a focused mind than a passive presence, if you know what you're looking for." Blot shut her eyes and focused.

Almost immediately, they shot open and she curled around to the back of the seat.

"What's going on?" Alan asked.

"About seven cars back, left lane. We've been too distracted."

Alan squinted into the rearview mirror. A familiar car with one headlight and trash bags on the windows was at the very limits of visibility. "Todd. How long has he been following us?"

"No way to know. Could just be for this ride. Could be almost since we lost him the last time," she said.

"Couldn't be that long. We've left ourselves wide open plenty of times."

"He's not trying to kill us, he's trying to keep an eye on us. Or at least Rive is. Todd's mostly just getting drunk and getting belligerent, I suppose."

"I refuse to believe we could have missed them for much longer than this car ride."

"We've had a lot on our minds."

He squeezed the steering wheel. "If he's been following us for long enough, he knows where Jessie lives. And he knows where the garden is."

"For all we know, they already knew where the garden was. Look, it doesn't matter. If he keeps his distance, then we'll just call that a problem for another time."

Alan glared at the rearview mirror.

"Alan, we really don't need one of your 'they're threatening my friends' overreactions. Especially if we don't know there's an actual threat."

He gritted his teeth.

"Jessie is a cop. She can defend herself better than you can, especially against him. You can spot him as someone up to no good from a mile away."

He took a slow, seething breath but eased his grip.

"Let's focus on what counts. We drop off the shadow with the gardener. Then what?"

"We're going to need to get Marsha, and separate her from the Ghoul, while they're close enough to get her to Gladys for her to be saved."

"That basically means getting the Ghoul and her to the garden. You were holding on to a Shard of Shadow and you still barely made it more than five minutes without me," Blot said.

"Regardless, we'll have to find them. And we should warn Jessie about what's going on. Get my phone and call her."

Blot fished out Alan's phone and quickly tapped the screen.

"Hey, Alan. How's it coming?" Jessie said, answering before the second ring.

"We've got the shadow. How goes it with the search for Marsha?"

"I managed to get out there to canvas the area. A couple of locals know the woman in the anonymous tip, but I'm having a little trouble getting them to cooperate. This is a community that isn't comfortable with the concept of snitching. But I might have a lead. Heading there now."

"Alone?"

"The neighborhood has six squad cars. I've never been less alone."

"But none of them are going to be able to do much about the Ghoul."

"I've got Frightful tagging along."

"What?"

"That's the bird. I'm calling her Frightful. You were right, she needed a name."

"That was Blot who wrote that, actually. But having her around probably isn't going to do much more than help you see what's really going on."

"True. When's your next shift? Maybe we can get them to—hold on. I've got something coming over on the radio."

Alan could barely make out some distant, distorted voice.

"Copy that," she said. "Alan, there's a motel on the north side of town. The owner saw the news reports and says someone checked in with the girl's description twenty minutes ago. Get ready for the address, but for god's sake keep your distance unless something shadowy starts to happen."

Alan pulled to a stop a few intersections away from the motel and sat tensely with his hands on the wheel. He could see the flashing lights and hear the sirens. From the looks of it, six police cars and an ambulance were on-scene. Someone on a bullhorn was delivering orders that were destined to be ignored.

"Things are moving too fast," Alan said. "What the hell are we going to do about the Ghoul here? Is there any way to incapacitate a shade?"

"The best option available to us is a flash-bang, but even at point-blank I can't imagine it would do much more than daze the Ghoul for a few minutes," Blot said. "We're reaching the point where you might have to answer an unpleasant question, Alan. If bullets and knives start flying, I'm okay with the Ghoul dying. It's had a good run, and misguided or not, it's spent it killing people pointlessly. But you're going to have to decide if you're willing to let the girl die."

"We're not letting her die."

"Then you're going to have to get clever in a hurry, because I'm out of ideas."

Alan's grip creaked against the steering wheel. His mind raced in tight circles. Then, ahead, he saw some sort of commotion. The ambulance doors flew open. His phone rang. It was Jessie.

"Alan, we forced its hand. The victim must have recognized the woman and tried to make a break for it. There's blood but it looks like we got in there before the killing blow. But there's no sign of the Ghoul and no obvious means of escape. Have you seen anything?"

"Nothing but..." Alan turned to the window at the glimpse of movement.

Chu-chu strutted into view, cast from the base of the nearest parking meter. The vacant, vaguely crazed look normally present in his gaze was replaced by a piercing, intent stare. It wasn't a would-be pet waiting to play. It was a wild animal that had spotted a meal.

"I don't think the rikt is here because it likes us, Blot. I think it's here for the other reason."

"What?" Jessie said over the phone. "Alan, where are you?"

"Three streets west of the motel. I think the suspect is about to show up."

"I don't feel the Ghoul, Alan. If it was close, I should be getting *some* sense of it."

Alan looked to Chu-chu again. The creature blinked once, then cocked his head to the side, gazing upward. A moment later, the two nearest streetlights went dark amid the sound of shattering glass.

Something smashed down on his roof hard enough to break one of the rear windows. There was the horrid screech of metal on metal. Blades punched through the roof of the car. Blot snatched the shadow stone and anything else she could reach in the back seat as Alan wrenched the door open and tumbled out of the car.

He scrambled backward. A writhing mass of black, gleaming around the edges with clutched blades and shards of glass, glared down at him with its unblinking round eyes. Clutched in the center of the mass, like a doll held to its chest, was the trembling form of the Ghoul's young host. She was beside herself with fear, tears streaming from her tightly shut eyes.

"The ritual..." the thing breathed. "Ruined..."

"We're not going to let you kill anyone else," Alan said, climbing to his feet and pulling his flashlight.

Three limbs whipped toward him, lashing their weapons. Blot surged up and vanished the blades before they could reach him.

"And that goes double for Alan," she said.

He shined the flashlight at the Ghoul. The powerful light tore its dimension from it, casting it forcefully onto the front of the apartment building. Marsha fell to the roof of the car.

"He'll kill you," she sobbed. "He'll kill everyone."

Sirens echoed up the street. Blaring headlights overpowered Alan's flashlight, casting the Ghoul down the road. A lashing limb yanked his host into the shadows with him. The shifting mass of limbs streaked along the road, forced along ahead of the cars and bounced between traffic lights.

Alan crouched down behind his car. "After him!"

Blot skipped the requisite warning to breathe deep and dragged him down to the shadows. The tide of light shoved them along at the speed of the arriving squad cars. They screeched to a stop at the car he'd left behind, causing Alan and Blot to slide onto a busy cross street. Fresh headlights shoved them hard toward the point of thrashing black sliding ahead of them.

A chaotic pursuit followed, with both sets of shades and humans attempting to use the various lights to keep their speed up and maintain some sort of course. Alan fought the urge to breathe and held tight to the shadowy arms that gripped him. The rush of light shoved and smashed them. The ghoul moved like he was born to flee in this way. With him choosing the direction, Alan and Blot were perpetually a turn behind, leaving them scrambling to stay on track. Blot nudged herself into the passing lane to gain ground. She dove for brighter lights to inch farther forward.

Ahead, the bits of asphalt started to spark and crackle against half-emerged blades. He was slowing, perhaps preparing for a clash with Blot in the middle of the street. Blot, it turned out, was ready and willing to oblige.

She didn't slow herself for a moment. Alan could feel her contorting her shape, twisting and stretching into her monstrous form. When she struck the Ghoul, she struck hard. The pair of them lurched off the road, and once they were free of direct headlights, they lurched out of the shadows.

Alan gasped for air as Blot wrapped around him, protecting him as best she could from the highway-speed tumble. The Ghoul did the same, though a surplus of limbs left it far more able to bring itself to a stop.

The shades and hosts both came to a rest a dozen yards apart on a stretch of grass as they struggled to get their wits about them.

Jessie climbed out of the squad car. Several years on the force had trained her to split her mind into two distinct parts: Cop Jessie and Civilian Jessie. Cop Jessie calmly reported her findings over the radio.

"We've got an abandoned vehicle. Severe damage to roof and windows. Puncture holes on the roof. No sign of owner or perpetrator. No sign of injury or blood," she stated.

While she ticked mechanically through her procedure, the other half of her brain tried to grapple with the concern for her friend and what manner of formerly impossible things might have happened to him.

The radio was cluttered with alerts. Disruptions on major roadways. Wild-animal sightings. Because of the concentration of police cars in the area, and the search for a potential escaping serial killer, every minor report in the area was being relayed in nearly real time. Jessie plotted them out in her mind. They were forming a rough line.

A few of the reports were almost certainly extraneous or false, but one glaring report that just came in trumped all the others.

She slid into the car, ready to call in her destination. "It's the worst place he could have ended up, so he'll be there."

The world was still spinning for Alan as he shakily got to his feet. Blot was only slightly further ahead of him in the process of unscrambling her brains, but she'd put that time to good use. She towered over him in her combat form, as large and formidable as he'd ever seen her assert herself. She stood between Alan and the Ghoul, who was similarly imposing himself on reality.

Alan tried to click the flashlight on, but not unlike half the things in his bag, and possibly one of his ribs, the flashlight was broken. He flipped it into "persuader" position.

"Where are we?" Marsha said.

Alan spared a glance around him. It felt like a public park, but it didn't smell like one. The air was heavy with the musky scent of large animals. His eyes settled on a sign clearly not intended to be viewed from his current vantage point.

"Kangaroo habitat," Alan said. "We're in the Philadelphia Zoo. You're kidding me..."

"Keep your head in the game, Alan," Blot said.

He turned. The Ghoul was advancing. Due to either a shortage of knives or the raw desire to use its own claws to get revenge on Alan and Blot, the thing was unarmed. Or at least, it was as unarmed as a nightmare like it could ever be.

"I don't know how this is going to go," Blot said.

"If it comes down to you and it..."

"Oh, it's going to be it. The question is if I'm going to be the one who makes that decision."

The Ghoul made the first move, charging toward the duo with its host reluctantly in tow. The battle was horribly pitched. Blot was weaker and less experienced. Only two things seemed to be in their favor. Blot was just as vicious as the Ghoul, and the Ghoul was wholly devoted to targeting Alan.

A panicked roll took Alan out of the path of the Ghoul's first flailing attack. Blot caught a stray limb and slammed the creature to the ground.

For a harrowing few seconds, the battle became a game of keep-away, with Alan as the target. Blot slashed and shredded at the Ghoul, but the Ghoul shrugged it all off and continued its monomaniacal attack. Distant sirens signaled the arrival of the police, though from the sound of it, at least one of the squad cars wasn't content to stop at the zoo's entrance.

Startled animals and smashing guardrails managed to briefly draw the attention of even the Ghoul, whose vacant white eyes came to rest on a vehicle charging up a pedestrian path. It wasn't a police car. It was a beat-up sedan, with fresh tires, and garbage bags flapping from the windows. The journey through the zoo had cost the car its one functional headlight, but it was just as well. Its graceless plunge into the kangaroo habitat made sure the thing had seen its last road trip.

The engine ground and puttered to a stop, then the door wrenched free. A shabby and not entirely human figure pulled itself out of the wreck.

"I'm supposed to be keeping an eye on you, hotshot," Todd said, his body stretching into a further unrecognizable, ogreish appearance as he stalked forward. "But once *this* guy showed up, you went and made Rive curious."

"You were not among our number," Rive hissed, jagged eyes fixed upon the writhing ball of limbs, who stared blankly back. "You hide yourself even from your brethren. Serve under Stigma and share your wisdom, or befall the same fate as this traitor."

Todd looked to the trembling woman huddled behind the Ghoul. "Evenin', ma'am," Todd said. "Won't be a minute."

Alan backed away. Blot had slid into the shadows again.

"I don't think there's a good outcome to this one, Alan," Blot said.

"No, but there's definitely a worst one. We can't let these two team up."

"Again, I don't know if we're going to have a choice in the matter," she said. "I don't have much left. That was a long slide and a rough fight. I don't know if I'm going to be able to stand back up for much longer."

Alan looked around him. In the distance, kangaroos with far better sense than him were keeping their distance. One of them had a familiar white eye staring from its shadow. Chu-chu was still waiting for what was increasingly likely to be a massive meal for the greedy scavenger.

"What's it going to be, big guy?" Todd asked, strutting his wiry form up to the Ghoul. "Fall in line or hit the ground?"

The Ghoul didn't reply. Todd turned to Marsha and crouched down.

"There some secret to getting through to it? Or maybe you've got a say in things?" He reached out to place a knobby mitt on her shoulder.

This act of perceived aggression was a step too far. Three ebony-clawed hands snapped around his wrist and hurled Todd like a rag doll. He tumbled to the ground but managed to slide to his feet.

"About time someone was willing to throw down," Todd said.

He charged in and hit the Ghoul in a clash that was easily a match for the collision on the roadway. He swatted away attempted strikes and countered hard. For all the haze of alcohol that perpetually hung over him, Todd was legitimately a worthy opponent, and finally getting the fight he'd been spoiling for.

Police finally started to organize themselves at the edge of the habitat. Alan hastily pulled his mask on. Voices echoed with shouted commands. There were lights in the habitat, and the police were shouting for the zoo officials to turn them on.

"This could get bad..." Blot said. "The Ghoul is barely a step above a wild animal, and it's about to be cornered."

"We'll just try to be ready," Alan said.

"Being ready for a psychotic shade to go on a killing spree isn't really going to help."

Alan flinched as the blows and struggles between Todd and the Ghoul became fiercer. The murderous shade didn't seem to be tiring.

"This is like a pileup of everyone who has been pulling my strings. Except... I have an idea, Blot."

Heavy power breakers thumped, and ancient floodlights slowly lit up. One by one, the Ghoul dropped down limbs to steady itself against the ground. The tide started to turn in favor of Todd with the pressure of brightening light forcing the Ghoul toward the ground.

"Ha! *Ha!*" Todd taunted. "This is why you send a shifter to do the bruising. No dark. No problem."

One of the officers hopped the rail, holding a gun low and a flashlight high. The closer he got, the lower the Ghoul dropped. Todd finally stopped throwing punches and leaned down at the now nearly entirely two-dimensional shade.

"You about ready to join the winning team and spill the beans?"

The response was certainly not in the affirmative. It wasn't even words. A bestial screech erupted from the twisted shadow, followed by a dozen hurled blades emerging from the darkness. Todd fell aside, the fastest dodge he could muster. None of them struck him, and a fraction of a second later it became clear why. Showers of sparks rained down as each of the powerful lights within range were shattered by the blades.

The Ghoul clawed itself back up to some semblance of depth, like a monster crawling out of the muck. Jagged bits of metal gleamed in each claw. And its white eyes fixed on the nearest of the police with the flashlight.

"Blot, drop the stealth!" Alan said.

"What?!"

"*Now!*" He turned his back. "*Drop it!*"

She slashed out a final rune on his back. A subtle tingle of mystic influence that had fallen into the back of his mind vanished. All three shades turned. Alan followed their gazes. Two white-suited individuals emerged from the feeding shed. Police shouted for them to keep their distance.

"Will everyone kindly keep quiet and hold still!" shouted Dina, her voice carrying effortlessly.

All within earshot obeyed. The Ghoul, Todd, Rive, Marsha, the police. Even the kangaroos at the edge of the habitat.

Gabriel and Dina took stately strides toward the center of the habitat.

"We should have known you would be at the center of this mess," Dina said.

"You have always had difficulty with subtlety," Gabriel said.

Dina peered at Todd. "Good heavens. You would choose to allow this to be made of you? Really!" she said.

"Clean yourself up. The law enforcement is on hand," Gabriel instructed him.

Todd's form eased back toward proper humanity, his clothes barely clinging to his body when he was finally himself.

Dina surveyed the Ghoul and Marsha. "So this is the Metro Ghoul."

"Not who we expected," Gabriel said.

"A rare failure of intuition."

"This is most certainly *not* one of Stigma's operatives."

"I do hope we haven't wasted our time on someone working independently."

Gabriel turned to Alan. "I suppose that remains to be seen."

Dina approached from the other side. "I understand you slipped Angel's gaze."

"And remained hidden for some time."

"That was *not* what you were instructed to do."

"Explain yourself, Mr. Fontaine."

"We followed the Ghoul. It led us to the thing you were looking for. We learned how Stigma and the others are hiding themselves," Alan said quickly.

"Did you?" Dina said.

"Do elaborate," Gabriel said.

"It's runes," Alan said. "Blot can write them down. Runes from the Dawn's magic."

Both of the Glints shut their eyes and tilted their heads back.

"Dawn magic..." Dina said.

"A painfully obvious solution."

"We should be ashamed for not coming to the conclusion ourselves, given the situation."

"What situation exactly?" Alan said.

"You are to answer questions, not ask them," Dina said.

"I trust you can provide the precise runes involved?" Gabriel said.

Alan held out his hand urgently. Blot produced a pad, flipped it to the proper page, and tore it free. Gabriel took the page and looked it over critically. He handed it to Dina, who gave it a cursory analysis.

"That will do," Dina said.

"At least with regard to the assigned task," Gabriel said.

"It does, however, leave us with the dreadful mess you've made of things."

"Police on the verge of witnessing unexplainable acts."

"Damage to public property."

"And the potential for numerous murders."

"This is substantial."

"But is it threatening to the balance?"

"The Metro Ghoul can stay. It is a part of culture at this point. Easily dismissed."

"And this shifter?"

"Clearly a fool."

"Not long for this world."

"A problem that will solve itself. Also easily dismissed."

"The witnesses?"

"This is a zoo. They've seen a drunk crash into an enclosure, to tangle with a wild animal."

"Which leaves Mr. Fontaine and his associate."

The twins steepled their fingers.

"Further interrogation *could* be called for," Dina said.

"There are some intriguing questions that are as yet unanswered."

"And there are some behaviors that really should not be encouraged."

"You have tread on the very precipice of disobedience, Mr. Fontaine."

"Something that, ideally, would be unachievable."

"But you have provided results in all cases that we have requested them."

"A valuable operative of our own?"

"Or a loose cannon likely to misfire at an inopportune time."

They looked to each other. After a few moments of silent consideration, Dina nodded.

"Noninterference," she said.

"If our boy survives, we will be able to ask questions at our leisure."

"And if he dies, the questions will be irrelevant."

"Sufficient."

They paced for the feeding shed.

"While officially your survival or demise are equivalent in the grand scheme of things..." Dina began.

"Which is the scale at which we choose to operate, mind you..." Gabriel added.

"Please be aware that I would prefer your survival."

"You get results."

"And if nothing else, you get along with Angel."

They lingered in the doorway.

"As you were, everyone."

Those not directly engaged by the Glints returned to their senses at varying speeds.

The first and most frantic recovery was the Ghoul. For the first time, its eyes showed raw terror. The blades dropped into the grass. The limbs spread and carved arcs into the ground.

"No... No, no, no!" Marsha cried. "It's trying to run. It's trying to open the door again!" She rushed to Alan. "Don't let me get away. It'll kill someone else! Don't let it happen again. I'd rather die than see that again. And it won't even let *that* happen."

A black limb slashed up and grabbed her, beginning to drag her down. Alan held her tight. Blot reached a hand up to clutch Alan's and dug the other into the ground.

Despite their best efforts, the Ghoul was successfully dragging the three of them in. Alan turned to the guardrail above the enclosure. Chaos reigned as the emergency responders tried to react to the smashed lights and Todd's smashed car, which had begun gushing fluids. Between the sparks and the gasoline, a fireball was imminent if something wasn't done.

Only one police officer had her eyes trained on the half-seen struggle in the middle of the enclosure. It was Jessie. She had her flashlight, and its glare made it difficult for Alan to see her expression. The circle of light fell not on him, but farther along the enclosure.

"Look out!" she shouted.

Fighting for his life, Blot's, and a terrified woman's required a lot of him, but when he turned, he still found the mental bandwidth necessary to pile a dollop of confusion onto the intensity.

Charging at him from the distance was not Todd or Rive. It was something that a less distracted person would have been worried about from the start, and what Alan had all but forgotten.

A single kangaroo had broken off from the others. Something had terrified it even more than the clash in the center of the enclosure and the sputtering sparks raining all around. That thing was the phantom talons of Chu-chu, which was fluttering behind the beast, clinging to its shadow.

The crazed creature bowled into Alan and the girl. Blot lost her grip on the ground. The whole chain of them slid through the gateway, with Chu-chu leaping in after.

Jessie lingered wide-eyed at the patch of grass a few steps ahead of her. She'd just seen two people and some half-seen black forms vanish through the ground. They were just... gone.

She turned. A fragrant and unsteady man who was one heroic strip of waistband away from being completely nude, gave her a halfhearted grin.

"Really something, huh? Funny little world we live in," Todd said.

"Where did they go?" Jessie demanded.

"Lady, I'm not even sure where I am now."

"That's 'officer,'" she corrected. "And I can see your shadow. I know you're like Alan, with a shade of your own."

"Ha! If you think I'm going to say anything about anything to *you*, you're crazy."

"I see. Well, then, I have some good news for you." She snatched the cuffs from her belt and clapped them around his wrists. "You have the right to remain silent."

"Are you serious?"

"Anything you say can and will be used against you in a court of law. You have the right to an attorney. If you cannot afford an attorney—"

"You know you're not going to be able to hold me, right?"

"*Let me finish,*" she snapped. "If you cannot afford an attorney, one will be provided for you. Do you understand the rights I have just read to you?"

"Yeah."

"Good, then listen up. You're going to jail."

"I don't think so."

"I *do* think so. You're going to go to jail, and you're going to go to prison, and when you get there, you're going to talk to the last cluster of shades and hosts who decided to tangle with Alan Fontaine." She leaned closer. "And believe me when I say this. Alan is a pussycat compared with me."

Jessie spoke the words with chilling certainty, particularly for someone who knew full well she was speaking to a supernatural entity, which, until a few moments ago would probably have been confused for a rogue gorilla.

"Now are you going to come with me quietly?"

Todd glanced at his shadow. Rive's attention was focused on the surly posture of Frightful, who was staring back with something approaching a predatory gaze that was every bit the match for Jessie's intensity. Todd looked back to her.

"Yes, ma'am."

Blot flailed and struggled as the world itself seemed to vanish. She was a shade, she was accustomed to the very nature of the world shifting. One moment a silhouette, another moment forcing oneself into reality. But this was different. Inside the gate, it didn't feel like she had any control over anything. There was nothing to control. This wasn't a place. It was somewhere between places. Around them was not darkness, but a void. A place where, if light existed anywhere, darkness might also exist. For now, there was only one thing here. Direction. They weren't somewhere, but they were *going* somewhere.

She tried to focus her eyes on Alan. She knew she was still connected to him. She could feel their connection. But she couldn't see him. And she certainly couldn't see the Ghoul or Marsha. But a point in the distance was approaching.

"Alan?" she called. Her voice made no sound. But she felt the faint flicker of a response through her link to him. "Brace yourself. Whatever is coming, it's coming fast."

Alan's mind felt like it was frozen. He could barely think, and he couldn't move at all. He would have been terrified, if not for the one solid constant in his life. The connection to Blot. What had started as a barely perceptible notion he couldn't hope to understand had come to be the thing that he clung to in order to maintain his sanity.

In a flash, the world painfully reasserted itself. For the second time that night, he tumbled to a stop. This time he narrowly missed striking a tree.

His brain was crackling with static, as if his senses had to take a moment to reorganize themselves. They gradually drip-fed him information. It was cool here. It was dark. There was grass, trees, bushes...

"Get up, Alan," Blot urged, her fingers weakly gripping his arm and helping him up.

"Where are we? This feels like..."

"It's the garden. He took us to the garden," she groaned. "And if that's how that gateway spell works every time, I don't think I want to learn it. I feel so weak."

Alan leaned against a tree and finally got his eyes to focus. "I don't feel much better."

He heaved himself upright and scanned his surroundings. They were quite near the column. Judging by the churned-up ground between them, the group had probably come tumbling out of the column itself. He didn't spot the Ghoul or Marsha, but a clear trail was left behind.

A stone beside him rattled. He turned to find Chu-chu looking upon him expectantly, cast from the stone. He was frustratingly free of the same lingering weakness. He squawked once, then shifted to his sprite form and curled through the air.

"Lead the way, Chu-chu!" Blot said. "I knew he'd be an asset, I *knew* it."

Alan limped along. All of these uncontrolled landings were starting to take their toll. "Tell me the Ghoul is going to be as weak as we are," he said.

"It opened the gateway. It's going to be weaker. But that's relative. Considering how powerful it was to start, we might still be outclassed."

Alan searched through his bag. He had nothing to defend himself with. His flashlight was broken, his cameras were in his trunk. The only things he had of any significance were the stone with Marsha's shadow and his phone.

"Have you got any backup flashlights?" he asked.

"Fresh out."

"What *do* you have? At this point, I'll take anything even remotely useful."

"Let's see..."

Blot was cast along the ground more by her will than any real light source. She reached her shadowy hands behind her back and, one by one, pulled them out with a vague shape in her grip. She listed the contents and let them pop back into reality.

"Sixty-five ballpoint pens... Fifty-one mechanical pencils... Thirty-two memo pads... A few hundred coffee stirrers... Seventy-three sugar packets. A couple hundred napkins..."

"Do you steal a handful of things every time we go to the coffee shop?"

"Those are complementary. It's not stealing," she said. "A big long hank of rope... Two ball-peen hammers..."

"Do you steal something from *every* store we go to?"

"Only when they aren't complementary. A sleeping bag... A silk handkerchief..."

"Now would be a really good time for you to have a spare flash-bang."

Blot hissed angrily. "I misplaced it."

"You what?"

"Hey, you don't know what it felt like to get hit by that thing. I started to get nervous carrying it around and I left it somewhere. Believe me, I'm really kicking myself about it now. But that's about everything I've got. ... Wait. What's this?" She produced a rod that appeared to be made from silver. It had a few small markings scattered along its length. "This looks... we were in Angel's lab at some point, weren't we?"

Alan searched his memory and found the dull residue of something suppressed.

"I... think? They must have made us forget. Like when we have to fight to remember there even *is* a lab."

"I *knew* I would have stolen something if I could," she said angrily. "Lousy Glints, making me forget when I put one over on them."

"Is it anything useful?"

She twirled it and caught it. "Not yet. It seems like it's just raw material. This is probably stock for making jewelry like that locket. It would have been good to know I had this the whole time. We might have been able to make something useful out of it."

"Looks like I'm going to be fighting an ancient murderer with my wits and cell phone," he said, preparing the phone in case he needed to use the flashlight. "And both of them are running a little low on battery."

"Here," Blot produced the locket. "Give this a try."

"Will it do any good?" Alan asked, slipping the silver necklace on.

"It didn't do *me* much good when I tried it with the Ghoul, but it seems like it does a lot more for humans than shades when it's not charged. Makes you more solid, in a metaphysical sense."

"More solid..." Alan crouched and fetched the rope. "I've got an idea. Tell me if this would work."

"Skaw," said Chu-chu, turning to the darkness just off the slate path.

The rikt fluttered from the ground to the branches of the nearest tree. He peered down with his head turned aside, one large eye surveying the path.

"Talk fast. I think the Ghoul isn't done being on the offensive."

After taking a few moments to finish the preparations for what Blot had dubbed "barely a plan," the pair of them waited for the Ghoul. There was no doubt in their minds that the monster would come for them. It hadn't retreated to this place because it was through fighting. It retreated to this place because it was frightened of the Glints, or at least the power they had over it. Even if it wasn't after revenge, Alan had cost it a kill for the ritual. The killer would want him as a replacement.

"Come on... This waiting is killing me," Alan said.

"Technically the killing is what you're waiting *for*," Blot said.

Chu-chu rattled the branch and produced an excited crow. In the distance, a darker form moved among the shadows. Two small eyes resolved, bounding toward them as the skittering monstrosity made its move. Blot remained in the shadows, but tensed. Alan held his ground, phone in hand, finger hovering over the flashlight icon on its screen. When he judged that the Ghoul was near enough, he tapped the button and held up his phone. He didn't bother shining it at the Ghoul. The paltry little LED wouldn't have done much more than irritate the raging beast. Instead, he turned the light to illuminate his own chest and hand. The locket caught the light and sparkled, and in his hand, the stolen silver rod gleamed.

The Ghoul came to a stop. Its host was still clutched close to it, carried like a struggling toddler. Small white eyes glared at the silver implements.

"That's right," Alan said. "I saw how terrified you were of the Glints." He tapped the locket with the rod. "They're the ones who sent me after you. Did you really think they wouldn't send me with a weapon?" Alan brandished the inert silver rod in what he hoped was a convincing way.

The Ghoul tipped its head, barely discernible from the rest of its inky body. It took a step closer. Alan took a step back.

"Don't push me. I don't want to kill you. But you've got to face justice for what you've done." He took another step back. "You may think it was a ritual, but it was never going to work. And the others are here now. There's no need to continue doing it."

The Ghoul took another step forward and reached a dark claw toward Alan.

"I'm warning you!" Alan said, raising the bar.

When the monster refused to back down, Alan swiped with the rod. It struck the Ghoul's claw with a pathetic clunk. The monster withdrew the afflicted claw, discovered it was unhurt, and lashed out again to knock the rod away. It surged toward Alan, but motion and a startled yelp behind it drew its attention.

Blot had popped up from the darkness and pulled a loop of rope tight around Marsha's waist. She cinched it securely, binding her against the tree, then knotted it.

"Trust me," she said to the woman. "Hold tight. It's the only way."

The Ghoul rushed back to its host. Blot dipped down into the shadows again and sank the fingers of one hand into a strip of shadow that joined the Ghoul to Marsha. She pulled hard, and reached a single hand out of the shadows. Alan dove for it, grabbed her wrist, and pulled.

It was a direct assault on the connection between host and shade, and the Ghoul knew it. Blot, mostly in the shadow, contorted herself into as powerful a form as she could muster. One hand still skewering the Ghoul, she shouldered him away while Alan hauled at her.

Panic started to seize the Ghoul as the connection was tested. With Blot mostly in shadow, the monster had to remain in shadow to resist her, but with Alan helping to pull her, the Ghoul would have to pull himself out into three-dimensions to try to stop him.

Alan knew all-too-well the soul-searing terror that came with having your shadow torn away. He'd faced it more times than most creatures would ever get a chance to. The fear and panic was raw and deep. It forced out logic and replaced it with desperation. Slashing claws jutted up out of the ground and gouged Alan's legs. Blot shook and shuddered with the blows she was absorbing in the shadows. But they ignored the attacks and dragged the Ghoul farther away. Finally, the connection was severed.

Marsha cried out and trembled, her eyes wide and terrified as she felt her connection to the world suddenly ripped away.

"Keep him away," Alan said, fighting with the knot.

"Easier said than done."

Desperation turned to frenzy. Weakened by the prolonged battle, the opening of the gate, and being torn from his host, the Ghoul wouldn't last long without an anchor. If they weren't already in the garden, it was just possible that the Ghoul would have succumbed already. As it was, it was a shrieking, slashing flurry, desperate to take Marsha back. For once, Blot had a strength advantage now, but the Ghoul didn't have to beat her, it just had to get past her.

Alan gave the stone and the locket to Marsha. "I know you feel cold and weak, but trust me, you've got some time. The locket will help. You just need to get to the gardener. Right at the end of this path. Give her the stone. She'll get you fixed up. Understand? You can do this. We'll keep the Ghoul at bay."

Marsha shut her eyes tight and gathered herself, then turned and dashed down the path. Alan turned back to the clash.

"It's not fighting," Blot grunted. "It's just struggling." She did her best to keep a grip on it. "Get ready to run. I can only go as fast as you can, and there's no way it's got the oomph to haul itself out of the shadows like this." She circled around and tried to hold the squirming mass of limbs back. "But it's just got to get its claws into her again. As weak as they are, pulling them apart a second time might kill both of them."

Alan dashed a few paces along the path and turned. He raised his phone again. Its meager flashlight was little more than an annoyance to Blot, but the Ghoul shuddered under its glow. Blot's efforts and the weak light were enough to keep the increasingly maddened shade back for a while, but an uncountable number of limbs flailing uncontrollably will not be denied. The Ghoul broke free and streaked down the path.

"No!" Alan said, dashing after the shifting form.

"One more deep breath, Alan," Blot said.

She reached up and tugged him down into the shadows and gave chase. They started to close the gap, but the weakened Marsha wasn't moving very quickly. At this rate, the Ghoul would reach her before they could reach it.

But there was one more player in this game. Someone who had been patiently watching and waiting.

The trees rattled and rumbled above them. Something was moving swiftly through them. With each tree closer to the Ghoul, more branches shook. Then something dropped down. Though still just a shape cast on the ground, the silhouette it cast was enormous, as large as a lion. It looked like a heraldic symbol, feathery mane that roiled like wind-blown fire. Four cunning, lean legs tipped with slashing talons. A fierce head gazing at them with focused, angular eyes.

"*SKAW!*" shrieked the beast, somehow making what had been a cute, curious sound into a terrifying battle cry.

It set upon the Ghoul. To call it a battle would have been generous. The hulking beast that Chu-chu had made of himself reduced the Ghoul to shreds. As a herald of death, the rikt had chosen to help things along for the sake of a quicker meal.

Blot released Alan. He slid back into reality just as Chu-chu finished his grim task and returned to his rooster-like form.

"Y-you full, little guy?" Blot said, sliding subtly behind Alan.

"You didn't tell me he could turn into a raging hell-beast."

"I mean, *I* have a battle form. It stands to reason he would. I'd just... never seen it before."

"Why do I get the feeling that this whole thing was *his* plan, not ours?" Alan said.

"Skaw," Chu-chu said.

"Let's go," Alan said. "We've got to see if Marsha is okay."

He gave the rikt a wide berth, then continued on his way. Chu-chu shifted to his sprite form and swirled and bounced his way along the path to join them.

"I suspect Grandmother was a bit backward," Blot said. "It's not so much good luck to feed a rikt as it is bad luck to let one get hungry..."

The pair reached the cottage at the end of the path. Marsha was reclining on a pile of blankets laid out on the porch, unconscious. The gardener sat on the porch beside her, open locket in hand. The stone sat on the sleeping woman's chest.

"You sent this girl running here?" Gladys said.

"Yes. Is she—" Alan began.

"Alone? With no shade and no shadow? What sort of a damn fool are you? You ought to know better. The girl could have slipped away. Two more minutes and she would have."

"We had our hands full fighting an ancient psychopath," Blot said.

"Mmm... As I recall, you wanted me to lock it up for you," the gardener said.

"Skaw," remarked Chu-chu.

Gladys glanced in the creature's direction. "Ah... So the rikt got a bit rambunctious. A shame. I'd hoped the Ghoul could be made useful again in the future, but I can't say it didn't earn that."

"Is she going to be okay?" Alan said.

Gladys leaned heavily on the ground to inspect Marsha. She plucked the stone from the young woman's chest. "No shadow on the stone," she said. "Do you have a light?"

He fished out his phone and shined it on Marsha. Sure enough, she cast a simple, accurate silhouette.

"There you have it. Back to normal," Gladys said.

Alan leaned close. "She's barely breathing."

"Of course she is. Her shadow was worn out, and you gave me a half-dead shard to work with. I'll put some more work into her, see if I can mend her a bit better, but whether she makes it is touch and go. The good news is, if she lives or dies, she'll do it with her own shadow."

"We've got to get her to a hospital," Alan said.

"What she's got isn't something they can fix, but you may as well. Give her some time before you move her out of here, though. If that shadow's loose, this place'll keep it in place a bit easier than out there." She handed over the locket. "And I wouldn't expect to pull that stunt again anytime soon with this shard. Give it another few months, and maybe. But I think you see why we need a few of them if this is going to be a regular thing."

Gladys reached out a hand. Her shadow helped her to her feet, then dragged one of the borrowed dining room chairs up so she could take a seat. She sighed. Her shadow continued ministering to Marsha.

"Do me a favor and bring me a fresher shadow next time. It's nice to know the spell works, but it won't do anyone any good if all I manage is to patch up folks who end up in a coma after."

"You don't seem terribly concerned about her."

"I hope she lives. I need her to live, if shades are going to have a shot at being anything but a blight in the eyes of humans. But I've been around a long time. I've seen an awful lot of young folk go before their time. You start to grow a callus after a while. Glad to know you haven't, yet. Hang on to that. A good heart'll get you through some tough times." She gave the pair a once-over. "And it looks to me you've had your share of tough times already. You two are a couple of scrappers, aren't you?"

"When you're facing nothing but uphill battles, it's that or die," Blot said.

"Truer words were never said. How are things with the Glints?"

"They sort of left us to die," Alan said. "And Blot stole some silver from them, which is lying on the forest floor somewhere."

"Did you now?"

Blot gave a cocky grin. "I even forgot I did it." Her grin faded. "But we had to hand over the secret to the Dawn-style stealth."

"I figured you would have to... And that leaves you out in the open for everyone."

"It was nice being able to hide while it lasted," Blot said.

The gardener rubbed her face. "You did some good work for me. And you proved this little trick here might be a winner... Tell you what. You leave that silver where you dropped it. And come back here once in a while to see if I need anything, now that a rikt tore up my old errand boy. For that, I'll get to work on something for you. Something specific for you. That way if you end up falling in with the wrong crowd, the rest of us will be safe. Sound good?"

Alan winced. "I've got enough gigs already. I'm not sure I want yet another supernatural entity giving me odd jobs."

"But this one's a good guy!" Blot said. "I vote yes."

He grumbled. "You aren't going to make us kill anyone, are you?"

"I didn't even want the Ghoul to die. There's enough of that going around already."

"Fine. We'll keep in touch."

"Grand." The gardener motioned to Marsha. "If you're going to get her to a doctor, I'd give her an hour with me and Mote. Let the patch settle a bit. Until then, coffee?"

"Always!" Blot said.

"In a minute," Alan amended. "I've got a phone call to make."

Epilogue

Alan turned his bleary eyes toward the road. There was no cell reception inside the garden, so he'd had to make a handful of hikes into and out of the place to make the proper arrangements. It had been more than an hour since Marsha's "procedure." She was still asleep, but the gardener said she'd stabilized enough for them to pull her out of the garden. Alan's limited medical expertise didn't give him much confidence in his assessment of her well-being. He'd set her on the bench of a picnic table near the hiking path not far from the gateway tree and listened to the slow approach of wailing sirens.

This was technically a victory, but Alan wasn't feeling terribly fortunate at the moment. He was alive, he may have saved the hapless host, and the murderous shade was dead. But he was also in a campsite in a state park forty-five minutes away from his car, and there was still some question of whether or not the "cure" of having a shade was anything more than a delayed death sentence.

Gravel crunched beneath the wheels of the first of two approaching emergency vehicles. Alan glanced up to see a squad car pull up. The door opened and out stepped Jessie. She assessed the situation with a very Officer Hearst expression and locked on to Marsha. She crouched down and illustrated that she was better at assessing health in seven seconds than Alan was in forty-five minutes.

"She's stable. Blood pressure is low. Pupils are responsive. No major trauma. The ambulance will be here in three minutes. Get in the back of the squad car."

"Shouldn't I—"

"I shouldn't be this far out of Philly, and you sure as heck don't need to be lingering around next to an unconscious woman. Better you at least appear to be in police custody to cut down on the questions that'll need answering."

"That's good thinking, Alan," Blot said.

He nodded and trudged to the car, grateful that for once someone seemed to know what was best.

Alan had watched from the back of the police car, hunched down, as Jessie skillfully oversaw the care of the sleeping girl. In the space of a few minutes, she'd been assessed, loaded onto a stretcher, and whisked off toward the nearest hospital. When they were gone, and Jessie had done the whole "nothing to see here" routine to the trio of campers who had been attracted by the commotion, she let Alan out of the back of the squad car.

Jessie brushed off his shoulders and looked him in the eye. Alan glanced down at her shadow, where the brooding form of her own personal rikt was giving Alan and Blot a critical glare. When he looked back, Officer

Hearst had melted away and Jessie nearly knocked him to the ground with an unexpectedly enthusiastic hug.

"You could have warned me you were going to do that whole disappearing act!" she said, squeezing him tight.

"Ow, ow, easy!" he said.

He stumbled a bit. Blot sluggishly propped him up.

"We took a beating," she said. "Be gentle."

Jessie backed away. "Are you two okay?"

"I've got some bumps and bruises," Alan said.

"You should see the other guy," Blot added.

Jessie motioned in the direction of the departed ambulance.

"Was *that* the other guy?" she whispered. "The shadow looked normal, but it isn't always so easy to see and hear this stuff. Frightful doesn't grip as tight as she should sometimes."

"The other guy was attached to her," Alan said.

"He's not anymore," Blot said. "He's not even attached to his own head anymore."

Some motion caused Jessie to jump, and coaxed a halfhearted crow from Frightful.

"What was that?" she asked, hand jumping to her gun.

"The other rikt," he said.

"Chu-chu," Blot corrected.

"Right. It seems like he's taken a shine to Blot. He followed us out."

"Don't make any sudden moves around him," Blot whispered. "You want to be on Chu-chu's good side."

"We've got a long ride ahead of us. You can fill me in then, but for the time being, the short version is that she's the human the murderer was hooked to, and the murderer is dead. Anything else I need to know?"

"That's plenty," Alan said.

"Okay... Good..." Jessie said. "So everything that remains has legal precedent. I did *not* want to have to figure out how to get the district attorney to accept that we were going to need some sort of magical special custody arrangement. The bail system was not created with demonic possession in mind."

"It's not technically demonic possession—" Alan began.

"Just let it slide, Alan," Blot said.

"How are things back in Philly?" Alan asked.

"I booked Todd, and you're going to see a lot of news stories talking about a gas leak at the zoo."

"There was a gas leak?"

"There was a whole squad of police officers with a gap in their memories, and when that happens, the easy explanation is gas leak. Come on. Let's get you home. If I get any farther away from Philly with this squad car, they're going to start making Smokey and the Bandit jokes about me."

Alan climbed into the front. Chu-chu picked some random object in the back seat to cling to and curled up.

"We're going to have to get a story together about you. I don't know if you noticed, but you are here and your car very much *isn't*."

"Oh, I noticed," Alan said.

"We're way ahead of you," Blot said.

"Fill me in on the way. But start with this, where does all this put you?" Jessie asked.

"I don't know. I'm pretty sure all but two shades want me dead, and one of them is attached to me. I haven't heard from the Dawn, and the Glints were hemming and hawing about whether they wanted to bother saving my life. They decided to let the dice fall where they may. So the list of allies is questionable at best."

Jessie patted his knee. "Eh. The ones you do have are pretty excellent. Not to toot my own horn. So what now?"

"I don't know. There's a whole lot of shades still out there, and most of them will be up to no good. And the suspect in that ambulance illustrates that under the right circumstances, there's a way to separate shades and hosts without killing either. At least... I hope. You're sure she was stable?"

"The paramedics didn't seem worried. She's not great, but I've seen worse pull through."

"So..." He rubbed his eyes. "Hell, I don't know."

Jessie nodded. "We'll figure it out."

They sat silently for a few moments.

"You booked *Todd*?" Blot said.

"Yeah. Drunk and disorderly. Public indecency. Breaking and entering. Reckless driving..."

"But you know what his deal is, right?"

"His deal is he was a criminal and I am a police officer. Though his shade seemed pretty iffy about facing me down once he saw Frightful."

Blot gave Alan a look from where she'd been cast on the passenger side door.

"I think I'm going to agree with Jessie on this one. If you could only have a couple of allies, you ended up with some good ones."

From The Author

Thank you for reading! If you liked this story, or perhaps if you found it lacking, I'd love to hear from you. You can find me online at my website, bookofdeacon.com. For **free stories** and important updates, join my newsletter.

DISCOVER OTHER TITLES BY JOSEPH R. LALLO

The Book of Deacon – an Epic Fantasy Series:

Book 1: *The Book of Deacon*

Book 2: *The Great Convergence*

Book 3: *The Battle of Verril*

Book 4: *The D'Karon Apprentice*

Book 5: *The Crescents*

Book 6: *The Coin of Kenvard*

Book of Deacon Anthology: Volume 1

Book of Deacon Anthology: Volume 2

Other stories in the same setting:

The Rise of the Red Shadow

The Story of Sorrel

Entwell Origins: Anya
The Redemption of Desmeres
The Adventures of Rustle and Eddy
Jade
Halifax
The Stump and the Spire

The Big Sigma Series – a Sci-fi/Space Opera Series:

Book 1: *Bypass Gemini*
Book 2: *Unstable Prototypes*
Book 3: *Artificial Evolution*
Book 4: *Temporal Contingency*
Book 5: *Indra Station*
Book 6: *Nova Igniter*
Book 7: *Quantum Shift*
Beta Testers
Big Sigma Collection: Volume 1
Big Sigma Collection: Volume 2

The Free-Wrench – Steampunk Adventure Series:

Book 1: *Free-Wrench*
Book 2: *Skykeep*
Book 3: *Ichor Well*
Book 4: *The Calderan Problem*
Book 5: *Cipher Hill*
Book 6: *Contaminant Six*

Free Wrench Collection: Volume 1
Free Wrench Collection: Volume 2

The Shards of Shadow Series:

Book 1: *A Traitor in the Shadows*
Book 2: *The Prison of Shadows*
Book 3: *The Balance of Shadows*
Book 4: *The Clash of Shadows*

The Greater Lands Series:

Book 1: *The Bygone Dagger*
Book 2: *The Bygone Archive*
Book 3: *The Bygone Mask*
Book 4: *The Bygone Caper*
Book 5: *The Bygone Plague*
Book 6: *The Bygone Way*

Other Stories:

Between
Fallen Empire: Rogue Derelict
Top Level Player
The Other Eight
Structophis
Between
Paradoxes and Dragons: Volume 1

Paradoxes and Dragons: Volume 2
Paradoxes and Dragons: Volume 3

www.ingramcontent.com/pod-product-compliance
Lightning Source LLC
Chambersburg PA
CBHW011738010726
47496CB00010B/2986